D.L. Hodges is married and the father of four boys, living in Barrie, Canada. When not working he enjoys listening to music, hiking, travel but mostly, time with his wife, Nadia. *Fissures* is his first novel.

Fissures

D.L. Hodges

This title is a work of fiction. Names, characters, places and events are fictitious and any resemblance to actual persons, living or deceased, places or events is coincidental.

ISBN: 0991914309

ISBN-13: 978-0991914302

ACKNOWLEDGMENTS

I would like to thank the many people who assisted, guided and helped me in the completion of this novel.

- My wife, Nadia, my sounding board through every rewrite and the many edits.
- Patricia Montgomery, who was not only my editor but my head cheerleader. This would not have been possible without your guidance.
- Brendan Hodges, who designed and produced the cover art.
- Hyun Sook Ham and Marsha Bloom who gave me invaluable feedback.

Prologue

The grandfather clock towered majestically in the corner; its ticking provided the only sound, the pendulum swing the only motion, as it steadily counted away the seconds, indifferent to the events unfolding before it.

Standing in the living room, they faced each other. Two narratives: one pleading, the other expressionless.

Staring into his empty eyes, she wished, beyond hope, that she could help him. He looked so young, so vulnerable; a lost child needing protection; a hug; a mother's loving arms. That was not an option, she knew. Not now. But could she get through to him? Could she make him understand? To see that he had an alternative to the path he hadn't, yet, taken.

"Think about what you are doing," she pleaded, keeping her voice calm, fighting the urge to scream out *'Please don't do this!'*

She clasped her hands, fingers interlaced, and raised them to her chin, in prayer to a God she hoped would listen.

If I can just get him to say something, anything...I can make a connection... Please, God, please, give me the words....

A mask of anguish began to contort her face; lips slightly parted, teeth clenched and eyes pleading. She fought back the tears. Breathing became shuddered, her head light. Her view of the room distorted, like heat waves rising from scorched asphalt. Taking a deep breath she, again, struggled to calm herself.

She opened her mouth to speak. He shook his head slightly and, stepping forward, put his index finger up to her lips.

"Shhh, shhh, shhh."

Then he stepped back. Seconds passed. He kept his vacant eyes locked on hers.

Demanding attention, a kettle on the stove in the kitchen screamed out, shattering the silence. She glanced over to the kitchen door and back. The handgun was no longer at his side. The look in his eyes had changed to one of resolve.

Swiftly, he raised the gun. There was no time to move; no time to defend; no time to react but for a scream, drowned out by the sudden explosion. The muzzle flash trailed the bullet as it pierced skin, penetrated bone and brain and exited the skull, stealing with it fragments, and a life.

A single tear trickled down her cheek as she slumped to the floor.

CHAPTER ONE

"Here are your things, Andrew," said Vincent, the hulking prison guard with the quick smile, as he handed over the package of meager belongings.

"The name is Drew. Could you, please, just this once, call me by that name?" Drew pleaded as he opened the package and took stock of the belongings inside: wallet with ID; keys; necklace; the picture. From his pocket Drew removed his Prison Discharge Slip and a piece of scrap paper with a phone number scribbled on it and placed them in his wallet.

"Only my mother calls me Andrew."

Vincent looked at him for several moments before he obliged, "Okay, Drew," he mocked, with a broad smirk, "I remember you from the first day you arrived here; you corrected me that day too, you cocky little prick. I thought to myself: 'Shit, this one is going to be a handful.' Fortunately, I was wrong about you. You have really turned into a good man, Andrew, and I hope never to see you here again."

During the five years he had spent at the penitentiary, after two years in juvenile detention, Drew and the guards had come to a mutual respect. When dealing with the prison staff he was courteous and obedient; in turn, they treated him with civility.

As the two men shook hands, Drew recalled, with a pang of remorse, the compassion Vincent's vice-like grip could also offer.

"I wish you nothing but the best of luck, Drew."

The inner exit door crept open, its grinding wheels agonizingly screeched out every inch as Drew waited impatiently. Drew passed through then had to wait for it to shut. The heavy crashing of metal on metal as the door struck the frame, which had always meant confinement to him, today signalled freedom. When the outer door opened sunlight edged in and caressed his face. He smiled and stretched his arms out to his sides to receive its brilliant warmth and, with no intention of looking back, Drew walked out of prison.

At six feet tall, with a lean, muscular build and a bronzed, Mediterranean complexion, Andrew David Parsons looked older than his twenty-three years. His face was slender with hollow cheeks and a taut jaw line. His chestnut brown eyes, positioned just above his high cheekbones, were scrutinizing and cynical. Drew's short, wavy, brown hair was well groomed. The only blemish was a J-shaped scar which extended from the left side of his mouth curving down and under his bottom lip. The constant five o'clock shadow he wore only added to his mature appearance; a model's good looks.

Walking out to the main parking area, Drew was captivated by his surrounds. On the opposite side of the road from the penitentiary, a large watercolour boreal forest stood resplendent, its radiance enhanced by the mid-day, October sun. The rich, melodious songs of the Rose-Breasted Grosbeaks, which perched on the branches of the trees, filled the otherwise hushed afternoon while wisps of diaphanous, placid white clouds wandered languorously across the azure blue sky. The dry, crisp air tasted refreshing as he filled his lungs with deep breaths, and the lightly gusting northwest wind had the leaves tap dancing along the pavement, escorting him to the waiting car.

Jean Parsons, his adoptive mother, stood beside the vehicle wonderfully clad in a flower-print dress which seemed almost too light for the cool temperature. Her sombre eyes and submissive posture belied the welcoming smile she presented. As Drew approached her, Jean opened her arms to greet him. The two hugged. She smelled of the home he yearned to remember: the scent of laundry fresh off the clothes line and of lavender; her favourite flower. It was a long, lingering embrace that neither of them was desirous to relinquish. When they eventually separated, Drew reached out both hands and, with his thumbs, wiped away the tears that glistened on his mother's cheeks. He stood there for several moments, his hands cupping her face, and smiled; no words needed to be spoken.

William Parsons, Jean's husband, and Drew's adoptive father was absent.

"I am sorry, your father could not be here, Andrew, he was up late last night and was not able to get out of bed before I left at noon," Jean said contritely, her eyes fixed on the ground between them.

"It's okay, mom, you told me he likely wouldn't make it. I understand."

He couldn't even make the effort to be here. Why am I not surprised?

As they entered the car, Drew shook his head and released a huffing, disgusted sigh.

The same old shit-box; all these years and the old man still hasn't bothered to get her a new one.

What had been a midnight-blue paint coat, was now sprayed black, and pocked with fibreglass filler, rust holes and corroded metal; the car shed weight with every bump or pot hole it encountered. Inside the vehicle a forest of evergreen-shaped air fresheners hung in a desperate attempt to conceal the pungent smell of wet dogs and cigarettes. While his mother didn't smoke, his father was seldom seen without a cigarette in his hand. Beaded seat covers and duct tape provided the interior finish; the heater barely worked, air didn't blow but drifted from the vents to the floor which was beginning to show signs of rusting through.

Before she started the car, Jean turned in her seat towards Drew, her eyes gazing down at her hands.

"I am sure you are disappointed that your father could not be here, Andrew, and I really wanted him to be here too, but, unfortunately my repeated requests for him to get up fell on deaf ears. I guess he was just too tired."

"Really, it's okay, I'm glad you could come," he reassured, putting his hand on hers.

She smiled a sad, meager smile. Drew felt sympathy as her eyes remained focused on her hands.

His mother looked old, much older than her forty-nine years; a personification of the car she drove: once radiant, her complexion was now pasty with ruddy blemishes. At five and a half feet tall, she carried a portly frame which pushed against the seams of her clothing, while her once thick, black hair now appeared thinning and grizzled with an Amish-like bun set at the back of her head. Her eyes, which at one time had reflected her strength, looked mournful. As she reached for the ignition and steering wheel, flab sagged from her upper arms.

"We are very happy you decided to come home so we can help you get back on your feet." Her voice was faint, almost inaudible above the sound of the engine. "Your father said he may be able to get you a job working as a night cleaner at the office tower where he works. And once you start working, the rent will be reasonable enough for you to put some money away. We want you to do well, Andrew, so we hope you can abide by our rules and stay out of trouble. We will sit down with you and go over the rules we want you to follow." Her voice now started to rise in a nervous prattle. "They should not be a burden to you but we need to set some sort of boundaries. Oh, and by the way, those other boys you were friends with, you need to stay away from them. They are nothing but trouble."

Drew groaned, rolling his eyes.

"Please, mom, I have spent the last seven years in confinement, following rules; being told when to stand and when to sit, when to sleep and when to wake, when to eat and when to shit!"

"Andrew, please! There is no need for you to use vulgarities."

"Sorry, but I didn't leave prison to be locked up in my own home by you and dad. Your concern is understandable but you're going to need to give me some time and, maybe, some space to acclimatize to being out and back home. You get used to a particular way things are done when you are imprisoned and getting released is a form of culture shock. I need to find my way back into society."

"We understand that, Andrew, and irrespective of what you may believe, that is why your father and I feel that if we set some boundaries, it will give you an opportunity to accustom yourself to being out of jail. Knowing that you have been strictly controlled during the past seven years, we are concerned that you could become intoxicated with the rediscovered freedom."

Drew didn't respond. For several minutes the only sounds were the screeching of a loose fan belt and the monotonous humming of the car's engine.

He stared out the window at the countryside as they passed. A countryside he hadn't seen in several years, but one that hadn't changed significantly. Farmers' fields, a golden-brown sea of corn stocks waving, obeisant to the demands of the wind. Leaves falling like thousands of paint flecks from the canvas of tall maple and oak trees, standing ceremoniously on either side of the road; spears of light penetrating through their newly barren branches. Cattle, paying no attention to or looking lackadaisically at the passing traffic, chewed grass at their leisure.

And as Drew sat in the front seat gazing out his window, the view of a world he had been excluded from for so long assuaged and comforted him. He turned back to his mother deferentially.

"Mom, I've had a lot of time to think about my life. I mean not to return to that place. There was too much to deal with, too much seen while inside; things I never want to see again.

"Yes, I screwed up, but you cannot treat me like the delinquent sixteen year old who went to jail. That's all behind me now. And I refuse to look back at the terrible choices made and the consequences suffered. I took classes, graduated from high school and started working towards a university degree; grew up in there, made a lot of decisions about my life, amended my ways and have learned from my mistakes. Before you is a different person - one who has aspirations; a vision for a future. There are things I must do to get my life in order and just need some time to adjust to getting back to the outside world and to get my head together. I'm sure you have different ideas about what needs to be done, but hope you and dad can accept this."

Jean glanced over at Drew and gave a resigned nod but said nothing. The remainder of the drive home was silent and Drew eventually fell asleep.

CHAPTER TWO

Drew woke early the morning of his sixth birthday to brilliant sunlight coming through his window, exposing the dust particles as they wafted about his room like schools of fish in the ocean. As with the bedrooms of many six-year-old boys, Drew's was filled with pictures of sports heroes and cartoon characters. His favourite, a limited edition Bugs Bunny print, hung on the wall above the head of his bed. It was his prized possession, a gift his father gave him at a cartoon and comic book convention. The floor was awash with toys and dirty clothes which hid the smoke-grey carpet underneath. Beside his bed, under the window, stood a night table and on the opposite side of the window, across from the bed, was his dresser, its drawers unburdened as piles of folded clothes sat on top. Kitty-corner to the bed was his closet. Situated directly to the right of the closet was the bedroom door.

On the main floor, his mother sang along with a Red Hot Chili Peppers song on the radio in the kitchen as she prepared for Drew's afternoon birthday party with five friends.

As he scuttled from the bed and began dressing, Drew became aware of his mouth watering in response to the chocolate perfume from his birthday cake which permeated the room. Making his way to the bathroom Drew heard the shower running. His father was awake. Drew wanted to wait for his father to finish in the bathroom but all his dancing around in the hallway wasn't enough to stop the urge to pee. Slowly he opened the door.

"Daddy?" he stammered, "Can I come in and pee? I really have to go."

"Okay, son, but don't flush. I'll do it when I'm finished my shower."

The deep, heavy voice of his father had always intimidated Drew, even now sending a shiver down his spine.

William Parsons was taciturn, and churlish; with a fury unrelenting in its need to be satisfied. Though short in stature, standing slightly taller than Jean, he was burly, having very little fat on him. With a receding light brown hairline, blue eyes and an oft-broken nose, William would sooner negotiate with his fists than his words. His infrequent smiles weren't the nice-to-see-you type, as much as they were, you-just-wait sneers. After losing his job at the textile factory, William had found employment as a security guard, a job he did with palpable disdain. When he wasn't working shifts at a large office tower in the city, he often spent time with friends at the local bar. Most days the house had to remain funeral home silent while William slept. Drew's mother often explained the need for quiet as his father was recovering from work or drink. It wasn't unusual on the weekends for him to be sitting out on the back stoop holding a beer and cigarette in hand, when not down at the bar.

Drew lifted the seat and felt relief as the water drained from him. With that worry off his mind, he drifted back to thoughts of the presents he would receive, the special lunch his mother was preparing and the double chocolate cake waiting to be devoured. Yes, he was going to have a great day.

Drew shook out the last bit of dribble and zipped up his pants. Flushing the toilet, he immediately realized what he had done. His father yelled out as the hot water poured over his skin.

"God damn it, Drew, what the hell'd I just tell you!" he shouted as he turned the shower off.

"I'm sorry daddy," Drew's voice trembled.

"*You're sorry? You're sorry?* You're always bloody sorry! Can't you do nothin' right?"

For several moments Drew stood paralyzed. He looked in the direction of the shower through the blur of tears.

"I'll deal with you after," his father rumbled in a low, measured voice.

By the time Drew reached the main floor, tears had formed rivulets down his face and his nose dribbled a sap-like flow over his lips to his chin.

His mother, still singing in the kitchen, had not heard the incident in the bathroom over the sound of the radio. As Drew stood in the doorway she turned to him. Her smile faded and she rushed over and wrapped him in her arms.

"What is wrong, Andrew? What happened?"

Through choppy breaths Drew tried to explain. Hearing his father exiting the bathroom, he plunged his face into his mother's chest, and held her tight, his entire body shaking uncontrollably. Jean picked him up and carried him over to the kitchen sink to wash his face and settle him down.

"It is alright, my baby; everything will be just fine."

William charged down the stairs and into the kitchen.

"Where is the little bastard?" he growled.

Jean turned to face William, defiant, her eyes fixed on him, her hands holding Drew steady behind her.

"William, you are not being rational, it was an accident. He did not mean to flush; it is just that he was so excited about the birthday party."

"Bullshit!" he retorted, his outrage disproportionate to the situation, "I just finished fucking-well telling him not to flush and the next thing I know the water is scalding me. Jesus Christ," he unbuttoned his shirt to expose a faintly reddened chest, "look at this."

As William crossed the room, Jean backed away, keeping herself between him and Drew.

"William, it is his birthday. Could you please calm down?"

"I'll calm down soon enough," he fumed, brushing Jean aside like a minor inconvenience and grabbing Drew by the arm.

Drew let out a shrill scream. "No daddy, no...I'm sorry..."

From the floor where she had fallen, Jean, grabbed for William's leg. Light flashed in her eyes and severe pain shot through Jean's head as his heel slammed against the bridge of her nose. Everything went dark.

As they approached the sliding glass doors to the back yard Drew tried to pull away from his father. William, still holding Drew's left arm, grabbed him by the nape of the neck and threw him forward as though he were tossing fishing net. Drew turned his face away just before striking the door. The pane of glass exploded, surrendering to the force of the impact, and Drew tumbled through, landing on the porch with glass cascading down around him. He rolled onto his back revealing shards and specks of glass covering his face and body, shining like a million distant stars as they reflected the morning sunlight. A deep gash extended from the left side of his mouth to curve down under his lip and blood spewed forth like an open tap, running down his cheek and into his ear before continuing down and pooling on the two by four surface of the porch. Drew did not respond to the brutality, stunned by the impact.

"Ahhh, shit!" William blurted.

With panicked eyes, he raced over to the kitchen sink, grabbing a towel. Returning, he passed the towel to Drew.

"Here, hold this tight against the cut."

Carefully standing Drew up, William began to slowly remove the glistening clothing.

"I'm sorry," William whispered, "but if you hadn't made me so angry, none of this would have happened. Look at your mother, she is hurt, too."

Drew glanced over at his mother as she rose to her feet unsteadily and leaned against the counter. Guilt overwhelmed him.

"I'm sorry, daddy...I'm sorry I made you mad and made mommy get hurt."

Again the tears flowed.

"We can't worry about that right now, son, we have to clean you up and get to the hospital."

William lifted Drew into the kitchen. At the sink, he washed water over Drew's face to remove the fine shards. Jean looked on, nonplussed. After he had cleaned Drew's face, William carried him up the staircase to the bathroom at the top. Turning on the faucet William had Drew get down on his knees in the tub and position his head under the running water.

"Stay there, son, I'll be back soon. I am going to see how your mother is doing."

Drew did not respond, unable to hear his father's voice over the flow of the water spilling and lost in the thought of how his actions had hurt his mother.

In the kitchen William found Jean cleaning the shattered glass from the floor. As he approached she turned, a disgusted look in her eyes.

"What did you do to my baby?"

William could hear the bathtub water still running.

"*Me? Nothing.* Drew pulled away from me and ran into the door. I guess he didn't realize it was still closed," William defended himself with feigned sincerity.

Jean furrowed her eyebrows, sneering at him. William stared back nonchalantly.

"You look a little pale. You should go lie down on the couch. I'll take Drew to the hospital and when I get back I'll clean things up. Oh," he chirped, almost as an afterthought, "might I suggest, when you are feeling better of course, you call all the parents and tell them that the party has been cancelled."

Jean didn't want to lie down but knew the feeling of light-headedness could get worse if she wasn't careful. Discouraged, she walked into the living room and lay on the sofa, placing a cold cloth over her forehead.

William went back up the stairs to the bathroom and shut off the water. The cloth Drew was holding to his face secreted none of its original colours; it was drenched in a dark red hue. William replaced it with a clean towel and tossed the bloodied cloth in the garbage. He towelled off Drew's hair and escorted him to his room, sitting him on the bed.

"Wait here."

William left the bedroom only to return moments later, carrying a large box. It was gift wrapped, footballs and baseballs on a red background, and topped with a blue ribbon.

"Happy Birthday, son," William handed the gift to him. "Go on, open it."

It took great effort for Drew to open the present while still holding the towel to his face. William stood over him with a crooked smile, oblivious to the struggle. When the paper was finally removed, Drew lifted the box lid. Inside he saw a new button up shirt and a pair of blue jeans.

"A perfect gift!" William clapped his hands with a piercing slap.

With resignation in his eyes, Drew looked up at his father and softly acknowledged him. "Thank you, daddy."

Having helped Drew get dressed into his new clothes, William drove him to the hospital. Drew was quiet the entire drive as he sat in the back seat concentrating on keeping the towel over the gash and stifling the cries caused by the tenderness of his face. William listened to and sang along with the classic songs on the radio. When they arrived at the hospital, Drew was admitted immediately.

In the suture room, Drew was examined by Dr. Pritchett, a tall man, in his mid-forties, who carried himself with an innocuous self-confidence and a quiet, gentle manner. Removing the towel he inspected the wound. Drew looked up at him with tears in his eyes.

"I'm sorry. I'm so sorry. I didn't mean to do it," Drew said, his voice distressed.

"There is no need for that, Andrew. Can you tell me what happened?" Dr. Pritchett's voice was gentle and caring.

Drew refused to say anything more; choosing instead to curl his lips between his teeth and bite down on them despite the tremendous discomfort it caused him.

Dr. Pritchett studied Drew. Discerning the fear in him Dr. Pritchett made up his mind to move on with the examination.

"Okay, Drew, I am going to freeze the area around your cut and once it has started to work, I will stitch you up. We will use this gooey stuff that will make your skin feel funny but it will stop the pain while I am working on your cut. Do you understand?"

Drew nodded his head.

"Good. We will first have to clean out the cut so none of the glass is left inside of it."

Drew looked up at Dr. Pritchett, his eyes still red from the crying.

"I want you to relax. I am going to put a cloth over your eyes while I fix the cut. That will protect them from the thread and anything else I may use. So just close your eyes and relax, I will be done before you know it."

After waiting for the freezing to take effect, Dr. Pritchett began suturing Drew's face.

"So Drew, how did you get hurt? Your father said you ran into a sliding door, is that true?"

"I'm sorry, doctor, I didn't mean to, it was an accident."

"I know Drew, but *is* that how the accident really happened?"

Drew's breathing stuttered as he thought about the incident. Despair framed his face but no more words passed his lips.

"It's okay Drew, I will talk to your daddy when we are finished here. You can wait here until we have spoken. We will have a treat for you. Does that sound like a good idca?"

Drew gave a faint smile.

William waited outside the front doors of the emergency department, nervously smoking, while the doctor tended to Drew's injury in the suture room. Lighting his third cigarette, he noticed the early morning chill had given way to sunny warmth. A short time later Dr. Pritchett approached William, alone.

"Mr. Parsons, may we speak?"

"What's wrong? Is Drew alright?"

"Yes, he is fine. The laceration has been sutured but there will be significant scarring. He is lucky it was only a cut. His cheek or jaw could easily have been broken. I'm amazed he didn't even lose any teeth. He is waiting in the suture room until I have had a chance to speak with you."

His soothing tone and manner did nothing to relieve William's anxiety.

"Mr. Parsons, I spoke to Andrew while tending to him. He kept saying he was sorry; that he didn't mean to. Unfortunately he wouldn't say anything more. Can you tell me what he was talking about?"

William took a long drag of his cigarette. Turning his head away from Dr. Pritchett he slowly blew smoke rings before finally responding.

"Yeah, doctor, he was running around the kitchen and slammed into the sliding doors. He smashed the glass. That's how he got the cut. Pretty stupid, really."

Dr. Pritchett looked at William considering his words.

"Yes, so you said when you first brought him in. But my concern is also based on the red marks on his left arm. It is quite plain to see he's been grabbed there. There will be some bruising. When asked about it he still refused to answer, except to say sorry. He seems very scared, not just sorry. What can you tell me about how he got the marks?"

William felt his face colour. His eyes narrowed and he pointed at Dr. Pritchett with the fingers holding his cigarette.

"Look, when he was lying on the back porch I grabbed him by the arm to get him away from the glass. Maybe the grab was a little too hard, but my adrenalin was rushing. Are you suggesting that I had anything to do with the accident? I'm the guy who has to take time out of my day to clean up this mess. And, maybe the reason he is scared is because his mother cut her foot on some of the glass and he is afraid of what will happen to him when he gets home. So don't look down your nose at me, doc."

Dr. Pritchett's expression and manner did not change.

"Mr. Parsons, I made no such accusations but do have an obligation to question suspicious injuries when children are involved. My job includes ensuring your child's protection not to look down my nose at anyone. I hope you understand."

William, taking another draw of the cigarette, masked his anger with a calmer voice.

"Sorry, Dr. Pritchett, I guess this whole thing has me a little stressed. And it was to be his birthday party today, too."

"Yes," Dr. Pritchett continued, "that leads me to another question. Do I understand correctly that Drew is adopted and was previously a ward of the state?"

"Yeah, my wife and me were his guardians and adopted him when he was two." Pre-emptively he added, "And no, we haven't told him."

"Mr. Parsons, because Andrew is a child, I must send a report to Social Services. The report will include my observations and the information you have given me. I do appreciate you shedding light on the cause of Andrew's injuries."

"I know the procedure, doc," William replied acerbically. "When he was four, he fell off his bike and got a bad knock on his head. The hospital notified Social Services then, as well. They did a phone interview a few weeks later. Do what you have to do. In the meantime, let me get my son and get outta this place."

As they re-entered the hospital, William, ignoring an ashtray, flicked his burning cigarette butt towards some shrubs, not quite reaching them, and walked passed as it rolled back towards the entrance doors, its thin grey braid of smoke carrying into the hospital foyer.

Dr. Pritchett led him to the room where his son waited. Drew was sitting on a gurney, still working on a Popsicle the nurse had given him, sporting a large, customized pad of gauze spanning his left cheek, around his mouth and to his chin. The cut underneath had required several stitches to close. As Drew climbed down from the gurney, William put an arm around his shoulder and walked him out of the hospital.

Drew spent the remainder of his birthday rocking quietly in his mother's arms, exhausted; a combination of the day's trauma and painkillers.

William cleaned the kitchen and back porch, scrubbing the deck to remove the dried blood. The other children's parents had been contacted and had dropped off Drew's gifts. The gifts remained by the front door, unopened.

By early evening, Drew had fallen into a deep sleep. The left side of his face was showing the signs of trauma from the impact against the door and his arm showed bruising from his father's grip. Jean carried him up to his room and laid him in his bed, new clothes still on, and placed a small gift in his shirt pocket. Then she lay down beside Drew, her head still throbbing from the kick, and, putting her arms around him, let herself slip into the dark void of sleep.

Social Services never called.

CHAPTER THREE

As Jean drove into town, Drew awoke and looked at the buildings as they passed. The town of Drury – called Dreary by many who lived there - was painfully unexceptional. Located approximately one and a half hours from the nearest city, it was home to a dwindling community of barely four thousand residents; down by nearly half from a few years before. The population had decreased significantly after the largest business, a textile manufacturer on the outskirts of town, moved its company to Mexico to take advantage of free trade and cheaper labour. In response to that, many families moved to be closer to the city where jobs were available. Numerous homes had fallen into disrepair, a consequence of the owners, unable to sell, abandoning or renting their properties when they moved out of town.

The main street was lined with nondescript and dilapidated buildings housing a variety of small, unremarkable businesses, 'For Lease' signs or boards covering their windows. Many of the building fronts were also crumbling from neglect. A local bar, Mack's Pub, was the only establishment which flourished.

By eight o'clock in the evening the streets were virtually barren. Mack's Pub, located in the middle of town, would fill with young men drinking to celebrate their youth or old men drinking to remember their past. Beyond the main boulevard, the only sounds were the crashing of garbage cans being savaged by racoons and the howling of dogs aroused by them.

At five o'clock Jean pulled the car into the driveway of seventeen Mississauga Avenue. Light and shadow wrestled for position as the late afternoon sun began its descent towards the horizon, its brightness intermittently obstructed by wisps of clouds. Drew peered up at the one and a half storey house which, for most of his life, he called home. It was typical of the homogenous, post-war cookie-cutter houses found throughout the town. The peaked roof of rust-coloured shingles, its eaves trough overloaded with leaves, was positioned on top of a rectangular façade of light-brown bricks; though his mother preferred to call the colour sepia, apparently in an effort to elevate it to a more patrician status. Two large windows at the front of the house, with mock shutters framing them, were located on either side of a black front door. A small cement porch raised four steps above a lawn blanketed with bright red, an offering from the large maple tree in front which had surrendered her leaves to the season.

The only thing exceptional about the house was the front garden, his mother's domain. She was fastidious, spending weeks every spring and fall meticulously planning and planting flowers and shrubs for the season only to change the layout the following season. The few perennials she grew were simply used as a backdrop for the annual creations she fashioned. Even now, in late autumn, it was pulsating with seasonal blooms of violet and ochre. This was her spiritual centre: a place to come and rejuvenate, to feel alive – body and soul, to get lost in her thoughts and release whatever burdens she carried; her sanctuary.

Exiting the car, a thought struck Drew: *If gardening were art, the front garden acts as her canvas and Jean Parsons is Monet.*

As they approached the door, Drew stopped, noticing the unnatural silence, and looked around.

"Where are the dogs?"

"Sasha died about six months ago and Spartacus a month later. Those two were so close I think Spartacus died from heartbreak."

"You visited me three times since then and you didn't think to tell me?"

"I thought you had enough to deal with, that you did not need anything else to worry about. What would have been the point?"

The point is I could have mourned. The point is I'm a man now and you can't go on protecting me forever!

Drew held the front door open, allowing his mother to walk through. They hung their jackets in the front closet and placed their shoes on the mat.

"William, we are home."

There was no response. Jean walked from the living room to the kitchen then to the stairs leading to the second floor. Drew followed.

"William?"

She was surprised that he hadn't met them when they arrived home but this was even more confusing. They climbed the stairs to the landing.

"William, are you still in bed?"

Making her way up the remainder of the stairs she peeked around the corner into their bedroom. The bed was empty. Just then they heard the back door slide open and the heavy steps of William as he entered the kitchen. They joined him there as he was taking his boots off.

Jean looked at him.

"Good, you are home," relief in her voice.

"Where else would I be?"

Drew noticed that Jean glanced at him before she lowered eyes and her voice trailed off.

"I just thought..."

William stood, his annoyance evidenced in his eyes which remained fixed on her.

"You thought what? That I wouldn't be here when our son came home from prison? What do you think I am? I only wish I could've gone with you to pick him up."

"Dad, I'm glad to see you. It's been a long time." Drew interjected.

William continued to glare at Jean for several moments before turning his focus to Drew. With a slight smile, William extended his hand and the men shook.

"It's good to see you."

Unlike his mother, Drew's dad hadn't changed that much. He looked a few years older, had put on some weight and kept his head shaved bald. However, the most significant difference was that Drew had grown taller than him by several inches and his father no longer seemed so intimidating.

William walked over to the fridge.

"Beer, son?"

Son, almost never Drew. That was what his dad called him, except when he was angry. Drew was always alerted by the way his dad addressed him as to whether or not he needed to be concerned. And, even then, it was by degrees: son was good; *boy* was bad; *Drew,* worse; *you bastard,* terrible. Of all the monikers, though, Drew disliked 'boy' and always had. Now he wasn't a boy and hadn't been for a long time.

"Not right now, dad, I have to get washed up. Mom, is my room still upstairs?"

"For now, Andrew. We are going to move you to the main floor bedroom once it has been prepared. That should be a couple of weeks."

He smiled at her then walked from the kitchen and made his way upstairs.

After washing, Drew exited the bathroom and walked down the hall to his old bedroom. Entering the room he could smell the lavender scent from the flowers his mother had cut from the garden and placed in a vase on his dresser. The room was how he remembered it, except it seemed much smaller. There was even the hook protruding from the wall over his bed where the Bugs Bunny print had hung. From deep inside his stomach he felt a twinge of sadness. Drew removed the items from his pockets, placing his wallet, brush and keys on the dresser.

Sitting on the bed with his back against the headboard and his knees pulled up, he held the picture and gazed at it.

It was wrinkled and worn from years of being stored in his wallet and carried about, but Drew was able to clearly make out the subject: a baby, not much more than one year old, sitting on the lap of a man; who was, himself, just a thin boy, really, in his teens, with a tan complexion and short, brown hair. His face was twisted, his eyes squinting in the sunlight. They sat on the steps of a white wooden porch. Along the right side of the picture Drew could just make out the beige colour of an aluminum-sided house. Drew recognized the baby as himself from family pictures that had been taken with his adoptive parents but didn't know who the teenager was, though he assumed it was his biological father. The shadow of the photographer, stretching toward them, was that of a female, her skirt clearly defined.

Drew had looked at the picture so often over the years that the image of it was like an old tattoo in his memory; faded yet still imprinted. Nevertheless, every time he stared at it he felt an indescribable warmth sooth him. He didn't know where the picture had come from or how he got it but, as far back as Drew could remember, it was his.

Tenderly, he ran his right index finger over the wrinkled surface as if trying to feel the people and the moment the photograph was taken.

"Son, you asleep up there?"

The boom of his father's voice startled Drew. He noticed the room was illuminated by the golden aura of the setting sun. Looking at the clock he realized that he had been up stairs for almost an hour.

"I'll be right down."

When Drew entered the kitchen his father tossed him a can of beer.

"Come on, son, you're already behind."

"William, this is not a competition."

His scowl forced Jean back to her preparations.

"Jesus Christ, you making dinner or trying to make trouble? I'm just kidding around with him, if that is okay with you. Do you have to pamper him all the time?"

"It's been a long time since I have had any alcohol, dad, so I will need to ease back into it." Looking at his mother Drew continued, "How about if you and I go onto the back porch and get out of mom's way. It'll give us a chance to talk."

William walked to the door and opened it.

"After you, son."

On the porch, Drew looked out over the back yard while he waited for his dad to grab the lawn chairs. Unlike the front, the back lawn was in shambles. Though it was wide and deep, years of the dogs using the yard as a personal latrine had left the grass brown and patchy. Where the lawn wasn't patchy it was covered in car parts. Walking through the yard at night was akin to traversing a minefield: best done carefully.

William exited the shed with two chairs in hand. Placing them on the porch the two men sat down. The last remnants of daylight were giving way to the evening blue. The sky was cloudless and the air quickly began to cool.

William lit a cigarette and held up his beer.

"Cheers son and welcome home."

He threw his head back, quaffing the contents in their entirety and crushed the aluminum can in his hand before dropping it on the porch.

"So, son, what's next?" he asked, after wiping his mouth with the sleeve of his shirt.

"I have a general idea of what I want to do, but tomorrow I am going to sit down and draw up a concrete plan."

His dad gave a skeptical look but Drew continued.

"Needless to say, the first thing I am going to do is get in touch with the parole office. Actually, there is something I want to talk to you and mom about but that can also wait until later."

William ignored the last part.

"I hope this plan," said William, making quotation marks with his fingers for emphasis, "includes getting a job. This ain't a free ride. You have to pay rent, like a regular working man. I don't know if your mother mentioned it, but I have been speaking to some people down at the tower, where I work, about you working there as a night cleaner."

"I'm keenly aware of that, dad. Mom already spoke to me about it but as I mentioned to her, I have to take care of some things, first, before I can...."

Before Drew finished, William flicked away the cigarette butt and got up from his chair to get himself another beer. As he reached the door, Jean opened it to call them to dinner.

After the dreadful meals Drew had to endure while incarcerated, his mother's great cooking was an appetizing and fragrant reminder of how good life could be. For the appetizer, Jean served bacon-wrapped scallops set on lime slices. The main course was chicken cacciatore on a bed of vermicelli with an Asiago and garlic tomato sauce followed by a garden salad with raspberry vinaigrette. For Drew the meal experience was almost transcendental. With every morsel he paid homage, producing a soft sigh and taking pleasure in each moment.

However, as delicious as the dinner was, it was simply the prelude. For the apogee of his first meal as a newly released man was when his mother placed a platter in the middle of the table and, removing the lid, revealed the double-chocolate cake. Drew could not contain himself. With eyes as round as saucers staring at a found treasure, and a Cheshire grin, he was the little boy on Christmas morning opening presents.

Jean had hoped the dinner would act as a lubricant for conversation and looked forward to the evening as the family reconnected after so long. The meal was accompanied by enthusiastic discussions and stories between Andrew and her. William sat there quietly, periodically nodding or offering a word to the conversation. Mostly, though, he smoked and drank his beer, paying little attention to the two of them. Jean, however, lavished Drew with her attention, virtually ignoring William.

As the meal neared its conclusion, the telephone rang and William rose to answer it. Jean looked on, unhappiness displayed on her face, knowing what was to come next. William turned his back to the two of them while he spoke and, after a few muffled words, hung up.

"I gotta go down to Mack's."

"It is Andrew's first night home."

"And? It isn't like I've been any part of today's reunion. Anyway, it was Jake, he wants to meet me. He has something important to talk to me about. I would really like to stay and listen to you two yammer on but..."

"Can he not talk to you tomorrow?"

"He said it's important, I gotta go. Besides, I'll have lots of time to visit with him," he said, giving a slight nod towards Drew.

Jean stood up from the table and began removing the remnants from dinner refusing to look as William readied himself to leave.

"Son, you want to come out with me? The guys haven't seen you for a while and it would be a nice surprise."

"Thanks dad, but no. I'm going to help mom clean up around here then hit the sack. It's been a long day and I'm completely exhausted. Maybe we can do it some other time, when I'm not so tired."

"Sure, maybe some other time," William replied with an undertone of skepticism in his voice.

With that William grabbed his jacket, ambled from the kitchen and out of the front door. Seconds later a flash of light glanced through the windows as he backed his car out of the driveway and headed to the bar.

Drew looked over to where his mother stood by the sink, her head lowered, and her shoulders heaving slightly. He wished he could make everything better for her but as long as his dad was in her life, he knew that she would continue to suffer. He walked over and placed his hand on her back, gently rubbing in a circular motion. She turned, red rimmed eyes staring up at him, pleading.

"Please, Andrew, do not leave me again. He will be at the bar for hours, then when he gets home..."

She put her arms around his waist and pulled him close, squeezing tightly, her head pressed against his chest. Drew put his arms around his mother and kissed the top of her head. They slowly rocked for several minutes.

When Jean collected herself she backed away, smoothing her apron before she removed a tissue from her pocket and wiped her eyes and nose.

"I am sorry, that was silly of me."

She turned back to the sink and began washing the dishes.

"Mom, you don't have to apologize. I was hoping we would have a nice evening as well. There will be other nights to visit with dad."

They finished cleaning the table and washing the dishes without speaking another word. When they were done, Drew kissed his mother good night and went up to his bedroom.

Later that night, Drew awoke to the sound of his father walking up the stairs. The rasping sound of his body leaning against the stairwell wall as he climbed, suggested he was drunk. At the top of the stairs William paused, let out a loud belch, and then made his way into their bedroom. Moments later Drew could hear the muffled voices of his parents. As he lay in his bed the tone became more strained.

"Please, William, Andrew is just down the hall. I do not want him to hear this."

The bed could be heard rustling.

"No, William..." his mother's voice fell silent.

Seconds later their bed began to squeak rhythmically followed by a guttural groan from his father. And silence.

A short time after, Drew, though he wasn't certain, thought he could just make out the sound of weeping between his father's snores.

CHAPTER FOUR

Arriving home at two forty-five, after his first day of grade nine, Drew called out to his parents. There was no answer. Jean had taken a job as a secretary at the elementary school when Drew entered grade one. He had always walked to school with her in the morning and waited for her after the school day ended and they would walk back home together. But, now that he was in high school, he would be alone for the next two hours. The house seemed empty. His father was between night shifts so would be in bed and likely wouldn't get up until five.

Drew went up to his bedroom and closed the door. Using the small deadbolt, he locked it and walked over to his dresser. His parents always made him wear nice clothes on his first day of school and he couldn't wait to get out of them.

As he stripped down, Drew caught a glimpse of himself in the mirror. At fourteen years old, he was changing, both physically and emotionally. Standing there he was aware of the thicker hair on his legs and new growth under his arms and on his chest and face. His physique had become lean and muscular, his pre-pubescent fat gone. Still looking at himself, he posed, arms flexed. Other poses followed as Drew imagined himself a body-builder. Continuing to admire his physique, he thought about the gift his friend, Jim, had given him a few days before school started. It was the first adult magazine Drew had ever seen. Jim had stolen it from his father's stash which was hidden in his parents' attic.

Drew walked over to the bed and slowly removed his Bugs Bunny print from the wall above it. Turning the print over, he dislodged the magazine from where he had hidden it; wedged into the back frame. After removing the magazine he carefully replaced the picture back on the wall. Drew reclined on the bed, opening up the magazine to the middle spread.

He examined every inch of the nude. She had straight jet-black hair and dark chocolate brown eyes that met his stare like an intercessor inviting him into a picture. As he gazed upon her perfect breasts, rounded ass and finely manicured mound his breathing became stuttered. Drew felt a bizarre new sensation in his stomach. It felt mildly nauseous and, at the same time, incredibly exhilarating. The intensity was almost unbearable and yet he didn't want it to stop. As he moved on the bed, the rub of his underwear against his erection caused a stir that made him jolt, his stomach muscles to tense up. Drew shifted the magazine and looked down to see the glans of his penis extending beyond the top of his briefs. Setting the magazine aside, he moved his hands down past his waist and pushed his underwear to his thighs. His left hand returned to pick up the magazine while his right slowly caressed his erection. With each movement of his hand the pleasure increased. Stroking the full length more vigorously, Drew stared into the model's rich, sultry brown eyes, visualizing himself with her, kissing her lips, fondling her tits and finally fucking her. He imagined it was her hand, not his, stroking him. And at that moment he instinctively closed his eyes and felt the release, aware of his entire body; the burst of colours in his eyes, the strain in his neck and jaw, the rigidness of his stomach and the pulsing of his erection as it ejaculated, sending white droplets across his stomach and onto his sheets. He continued stroking himself until the intensity subsided.

For several minutes he lay there enjoying the feeling of pleasure and fulfilment; the satisfaction of his first orgasm.

When his serenity was intruded upon by the sound of his parents' bedroom door opening down the hall,

Drew's eyes opened as if spring-loaded. Jumping from the bed, he grabbed tissues from the box on his night table and began wiping the semen off his stomach while hurrying to the dresser to get his clothes.

His father walked down the hall and knocked on the door before trying to open it.

"Son, are you in there?"

"Yeah, dad, I'm busy, though."

"Son, open the door."

Drew had his pants on and was struggling to get the shirt over his head.

"Boy, did you hear me? I said open this door."

"Hold on a minute, dad."

He lunged for the magazine on the bed and hurriedly tucked it behind the print on the wall. The entire time his father listened to the frenzied movement from the other side of the door, becoming more suspicious and impatient.

As his father knocked again, Drew opened the door.

"Hi dad, I was just getting dressed out of my good clothes and putting on something more comfortable. You know how I hate wearing good clothes to school."

His father looked at him suspiciously; eyes questioning, lips pursed. Then he noticed the clothes lying on the floor and his expression changed.

"Okay, son. Clean your clothes off the floor. And make your bed, it..." his dad's voice trailed off as his eyes became riveted to the slanted print above the bed. Drew's eyes widened as his father moved towards the bed.

He reached out. "I'll fix that, dad. I must have accidently hit it. I can do it after I finish making my bed."

But, it was too late; his father was at the picture and straightening it.

"Take care of this, son; it may be worth something one day."

William stepped back to ensure it was level. Satisfied, he smiled and winked at Drew.

"I came to see how your first day of scho..."

The picture shifted, again catching William's attention. As the frame continued to slowly tilt, the corner of a page became exposed as the magazine moved. William walked over and removed the print from the hook. The magazine dropped on the bed. He looked at the cover, then at Drew. Placing the picture on the floor beside the bed, William picked up the magazine. Drew could see his father's lips begin to quiver, almost turning to a snarl.

"You little bastard, this is what you were doing, why your door was locked!"

He looked at the sheets and noticed the stains and globules of Drew's discharge.

"What are you some kind of pervert? Spending your time looking at dirty magazines and touching yourself?" His face reddened with every word.

Drew was mortified. He wanted to hide. He started to respond but realized he had nothing to offer in his own defence. His stomach turned and, again, he felt nauseous, his mouth arid as a desert, his palms clammy as morning dew.

William tore the magazine in half, throwing the pages at Drew, who held his hands up in defense.

"You use this to hide your smut! You're a disgrace and you don't deserve it." William said, pointing at the print.

He picked the print up off the floor and walked past Drew towards the bedroom door. Turning, William stared with penetrating eyes. Drew was frozen, the colour drained from his face. He wanted to look away from his father but couldn't. In one evanescent motion, William, still glaring at Drew, raised his knee and brought the print down over it, snapping the frame like a popsicle stick. Drew moved forward but the calcified look in his father's eyes immobilized him. There he remained, in the middle of his bedroom, rooted by abject humiliation and fear.

Without looking away from Drew, William removed the print from the frame and tore it in half. Then by half again. And again. And again. When he was finished, on the floor near the bedroom door lay a jigsaw puzzle of what was once Drew's prized possession. Without saying another word, William turned and walked out of the room and back into his own bedroom, slamming the door behind him.

Drew stood there, devastated by everything that had happened. Slowly he walked over to the pile of debris. Falling to his knees he started to pick up the tattered pieces before letting them slip through his fingers to take their place back on the floor. The tears that filled his eyes were not of anguish but of resentment. White hot rage coursed through him as his face turned cerise.

You prick! This was my picture, my frame, mine.

Drew stood up from the remains, seething.

"You prick! You fucking prick!" he screamed out, neck muscles straining and his body tense.

In an instant, William was back in the bedroom, his eyes feral; his face rabid. Drew stood as tall as his father, now, but was outweighed by a hundred pounds. Before he could defend, William tackled him, landing on Drew's chest with tremendous force and crushing the breath from his body. Drew went limp as his father straddled him. He was defenceless; his arms pinned under his father's shins as William began punching him in the face like a boxer would a speed bag. With each strike of his fist, William reprimanded Drew, his voice growling.

"You fucking piece of shit. You dare talk to me like that? Next time you better be ready for the consequences, because next time you talk to me with such disrespect will be the last time."

After a several punches, William rose.

Drew did not move. Blood ran from his mouth, his breathing produced a procession of reddish, translucent bubbles which gurgled and popped from his nose. His eyes were already beginning to swell shut and from his throat came a shallow groan.

"I thank God that you are not of my blood. No true son of mine would do that!"

Drew was scarcely able to open his eyes but managed to look at his father, bewildered.

"You heard me, you fucking bastard, you are not my son; you're an abomination. We adopted you. Your real parents abandoned you and we picked up the scraps. They knew what they were doing. We were the fools. I should've followed my instincts and said 'No', but I gave into your mother's wishes and your presence has been my burden ever since, stealing her...My God you disgust me and you shame this family; the Parsons name."

Each word punished Drew more than any of the punches he had just suffered. The divulgement of his adoption produced from within him an involuntary, primordial wail.

William stepped over Drew's supine form and exited the room. He went to the bathroom and washed the blood off his knuckles, walked down to the main floor, wrote a note for Jean and left the house.

Drew lay on the floor. He listened as his father left the house before he forced himself to get up. By this time his head was throbbing, his eyes were all but swollen shut; he needed to reach his hands out before him to feel along the wall as he made his way to the washroom. Once there, he washed and dried his face, leaving a blood-stained face cloth and towel on the floor beside the hamper. Taking a second hand-towel, Drew leaned forward over the sink and pinched his nose to stem the blood flow. Several times he snorted back and spat thick, red phlegm which splashed in the rinse water before being washed down the drain. Feeling his way back along the wall to his bedroom, he considered cleaning the floor of the blood he knew was there but realized any attempt would be futile. Making his way to the bed, Drew ripped the sheets off of it, tossing them on the floor along with his pillows, and collapsed onto the bare mattress. Grabbing for the facial tissues he gagged and spat more bloody phlegm fearing he would vomit on it as it trickled down his throat. Using the towel he had brought from the bathroom as a pillow, Drew lay down and fell asleep.

Jean arrived home at four-thirty excited to hear how Drew's first day of high school had gone. Walking through the front door she was sure he would meet her, like a dog does its master, and regale her with stories of his bus ride to school, new classmates and teachers. When he didn't appear she assumed he was out with his friend, Jim. The house was still. After putting her shoes and jacket away in the front closet she walked to the kitchen to begin the dinner preparation. Turning on the light she saw the note William had left. It simply said:

'I've gone out for the evening and will be going directly to work. You will want to tend to our precious little pervert.'

With dread washing over her, Jean started up the stairs, her stomach tight as a drum.

A blood mottled bathroom appeared before her as she reached the top floor. In it lay crimson stained washcloths and towels and the splatter of bloody rinse-water covered the sink.

Leaving the washroom, Jean followed the blood smeared trail along the wall in the hallway to Drew's bedroom. She stood at the entrance to the bedroom looking at a large bloody mess on the floor, the scraps of the magazine, and the remains of the print which lay at the bedroom entrance and Drew asleep on the bed; a bloodied towel under his face, bloodied tissues obtruding from his nose and the blood-stained carpet. She noticed he had removed all the bedding and left it in a pile near his dresser. Jean returned to the bathroom and wet a face cloth with soap and warm water before returning to Drew's room.

As his mother touched his hair to move it away from his face, Drew awoke. Through swollen eyes he looked at her, confused. He strained to speak.

"Is it true?"

Jean instinctively knew exactly what he was asking. Gently she brushed the hair from his forehead.

"That you are adopted, yes."

She paused, looking at him, pain wrenched through her.

Why did you tell him, William? What of our agreement? Andrew did not need to know.

Using the soapy face cloth Jean began to clean the dried blood on his face. Throwing the tissue from his nose into the waste basket, she wiped the crusted area around his nostrils. Finally, she wiped Drew's blood matted hair which had adhered to his cheek. As she did, Jean tried to sooth him.

"Andrew, you may find this difficult to believe right now, but, the fact you are adopted does not mean that you are not loved. I love you, it is just that your father..."

"Look at my face, mom," Drew interrupted, "Where is the love? Dad said he thanked God I wasn't his blood and that you were fools for adopting me. Is *that* love? This," he pointed to his face, almost hysterical, his voice quivering with anger, "this is my life. This is *our* lives! Is *this* what love is? Is *this* love? Tell me mom, is it?"

Drew raised a fist toward her before slamming it into the mattress.

When his mother reached out to embrace him Drew pulled away.

"Not this time mom. You can't hold me and make believe that everything'll be alright."

He rolled over facing the wall, his back to her. He did not want her there; he did not want to be there.

"Please, mom, leave me alone," he whispered, his tears unbridled.

She felt the drag of sadness overwhelm her heart. There was nothing more to be said. Jean was in a state of shock. Though she wanted to lie beside him and hold him in her arms, Jean got up from the bed and walked out of the room. Back in the kitchen she sat at the table, lost and despondent.

My boy, my baby. Someday, I promise, we will be away from that monster, together, just the two of us. Then everything will *be alright,* she thought to herself.

Jean made herself a light dinner before returning upstairs to clean the bloodied bathroom and hallway. She didn't finish until the early hours of the following morning. Drew never left his bedroom.

For several hours he lay in his bed thinking about all the beatings he had endured throughout his life, all the abuse he and his mother had taken; all at the hands of a repulsive, angry oppressor - his *adoptive* father. From that day forward, he would never look at his parents the same way and the anger which emerged from that afternoon would stay engrained within him like forged steel.

CHAPTER FIVE

For several days following his discharge, Drew attended to the administrative requirements of prison release: re-opening his dormant bank account; making appointments with agencies that assist with the various aspects of an ex-convict's reintegration into the community and attending the parole office where, though he had served his maximum sentence, he still needed to notify an officer of his release. Every day was consumed by the same routine: taking the bus to the city, filling forms, waiting to be seen by the appropriate personnel, filling more forms and returning home on the bus. Each evening was spent eating dinner, going for a short walk, watching television and, exhausted, heading off to bed. And, every night, Drew would give thanks for his friend John, and that he was no longer in prison.

On his tenth day back home, Drew was startled awake to a tremendous crack of thunder. Looking out his bedroom window the neighbourhood looked like a ship in a storm. An onslaught of deep turquoise clouds had arrived bringing with them tempestuous winds, blowing sheet after sheet of horizontal rainfall, with drops exploding into the puddles as though they were depth charges. Eddies formed in the air, shaped by ferocious winds and precipitation washing manically over parked cars. Strobe lightning flashed through the atmosphere over the town; the ensuing thunder moaned and cracked producing tremors through the house.

Drew dressed and made his way down to the kitchen for breakfast. Sitting at the table he looked out the water-blurred window to the inhospitable weather. He considered going into the city but chose to wait until the storm subsided.

After breakfast he sat at the computer and, only then, discovered the power had gone out - the result of a downed tree striking a generator.

The rains lasted all day, cancelling Drew's plans. Rather than sitting about waiting for the power to come back on, Drew passed the time wandering about the house, reacquainting himself with its history. As he did, memories flooded him with the warmth and comfort one feels upon meeting an old friend: sitting in the kitchen while his mother made delicious meals and desserts; the quiet pleasure of hanging around on the upstairs landing reading comic books with his friends; the excitement of building a track and running his Hot Wheels cars from the valance in the dining room, down the hall.

In the living room Drew walked over to the shelving unit and opened the doors to look at the compact disc collection. Nothing remained of them; replaced, instead, with an incohesive assortment of odds and ends collected by his parents over the years. He searched the main floor for the CDs but they were nowhere to be found. There was no place on the second floor to hold that many so, Drew concluded, the only other place they could be located was in the basement.

After retrieving a flashlight from the front closet Drew made his way downstairs. As he descended, each step creaked and complained under his weight while his shadow merged with the darkness below. The basement was how he remembered; unfinished and ethereal. Turning the flashlight on threw bizarre shadows as its light passed across assorted items haphazardly stored there. The concrete floor was cold under his feet, the air constricting and redolent of depression. A lone ceiling light, which was barely a shimmer against the darkness of the room when turned on, remained dormant in the power outage.

Drew thought about his hiding spot where he had so often retreated to as a child. Beneath the steps he located the long-forgotten storage space; his refuge; a place where he would conceal himself; a protective chamber when his parents argued – usually, his mother told him, the result of his father's drinking. Looking inside, the dark, elongated, narrow recess didn't seem to be that dissimilar from the cells he had occupied for the previous five years. With galvanic shock, Drew awoke to the fact that, one way or the other, he had been imprisoned his entire life. Without looking any further for the CDs, he returned upstairs as melancholy extinguished any pleasant memories Drew had earlier experienced.

Following dinner that evening, Drew went for a long walk. Descending the hill from his house, he looked to the scene below: a dull, despoiled mosaic of rooftops and houses which had lost their colours through neglect or time or vandalism; chimneys, like old stogies, disgorged cancerous smoke into the bleak, overcast sky. There was no movement, no pulse. The cityscape he saw sat sallow and skeletal, failing to conceal its necrosing underbelly.

It was just before seven o'clock when the last flickers of the late October sun finally broke through the dissipating cloud cover. Amber shafts of light illuminated the rain soaked street, giving it a marvellously iridescent appearance, the result of a wondrous mix of vehicle fluids and water. As the wind continued to howl in an effort to maintain its supremacy, Drew, buffeted by the incessant gusts, turned up his collar in defence.

Walking along the sidewalk on Main Street, Drew passed people with whom he had no connection - a stranger in a strange town. They were nothing to him and he nothing to them. Just as the physical appearance of Drury had changed during his absence, its people had long since become insignificant to him.

I belong in this shit-hole town no more than an animal belongs in a circus cage.

Drew walked through Drury until he found a sidewalk bench. Sitting down he watched as the town drifted off to its nightly slumber. The only movements were at Mack's Bar on the opposite side of the road and the streetlight above him flickering to life.

As he rose from the bench, a rowdy group of men turned the corner walking towards him. Drew paid no attention to them, instead staring down at the pavement before him.

"Drew?" a voice called out, "No fuckin' way!"

From the group an individual emerged, walking in the shadows beyond the reach of the street light's incandescence. Even as the figure walked nearer Drew couldn't make out who it was. Finally, he wandered into the lamp's glow; Drew recognized him immediately.

"Mickey! How the hell are you?" Drew extended his hand in greeting, a broad smile on his face.

Mickey gave a dubious look.

"Fuck that, man."

He slapped Drew's hand away and gave him a hug. After motioning for his friends to continue to the bar, Mickey turned back with an impish smile Drew remembered all too well.

"I'm doin' good! Fuck me, it's great to see you; how long you been out?"

"I was released early last week. Been back living at my parents' place."

"What the fuck! And you couldn't take the time to look up your old buddies?"

"Hey man, I have been so busy getting my shit back together," said Drew, defensively. "Besides, how am I supposed to know where everyone is? I doubt you're still living in the barn."

Mickey looked at him with a stern face that transformed into an easy laugh and, placing an arm across Drew's shoulders, nudged him towards the bar.

"Come on, I'll buy you a drink."

Drew didn't have an appetite for a drink, or the bar, but accepted the offer from his old friend.

As Mickey and Drew entered Mack's, the noise within spilled out onto the street, banishing the evening's peacefulness. Standing at the entrance they were enveloped by the hot, moist stench of beer and cigarettes mixed with the raucous sound of the stereo playing Led Zeppelin's 'Immigrant Song'. Mickey threw up his arms, bellowing like a ring announcer as he held up Drew's right hand.

"Hey, everyone, look who's back! Drew Parsons!"

Most of the patrons didn't take notice and, of those who did, many were not familiar to Drew. The smattering of greetings which came in reply was mixed with a few jeers.

"Ah, fuck them, let's get some beer," Mickey said pointing to a table.

Ignoring his other friends, Mickey led Drew to a table in the far corner, ordering two beers as they passed Jerry, the bartender. Sitting at the table, they wriggled off their jackets and stared at each other for several seconds, Mickey slowly shaking his head and displaying his oblique grin.

"Shit!"

"What?"

"I can't believe you're back. It has been a long, fucking, time."

Drew chortled, "Believe me, I know."

"Did you see much of Lorne while inside?"

Drew gave a vague shrug.

"In juvie I saw him around but we didn't spend a lot of time together. He got in with a group of guys who were a bunch of shit stains. I basically stayed to myself. Then, when I was transferred to The Pen, he was still under eighteen so he stayed behind. He never was transferred there. I don't know where he ended up."

There was another long pause.

"So, what have you been doing since I was sent away?"

"Oh, I've been doing this and that. I'm now living in town with my girl, Christa. We have a kid named Buck.

Working for a buddy doing lawn care and snow removal. Been fuckin' busy."

Natasha, their server, pirouetting with the ease of a music box dancer around the barroom tables and patrons, made her way to them.

"Two beers," she said, bending over and placing them on the table while shooting Mickey a mischievous smile, her tight shirt only just able to contain her abundant milky-white cleavage behind its strained buttons.

"Should I just run you and your handsome friend here a tab?"

Mickey winked, "And keep 'em coming."

"Oh, I'd like to," she smiled, looking at Drew.

The two of them laughed. Drew glanced back to Mickey, a little uncomfortable with the conversation.

As Natasha turned to leave, Mickey gave her a slap on the ass then ignored the steely look she threw at him before she dissolved back into the crowd.

"She pretends not to, but I know she likes my attention - and my cock." He laughed, grabbing his crotch.

Drew smiled. "I can buy my own, Mickey, I have..."

Mickey threw up his hand, palm toward Drew.

"I don't want to quibble," he retorted in a questionable British accent.

Mickey didn't seem that far removed from the boy Drew first met. Though taller, he was still diminutive, and his long, sandy hair remained as unkempt as Drew remembered. With eyes that dripped of seal pup innocence, he could get caught in the midst of stealing and give a look that would make his accusers question their own senses. His demeanour was loud and brash but sociable; he could start or calm a fight with equal efficacy.

Drew nursed each beer as long as possible not wanting to risk the inhibitions of drunkenness. Mickey felt no such restraint.

"So, what was it like in The Pen? I mean I did a bit of juvie time but, fuck, that's gotta be nothing like The House. Is it like what you hear about? You know, the gangs, guys getting stuck, little guys being big guys' fuckin' bitches? Jesus, just the thought of it makes my fuckin' skin crawl."

Drew gave a passing smile.

"Yeah, it had its share of shit but I tried to keep my nose clean. I can handle myself with fists but fists don't help much when the other guy has a shank."

Drew spoke some more about his time in the penitentiary while Mickey sat with his chin on his hand and looked at Drew, enthralled as a child listening to a grandparent telling stories of his time in the war.

"Luckily for me, I met a veteran in there who took me under his wing. Not Shawshank Redemption-style with sneaking stuff in, but a guy who made me see things straight and encouraged me to grow to my potential. He taught me that I have to take chances and, sometimes, fall down and that you can't learn from your successes without the balance of failure. But most importantly, to realize that prison was not where I wanted to be."

None of that seemed to interest Mickey.

"What was his name and what was he in for?"

"John. Armed robbery."

Drew stopped for a few moments; a contemplative look crossing his face. Then he continued.

"I took courses, got my grade twelve and started taking university classes, discovered a passion in something and want to find a job in that area. I am a different person than I was when I started my sentence."

"Uh-huh...sure," Mickey replied, blasé. Then his face brightened, "Hey, did you see any guys get killed? In The Pen, I mean."

"Yeah, but I don't want to talk about that."

Drew began stripping the label off his beer bottle, clenching his teeth and pursing his lips.

Mickey sensed his discomfort.

"Sorry, buddy. Fuck, I can guess it musta been scary shit."

Drew nodded.

Another awkward pause ensued.

"So, Muscles got arrested a few months ago for a bunch of abductions and rapes. It looks like he's in deep shit. Word is they got loads of DNA evidence against him. Could be lookin' at life if he gets convicted. That's fucked up, man."

Good, the misogynistic bastard deserves it. He's as guilty as sin, thought Drew.

"Yeah, brutal. Hey, what happened to Kat? She still around?"

"Naw, her parents up and moved about six months after you went to jail. Probably a good thing. Last I heard she was somewhere up north and going to university. That's almost as fucked up as Muscles. I mean, who would have thought Kat could be so smart?"

Drew cocked an eyebrow giving a disdainful look, a gesture Mickey took no notice of.

As the night wore on, Drew and Mickey reminisced about their times together and recounted their lives over the past seven years; Mickey with great details, Drew with very few, preferring to let Mickey do the talking. Much, yet little, had changed. Mickey was still involved in petty crime and even now talked about getting drunk on the weekends and fighting.

At twelve forty-five, Jerry gave last call.

As they stood to leave, Mickey lost his balance and only Drew's quick response prevented Mickey's face from hitting the floor.

"Fuck me, thanks man." he garbled, drool slipping out the side of his mouth.

"No problem. Do up your jacket, it's cool out."

Mickey's friends appeared and offered to take him off of Drew's hands with a promise to get him home. Drew nodded and handed him over relieved that they were around to help out.

As they walked toward the door of the bar, Mickey turned to Drew, his eyes devoid of focus.

"Fuck, Drew buddy, it's great seeing you. We'll have to get together and stir up some shit, just like the good old days," he slurred.

Drew offered an ambiguous smile and proceeded towards the exit.

Outside the bar, Drew looked on as Mickey's friends escorted him towards their waiting cars, all swaying the same dance of intoxication. Their shouts and laughter were soon absorbed by the damp, heavy air as they rounded the corner and went out of sight. The last voice Drew heard was Mickey's.

"Fuck..."

Just then it struck Drew that the bench he was sitting on earlier in the evening was the same one where he first met Mickey.

Much, yet very little, has changed.

Drew shook his head and with the twitch of a smile, turned up his collar and started heading home.

The night was starless; fog had rolled in after sunset, replacing the clouds, its opaqueness obscuring the sky above. The wind had dropped but so had the temperature. As he traipsed up the hill in the direction of his home, Drew's hot breath steamed from his mouth and dropped towards the ground under the weight of the miasma. The prickle of cold, clammy air coaxed him to pick up his pace. Halfway up the gradient, Drew stopped and took another glance back. Sadly, the town below looked even more beleaguered through the muted, monochromatic veil of mist.

When Drew entered the house he was confronted by his mother, arms crossed and stress displayed on her face.

"Where have you been?"

"Out. I told you I was going to be gone for a while."

"You did not tell us where or when you expected to be home. Andrew, I was worried sick. And your father was not very pleased when he left for work. It angered him to see me so troubled and upset by your absence."

Drew looked at her with his eyes opened wide and brows raised in absolute disbelief.

"Why? Is that his domain?"

"Andrew Parsons!"

"Jesus, mom, how can you defend him? With all the shit that has happened within these walls, the abuse that he has inflicted upon us, it's a wonder neither one of us has died."

"That is enough with the vulgarities. Your father may be..."

"My *adoptive* father! Remember, I am not of your blood, I'm the scraps you picked up."

As suddenly as he had blurted out the words, Drew felt a black guilt envelop him.

Tears spilled from his mother's eyes.

Drew reached out to her but she backed away as if disgusted by his gesture. He felt a boulder in his stomach.

"Mom, I'm so sorry, it's just that..."

"I do not want your excuses. I may not have birthed you but I have always loved you and protected you as if you *are* my flesh and blood. I would die for you. You are my son. Mine. No one else's. I am not stupid or ignorant of the failings of the family, and especially of your father. I am the buffer between you and him, the one who gives this household some semblance of normalcy. I am not here for your father, but for you, my son, knowing that you would return and that I would have to protect you again. But I am tired, so very tired. For so long I have not lived, but merely existed.

"And you may think your father is the only abuser in this house but you are wrong. Dropping out of school..." Jean hit her chest with the palm of her hand, "...the drinking and drugs..." now punching her chest with a closed fist. "The crimes you committed." More strikes to the chest. "All of those things you did and who was it you were hurting?"

She continued hitting her chest at a more frenetic tempo, sobbing uncontrollably. "It was me you abused, me....me...."

Drew moved quickly to grab her wrists. As he held on, his mother collapsed to the floor.

"Why? Why?" she cried out.

Jean emitted a moan that seemed to come from the depths of her being; the result of a lifetime of agony.

Drew kneeled on the floor and took her in his arms. Gently he kissed her on the forehead then on each cheek. Tenderly he spoke.

"I love you, mom, and am sorry for having been so terrible to you. My past can't be changed but the person before you, here, now, can. And I want you to realize that you don't have to protect me any longer. You have been there for me my entire life, but it's time to let me go; look after yourself. This household is not safe, not with him. It won't be easy but it's time for me to help and protect you. Please know that I will."

His mother did not respond but continued with an uncontrolled glottal sobbing that ripped at him.

Drew continued to hold his mother, delicately stroking her hair until she stopped crying and, eventually, fell asleep.

"Shhh...everything will be fine."

They remained entangled on the living room floor until the first gilded tentacles of daybreak emerged to burn away the enduring, grey night.

CHAPTER SIX

Disappointingly, the start of his second year in high school was a carry-over from grade nine during which Drew's grades suffered from his apathy and truancy. The hostile behaviour he demonstrated throughout his first year of high school was getting worse and his violent outbursts had driven away his friends. Even his closest friend, Jim, whom he had known since kindergarten, no longer wanted to be seen with Drew. He was now an outsider.

It was only the fifth week of grade ten and, though he had seldom attended classes, Drew had already been involved in several fights on the school grounds. In the most recent brawl he had broken the other student's nose.

At home, the situation was hardly better. Drew consistently ignored household rules and showed cold indifference or outright contempt to his parents. The few interactions he had with his father were fraught with anger and conflict. Drew often missed dinner, not returning home until late in the evenings, after his father had gone to work or the bar. The times he was home, Drew avoided him.

Drew had grown to nearly six feet tall and developed a sinewy, muscular build. He carried an aggression that was menacing. In the hallways of the school, students would avoid him, allowing a wide swath as he passed.

Drew and his parents sat outside the principal's office, having been summoned to deal with the most recent occurrences. The door opened to the principal's office and Mr. McMichael walked out to meet them.

He was a tall, heavy-set middle aged gentleman with a short, silver and pepper afro, a closely-cropped beard, and black, thick-rimmed glasses, and, though he smiled as he met them, Mr. McMichael was known for his serious but fair approach to discipline. He welcomed the Parsons, inviting them into the office.

"Please have a seat," he said, closing the door behind them.

"Mr. Parsons, Mrs. Parsons and Andrew, I'm going to get right to the point. We have come to a crossroad. Between the teachers and me, you have been contacted several times since the start of the school year about Drew's behaviour. He's been involved in numerous fights, is truant as often as he has been to class and hasn't been completing his homework or assignments. Starting today he will be suspended for one week as a result of the most recent fight he was involved in last Friday."

Drew sat hunched down in his seat stoic: arms crossed, looking at Principal McMichael with his eyelids half closed, a slight sneer to his lips and head tilted towards his right shoulder: A 'fuck you' look.

Principal McMichael turned to Drew.

"Andrew, I want you to take the time to think about what you want out of life. Your schooling is the foundation for what you do as an adult and, without those building blocks, success in life can be very difficult."

Drew continued to stare, unresponsive.

"I'm going to ask you to wait outside while I speak to your parents. You can sit in the chair in the office and your parents will be out in a few minutes. And, please, reflect on what I just said to you."

Drew stood up from the chair. As he sauntered from the office, he swung the door open and left it that way.

Principal McMichael rose from his chair and closed the door before returning to his seat.

"And what happens while he is out of school?" William snorted, "If truancy is a problem, how will a suspension benefit him? My wife works during the day and I work shifts; so either I'm not home or will be sleeping during the day between my night shifts. We won't be there to keep him in line."

"Mr. Parsons, it's not just about the truancy, it's about his attitude and disruptive behaviour in the school. He is an intimidating presence here, even for some of the teachers. Have you considered seeking therapy for Andrew?"

William let out a huff, crossing his arms as he leaned back in his chair.

"Therapy? He ain't crazy!"

Jean sat silent, nervously fussing with the tissue she had in her hands which rested on her lap.

"Mr. Parsons, it appears that something has happened to change Andrew. I have been in contact with the elementary school he attended and the report I received indicates he was an excellent student who was very intelligent and had good grades and no behaviour issues. Do you know what could have caused such a considerable change in his attitude and behaviour?"

William narrowed his eyes looking toward the ceiling while rubbing his chin between his thumb and index finger. Then he refocused on Principal McMichael.

"Nope, I can't think of nothing that could've caused this," he replied dismissively.

Hesitantly, Jean spoke.

"At the beginning of last school year, he found out that he was adopted. Not too long after, his behaviour started to change at home. He became more rebellious and combative, and his school studies began to suffer."

William looked at her, a stern expression on his face. Jean, feeling the weight of his glare, went back to fiddling with her tissue.

"No, he said he was fine with finding out that he was adopted. I think it has to do with this school and the kids who go here. This attitude didn't start until he began attending here."

"Yes, you are probably right," she replied demurely.

Principal McMichael leaned forward in his seat, interlacing his hands on the desk before him. A frown creased his brow; he looked over the rim of his glasses, focusing squarely on William.

"Mr. Parsons, to blame the school and the other students for Andrew's attitude and behaviour is disingenuous. This school fundamentally believes in, and teaches, respect and discipline and offers its students an open and welcoming learning environment. His behaviour has gone far beyond what we consider acceptable. During last school year and this year we have tried to assist him by offering alternative learning classes and visits from guidance but he rejects any assistance. Next spring he turns sixteen. If his bad behaviour continues, I will have no choice but to expel him. We have done what we can for Andrew; can you say the same thing?"

Without taking his eyes off of Principal McMichael, William stood, motioning at Jean to follow him.

"Come on, Jean, I believe this meeting is over."

Following William from the principal's office, Jean turned back to Principal McMichael, extending her hand to him, but was unable to look in his eyes.

"Thank you, we will have to consider what to do about Andrew."

Shaking Jean's hand, Principal McMichael looked at her, dolefully.

"Mrs. Parsons, if there is anything I can do to help you..."

She bowed her head slightly, before turning and disappearing out the door.

The drive back to their house was a continuation of what had gone on so often over the past year.

"You sure continue to make us proud, boy. What next, a school desk through a class window? How about you skip all the small stuff and go directly to burning the school to the ground?"

"I know, dad, I'm a disgrace to the family. Don't worry, it won't be long before you don't have to care for me anymore; when I'm sixteen you can kick me out of the house. Wipe your hands clean of your adoptive child. Like a wise man once told me, you 'picked up the scraps.' Soon you can toss them."

"Don't be a smart-ass, boy."

"It's better than being a dumb-ass, *dad.*"

William was red with anger but didn't respond.

Jean stared off into the distance, her eyes vacuous.

The remainder of the drive was done in strained silence.

Drew skipped dinner and, instead, wandered down to Main St. It was a moonless evening. While cool and clear, there was a heavy vaulted cloud cover which lurked in the west, blocking out the last vestiges of daylight and hastily bringing on the darkness.

Approaching the middle of town Drew came across a bench on the sidewalk. He sat down, withdrew a cigarette from the pack in his jacket pocket and lit it.

He had been sitting on the bench for a short while, immersed in thought, when he was brought back to the present by a strange voice.

"Hey man, you look lost."

Drew looked up to see a small, wiry kid.

"Mind if I sit here?" He flopped himself on the bench beside Drew as if he were exhausted.

"Do I have a choice?" Drew replied, rhetorically.

"My name is Brian, but my friends call me Mickey – after the mouse.

Drew didn't respond. There was a long pause as Mickey sat studying Drew, trying to figure out where he had seen him before.

"Hey, ain't you the guy who got into that fucking fight at school last week?"

"Yeah, why? You have an issue with that?"

"Whoa, fuck, no." Mickey threw his hands up in surrender. "I was there when it started. You beat the shit out of that poor fucker. Man it was sweet," Mickey sparred into the open space in front of him bobbing and weaving between punches. "You must've broke his fuckin' nose, there was so much blood. Fuck me, where you learn to fight like that?"

"My father."

Drew chuckled to himself as he thought about the absurdity of what he had just said.

"That's cool, wish my old man taught me to fight like that. Fuck!" Mickey continued sparring.

Drew didn't reply but remained staring ahead, blowing smoke into thc evening sky.

"Hey, can I bum a cigarette off ya? I ran out and I ain't got the fuckin' bucks to buy more."

Drew handed Mickey the pack and his lighter. Mickey took a cigarette out, lit it and handed both items back to Drew.

"Thanks. Hey, that's a wicked, fucking scar you got there. Was that from a fight, too?"

"You could say that. Obviously, I lost that one."

Silence. Minutes passed as both occupied themselves with their cigarettes.

"Well, as far as I'm concerned, fighting is the only fuckin' thing school is good for. I go but I don't, you know what I mean?"

Drew sat quietly.

Mickey continued, "My fuckin' parents are all over me about my skipping but I don't give a shit. I would rather hang out with my friends getting all fucked up. We hang out and drink or smoke up. Sometimes we stir up shit in the city when we need the money to keep the fuckin' bar stocked, if you get my drift."

Drew gave a slight nod and smile as he flicked his cigarette butt onto the roadway.

"Hey, you're pretty fucking cool, you want to come to the farm and meet my buddies? You'll like 'em, they're fuckin' chilled."

"The farm?"

"Yeah, we have this little farm, just outside of town that way," Mickey said while pointing west, "and we hang there. It ain't much but, fuck, it's better than nothing."

Though they had talked for less than half an hour, there was something about Mickey's enthusiastic personality that Drew liked. He considered the offer for only a few moments before agreeing to go.

They walked for fifteen minutes. Fifteen minutes of Mickey skipping along, prattling machinegun fast and accompanied by exaggerated gesticulating. Drew simply nodded periodically.

The lights of the town faded until they were no brighter than the stars above, shimmering celestially against the obsidian night sky.

In due course, as they approached an intersection, Mickey pointed.

"The farm is just ahead on the left."

Skirting past a large hedgerow which obstructed the sidewalk, the two turned up a driveway. Hidden behind five large spruce trees, a mansion materialized from the darkness. Though he had heard about it, Drew had never seen the house. It was at the top of a long circular driveway and stood poised with the majesty of a lion. On the front lawn rose a twenty foot tall Lateran obelisk fashioned after the famous monolith in Vatican City. Drenched by the floodlights at its base, it was an exact replica, from the encryptions along the four sides of its plinth up to the cross at its apex. Overlooking it was the extravagant manor. Sublime in its gaudiness, the estate had marble front steps, which fanned out at the bottom, leading to a portico of four Corinthian columns adorned with statues of nymphs. They supported a large gabled roof with a neoclassic sculpture depicting the last supper on the pediment above a marble terrace. The front double-doors had stained glass windows showing the hands of God and Adam; copied from the ceiling of the Sistine Chapel. The lights from inside the house emitted a translucent glow that gave the images on the door an even greater angelic quality. The windows on the main floor were large and arched with cherubs decorating the top of the arcs. Drew had never seen such architecture; he was mesmerized by it.

He felt a tug at his arm.

"Come on," Mickey urged, "I know all this shit must be real fuckin' fascinating, but we gotta get to the farm before the fuckin' rain starts."

Mickey led Drew past the mansion, through the autumn corn field and into a stand of more spruce trees. The night had become so black Drew had involuntarily opened his eyes wide in an attempt to see in front of himself. The only sounds he could hear were the rustling of the corn stocks and tree branches as they brushed against his clothing. Nestled amongst the trees, and in contrast to the mansion they had just passed, was a decrepit barn, scarcely illuminated by a nearby streetlight.

Looking at the structure, Drew wondered how it remained standing. Wooden walls were rotting and encumbered with vines snaking through the planks. The building leaned as if it was facing a strong wind and the windows had long been broken. Where the roof still remained, it drooped like a hydro wire between poles along the side of the road, and had gaps between its tresses. Inside was squalid, everything appeared covered in hay dust and smelling of feces and urine, which Drew hoped had come from the farm animals. Four candles occupied the corners offering diffused light. To the left of the entrance was a ladder that rose to a small loft where hay rested.

As Drew's eyes readjusted from the darkness to inside the barn, he noticed three individuals seated on makeshift chairs of old tires and wood slabs which encircled a small fire. They were passing around a joint.

Mickey cleared his throat to draw their attention.

"Guys, I want you to meet...Fuck, I don't know your name."

"Drew."

"Yeah," Mickey responded as though confirming it, while pointing a wagging finger at him.

"Guys, Drew. He's the guy I told you about who beat the shit out of some poor fucker at school. And he's a pretty fuckin' cool guy."

He turned to Drew and gave an impish smile.

"Let me introduce them, Drew."

Pointing to the slight figure on the right, Mickey introduced Lorne Jacoby. He had just taken a toke of the joint and was trying to casually suppress a cough. To Lorne's right was Steven Wilford. With the body of a Mr. Universe, he went by the uninspired nickname, Muscles. Finally, Mickey introduced Katherine "Kat" Clark. She was Muscles girlfriend.

All three acknowledged Drew before Muscles motioned for them to sit down.

The group talked - though Drew mostly just listened - and drank and smoked up through the night. Drew was able to make a quick assessment of the hierarchy within the group, immediately determining that Muscles was the group leader.

Muscles was glib and charming but, while his smile came easy, there was insincerity about him. Like Drew's father, Muscles seemed to anger quickly, especially, it seemed to Drew, when he was challenged by Kat. He was eighteen years old and stood slightly less than six feet tall with short bleach-blond hair and impenetrable, dark blue eyes. The mansion they had passed belonged to his parents, his father a renowned lawyer and his mother a popular news anchor. Muscles knew that his parents' standing in the community could be advantageous to him, and, as such, carried himself with the cocksureness of a prize fighter.

Drew recognized Kat from one of the few classes he had attended. She, too, was fifteen years old. Her long brown hair framed a pallid featureless face, save for her fern-green eyes. She carried a thin formless figure and had small breasts. She didn't say much but, when she did, Drew sensed that she was not obtuse. Kat had been Muscles girlfriend for four months. They met at a party and, after getting her drunk, Muscles brought her back to the barn where she had her first sexual experience; though, Kat would later admit, she remembered little of it.

Lorne Jacoby was fourteen years old though he would be turning fifteen in December. He was small, scrawny and ashen skinned with a pimply, freckled face and washed out green eyes which blinked neurotically. His auburn hair was cut short, military style. It seemed his involvement with the group was predicated on his ability to supply them with beer and marijuana that he would get from his older brother. Drew noticed that Lorne would often look to Muscles for acknowledgement or approval. Unfortunately, for Lorne, Muscles was indifferent and, in effect, didn't even respond to him. In vain attempts to impress, Lorne often made references to guns his family owned, which the others in the group off-handedly dismissed as empty rhetoric.

The cloud cover which had been far off when the night began was now directly overhead. A rumble of thunder introduced the impending storm. When the rain began it breached the barn through the gaping holes in the roof and hit the ground with the patter of mice scurrying across a wooden floor. Soon, however, it turned into a deluge. The only shelter the barn provided was under the loft where the group huddled together to stay dry. Though it didn't last long, the torrent was enough to extinguish the candles and small fire.

Muscles summoned Mickey and Drew.

"See if you can find some dry hay for a new fire. Lorne will get some wood. Kat and I will wait here."

Drew looked over at Kat who seemed as if she was at the point of passing out, an uncontrolled bob to her head.

Mickey grabbed Drew by the arm and left the protection of the loft to begin searching. Water was still trickling from the wood planks above.

"Let's go to the back of the barn, Drew," Mickey whispered. "Muscles wants some alone time with Kat."

"Alone time? She looks like she needs a night's sleep to sober up."

As they walked, Drew looked back and observed that Lorne, Muscles and Kat were nowhere to be seen. He continued to follow Mickey to the back of the barn.

Towards the rear wall, where wooden skeletons of stalls remained, Drew was barely able to make out a clump of hay on the dirt floor. As he lifted the top layer to determine whether any dry hay remained below it, he caught sight of something that made him jump back.

"What the fuck!"

On the ground lay the carcass of an eviscerated, decomposing cat, writhing with maggots, its fur sheared off and its stench gagging. Drew buried his nose in the crux of his elbow to ward off the assault.

Mickey laughed, though he too had to pinch off his nose against the smell.

"Relax; it's just a fucking cat...well, was a cat. Muscles told us he found it injured so he put it out of its misery."

"How did he do that, by skinning the fucking thing?"

Mickey shrugged then knelt closer to the body.

"Fucked if I know. Ah, Jesus, I just got a taste in my mouth."

He stood up, spat on the cat and walked away to look for more kindling.

Drew began searching around for a shovel to pick up the remains when he found the cat's pelt nailed to the back wall. He pulled it down from the wall and examined it, noticing that the skinning was done by a person who had perfected the craft. Drew tossed it on the floor near the carcass. He found a shovel in one of the stalls, scooped up the maggot-infested body and carried it along with the pelt out to the woods behind the barn where he buried them. As Drew would later discover, this was not the only animal remains which had been skinned.

When he returned, twenty minutes later, there was a fire going. Kat and Lorne were not there. Muscles and Mickey sat near the new fire.

"Where'd Kat and Lorne go?"

Without looking up from the fire Muscles responded indifferently, "In the loft."

Drew looked perplexed but Mickey signalled that he would explain later. Drew nodded and sat down.

From the loft, Lorne could be heard grunting; Kat didn't make a sound.

As the first pall of dawn broke through the blackness in the east, Drew left the barn and headed back home.

"Hey, can I crash at your place? I got no fuckin' way of getting home," Mickey asked.

Drew waved Mickey to join him.

As they arrived at the road, Drew turned to Mickey with the perplexed look back on his face.

"So, what was going on with Lorne and Kat?"

"After Muscles finishes fuckin' Kat, he will sometimes share her with us. Tonight was Lorne's turn."

"And she doesn't have a problem with that?"

Mickey snorted, "I've never heard her complain."

They walked for a while without speaking. Drew thought about the evening and the new acquaintances he had made and decided, for the most part, he liked them. There was still something about Muscles, though, which made Drew uneasy.

"Well, I'm guessin' that you can be part of our gang if you want to. I can tell you'll fit in good here, and you look like you would have fun doin' the shit we pull and you can really handle yourself; the fight I saw you in at school showed me that. Muscles seems to like you good enough and the others do too."

Drew gave no reply.

"Hey, if I got it figured out right, you're suspended for a while and I need some fuckin' vacation days off, so how 'bout we go stir up some shit in the city this week? Maybe we can hang out at the barn and get fuckin' wasted; just me, you and Muscles."

Mickey paused to allow Drew to respond. When he didn't Mickey continued.

"Muscles was saying we need to get some money because we are running out of beer and pot, and I know a few places we can hit where the money is easy fuckin' pickin's."

Drew nodded in agreement though he wasn't sure he was comfortable with the idea of committing theft.

As strands of golden sunlight inched above the horizon to illuminate the streets, Drew and Mickey entered Drew's house.

In Drew's bedroom, Mickey grabbed the top cover from the bed and lay down on the carpet. Before Drew was under the sheets Mickey fell asleep, mumbling between his light snores.

Drew looked at him and couldn't help but laugh.

Holy crap, even in his sleep.

CHAPTER SEVEN

"Mom. Dad. I want to talk to you about something; something that I have been thinking about for quite a while; something that I need to do." Drew looked at them with a suggestion of apprehension on his face.

Jean looked up from her breakfast wondering what Drew was talking about. William continued eating.

"What is it Andrew?" she asked.

Drew glanced down at his glass of juice, taking time to mull his words over carefully before he continued.

"I was once told by a friend in jail that a person's life is influenced by others he has in it. And, as an extension of that, when people who should be in his life are missing, a part of him is missing. He is incomplete."

Both of his parents were now looking at him with questioning expressions.

"I feel like I am incomplete, a part of me is missing. That part, I believe, is my biological parents. And I have come to the conclusion that that missing element of my life needs to be addressed. So it's my intention to discover who my biological parents are."

William and Jean's expressions transfigured from curiosity to stupefaction. Several seconds passed. Drew sat patiently waiting for them to grasp and reconcile what he had just said.

During the nine years since he had learned of his adoption, when he was fourteen, Drew hadn't so much as mentioned his biological parents, let alone asked anything about them.

At last, his father put his coffee cup down on the table.

"Why do you need to find them? It isn't like they were ever in your life. Remember, they are the ones who tossed you aside as a baby."

Jean still hadn't moved, shock and dread marking her face.

"That may be so, but it doesn't negate the fact they are still my parents; maybe not my mom and dad, but my parents none-the-less. Given that fact, I want to discover who I am, and knowing who my birth-parents are is part of that puzzle; because they are part of me; part of my history, my ancestry. Not having them in my life leaves a hole that needs to be filled. I'm uncertain how or if they will fill it but I will never know if I don't pursue this. What you, as my adoptive parents, have given me is an upbringing, but that doesn't answer the question of my history; doesn't fill that blank."

"And your upbringing isn't good enough for you? Without *that* upbringing you would have had no future," William said sternly. "We have provided you with a home. We put a roof over your head, food in your stomach and clothing on your back. We gave you opportunities to succeed and you threw it all away by getting involved with that bunch of bloody degenerates you called friends. Now you come back home and we welcome you with open arms, like the prodigal son. And this is how you repay all that? By telling us you want to find the people who abandoned you?"

"Don't think I'm not very appreciative of what you have done for me, dad," Drew said half in earnest, "but I need to know their circumstances. I need to find out why they felt it necessary to abandon me, to give me up for adoption. I need to know what their story is, their history, and I want to be a part of that and for that to be part of me."

"And, what about us, do we not matter? Have you not considered your mother and me in this equation, boy? How we'd feel about it?"

Drew lurched up from the table and walked away a few paces with his arms raised in frustration before turning toward his parents and dropping them down to his sides.

"Jesus Christ, dad, why do you have to make this about the two of you? This isn't about you at all. I need to do this. This is for me. Who was Andrew David Parsons before he was adopted by William and Jean Parsons? I'm not your son, remember? So, I should find out whose son I am. And I'm not asking for your blessing, this is going to happen whether you are supportive or not."

William looked over to Jean for support before turning back to Drew with an icy glare.

Jean stood up from the table and walked to Drew, placing her hands on his chest. In silence, William looked at her, rank with anger and disappointment.

"Andrew, you have to understand that what you just told us is so sudden."

"I do understand that, mom."

"We had no idea you wanted to do this. You have to give us time to come to terms with it. Your dad is just trying..."

"I don't need you speaking for me, woman," William interrupted, almost growling. "What I'm trying to do is to figure out what you expect to get out of this."

"What I expect? I just finished telling you. Christ, were you not listening?"

His father rose and took a step toward him but Drew did not flinch. William wouldn't intimidate him any longer. If he needed to, Drew would stand up to him no matter what came of it. Jean turned to William.

"Stop this now, both of you. You are both acting like little children. William, please, sit back down; Andrew, you as well. Go on, sit."

The two continued to glower for several moments before Drew, with a sigh, agreed to sit back at the table. William also sat back down. Jean took her seat between the two of them then turned and looked at Drew.

"Have you started to look for them?"

"No, I wanted to speak with the two of you first, to see if there is anything you can tell me about the adoption."

"Well, let me think about it. I am sure we can help you."

She looked to William for consent. William glanced at her disgusted before he peered down into his coffee cup, a frown on his face, shaking his head.

"Thanks mom, maybe you can help." Drew removed a lined sheet of paper from his shirt pocket, unfolded and began to examine it. The paper contained a list of information he was looking for.

"How about we start off with the basic questions; maybe at the beginning there is something you can tell me about them. Do you know their names? Where they lived? The hospital where I was born?"

"It was a long time ago," she chewed the corner of her bottom lip for a few seconds, her brow wrinkled.

"You were born at Grace Hospital. Their last name was Coburn, or something along those lines. I remember they were young and were going to get, or had just been, married, but neither of them was working and they weren't in a position to take care of you. She was a cute thing and he was taller than you but thinner. I think they came from the city, they were not local. As I recall, neither was a very nice person, and were often in trouble with the police. She, in particular, was not someone you would want to associate with. Unfortunately, my memory about the rest is foggy. We became your guardians when you were thirteen months old, then, about a year later, adopted you. The process was long but we had very little direct contact with them, especially me. Most of the procedure took place through the courts. I think you will have to go into the court records to find anything about them."

Drew pulled his wallet from his pocket, removed the picture and showed his mother.

"Is that him; is that my biological father?"

"Yes, that picture was taken when you were about thirteen months old. They had to give you up not too long after."

"And there is no picture of my birth mom?"

"No. They put two pictures in your file. The one of you and your mother was lost at some point but I kept this one. I placed it in your shirt pocket on the night of your sixth birthday as you lay asleep in your bed."

The memory of finding it the morning after his birthday, flashed in Drew's memory. He gave a reflective look at it before placing the picture back in his wallet.

"Why'd you give it to me?"

"I do not know, really. I just thought you would like the present. And you did, you were so excited the next morning when you showed it to me. When I mentioned that I gave it to you, you hugged me until I had to break away from you. When you asked me about whose lap you were on, I told you it was my younger brother. I felt you were too young to understand what being adopted meant. You just marched back up to your room and set it on your bedside table."

"You mean the brother who later died?"

"Yes."

Jean paused looking at William then continued talking to Drew.

"It was like the picture had lifted your spirits so much you forgot about the events of the day before and the pain you were suffering."

"When were you planning on telling me I was adopted? If not at six, or ten or even fourteen, what did you think would be the right age for me to learn of it?"

My intention was to tell you as an eighteenth birthday present. At that age you clearly understand what an adoption was. Of course your father's actions changed that plan."

Drew's smile evaporated, replaced by disdain as he looked over at his adoptive father and recalled the beatings he had taken. Immediately Drew felt a soupçon of resentment towards William.

William looked at Jean and shook his head in disbelief.

"Really? You had to bring all that up?" He gave a scornful, brusque laugh.

Jean ignored him and remained focused on Drew.

"Is there any more that you can remember, mom?"

"No, sorry. Your father might remember more. He did most of the communicating with social services and the agencies involved. He should still have the documents from the adoption. He used to keep them in a strong box."

"Dad, is there any more you can remember, or information you can give me?"

They both looked at William who didn't reply. Instead he continued to fixate on his mug, lightly circling the rim with his index finger, the scowl still on his face.

"Well, thanks anyway, *mom*." He hadn't taken his eyes off his father.

Drew got up from the table and pushed in his chair. Picking up the piece of paper he placed it back in his wallet. He walked out to the backyard, closing the kitchen door behind him.

The air was cold and the sharp chill gripped Drew's face as his breath steamed from his mouth. He folded his arms tightly across his chest in a futile attempt to repel the bitter morning air as he crossed the frosty back deck. The backyard sparkled in a pixie-dust layer of rime, a gift from the foggy, frigid night.

As the morning sun elevated above the eastern cloud cover, watery pearls formed and dripped from the leafless branches of the maple tree to the crystalline ground below, which remained in the shadows. The resulting sound reminded Drew of the splash of water drops as the background for a song in the movie 'Bambi'.

Sitting on a porch chair, Drew closed his eyes and let himself become draped in the warmth of the rising sun.

He took a deep breath, trying to clear his head and relax himself.

All the acrimony, all the tension that goes on within the framework of this family: the subjugation of mom; the unprovoked hostility shown by dad. I can't continue living in this situation. It's now time to shit or get off the pot. Drew laughed to himself. *Or, like dad's friend, Steve, use to say: 'It's time to defecate or abdicate.'*

Drew had made up his mind: he needed to move out of the house.

In the kitchen, William continued to nurse his coffee while Jean cleared the table, scraping the food leftovers from the dishes into the compost bin. Her silence was conspicuous, her bitterness acute.

"Why could you not give Andrew some information? It will tell him virtually nothing, but even a bit of insight would have satisfied him."

William looked up at Jean, truculent.

Have you remembered nothing about our pact? He thought.

"So you want to pamper the boy as usual."

William stared intently into Jean's eyes.

"Besides, what makes you think I even have the paperwork? Hell, for all you know I got rid of it years ago? I mean, it's not like we needed to keep it, given the situation."

Jean scoffed in disbelief despite her misgivings about William's assertion.

"Oh, please, stop being so dramatic, I am not pampering Andrew," Jean said dismissively, "Andrew is an adult, and will be a fine one at that."

"Yeah, of course, after all, we raised him." William chuckled.

"What? You have never been a real father to him. Even now, being, and God only knows why, so confrontational." Her undertone was indignant, "I raised him. I devoted my life to caring for that boy."

"Oh right," William said, a turbulence of anger beginning to boil in him, "Raised him; more like asphyxiated him. Besides, what information could I offer him? I remember no more than you. And don't forget our roles: Good cop, bad cop, eh! You're the angel; I'm the mean old bastard."

"Well, you have the angel and old bastard part right."

William didn't respond, but sat glaring at his mug.

"William Parsons would you get over yourself," Jean scorned, her pitch rising.

"William Parsons would you get over yourself," he mocked, with face contorted, his voice nasally and his head tilting side to side as he spoke.

Jean stared at him with no kindness in her gaze.

"Oh, you poor thing, what a sad life you must have had; a wife who loved you, a child you could mentor and protect, to show right from wrong. A little boy you could have loved, if you were not so self-absorbed. Instead, you have sulked and lashed out; you berated and beat that precious, little child. And what did you ever do to encourage him? Nothing. You forced him from this house with your bullying attitude to seek friendship with those boys and because of that he ended up in jail."

"Bullshit. You mean a wife who pit..."

Jean raised her voice, cutting him off.

"And you never gave him the time he deserved, were never around. You chose to spend most of your free time carousing with your friends down at Mack's bar and coming home late."

"Yeah, right, sure like I could have spent more time with him. It's all me. My drinking, my time with friends," William retorted, a loathsome tenor coming through fissures in his voice, "You have contrived against me at every opportunity."

"How? How have I contrived against you?"

Again William gawked at her with disbelief. He shook his head and looked down at his now cold coffee still sitting on the table.

William took in and expelled a long, deep breath. "What's the point of this, Jean?" William's tone was conciliatory. "Look, I know the miscarriages, the spontaneous abortion, took their toll on you; on us. Too many of our children lost. Add to that your brother. He was..."

"Do not dare talk about my little brother. Andrew was only a child; a child in my care. And I could not protect him from a world so full of dangers."

"Jean, you were a child yourself. Eleven years old and left with the responsibility of watching over a four-year-old. How could you have known ice on that river was so thin? You were eleven, for Christ's sake. At that age you aren't thinking in degrees. You saw the ice; you'd seen people on it in the past. How could you've known that it would be thinner than earlier in the winter? If you had gone out to try to save him you'd have died as well. No, you can't blame yourself forever."

"Enough." The sorrow in Jean's voice and eyes etched a picture of the guilt she carried from that day.

William studied Jean for a few seconds. He wanted to hold her; to let her know he would be there for her. But he knew that she would reject his offer; reject him as she so often had during the past twenty-two years.

"What I'm trying to say is all that didn't matter to me as long as we had each other. All I needed, all I've ever needed, was you. But that did matter to you. You saw our relationship as cursed and when Drew came to us our lives changed, and not necessarily for the better. Despite my wish that we not adopt him, you insisted and I gave in hoping it would end the suffering. And that decision was one I immediately regretted. I saw from the first day, Jean, saw the changes. And looking at him every day reminded me of that blight I had to endure.

"During these last twenty-two years I couldn't be like you, would not love him the way you have. But I tried to love *you*. And for that I have been rebuked. But I raised Drew. Twenty-two years of my life went into raising a child whose existence was a slap in the face; a wedge in our lives."

William took a sip of his coffee, grimacing as the cold liquid sluiced through his mouth before being swallowed. He stood up from the table and walked to the sink, pouring the remaining swill down the drain. He looked back at Jean.

"And now he returns from jail a new man and we offer him the opportunity; the help to get him back on his fect. And what does he do? He tosses us aside because suddenly his birth parents are so important to him. But how do you respond?" William paused; giving Jean a chance to furnish what he saw was the obvious answer. Instead she looked at him stolidly. He shook his head and let out a defeated sigh.

"You treated him in a manner that didn't and shouldn't have surprised me; immediately wanting to indulge him, effectively putting me into a corner and making me look like an asshole."

"You are an asshole," she blurted.

Jean covered her mouth in astonishment at what she'd said, though, in her heart she knew she meant it.

"Well Jean, if this asshole pays the freight and holds the key, he is the asshole to make the decisions around here. I would gladly give it to him but for your sake I say NO!"

"William, you are behaving like a spoilt child who acts out when he does not get what he wants."

Has she heard nothing? William stared incredulously at Jean as she continued.

"You know, I have often thought that is exactly what you are; a little brat. All you have ever done is look at what you perceive you do not have, rather than delighting in that which you do. And in response you have belly-ached and wallowed in self pity. My goodness, Andrew conducts himself like more of an adult than you ever have. Here is a chance for you to prove your love, to get close to him; but you chose to stymie him, to scowl in your chair."

"Do you hear yourself, what you are saying? 'Little brat?' 'Prove my love? 'I stymie him?' My God, how can you foist all this on me? How can I 'perceive' what is so obvious? And let's not start talking about perception, Jean."

Then a thought struck him; one that William was sure would make Jean agree with his position.

"So you aren't concerned he will toss us aside like yesterday's toy?" William paused and shrugged his shoulders before he continued in a facile tone. "Hey, if that is what you really want. Of course I don't have it but, if I did, I could give it to him. I took lots of notes and have a pretty good recollection of everything that happened. I can talk to him and give him whatever I can remember."

Jean stared at him not entirely sure what William's intentions were and was bothered by that uncertainty. She chewed on her lower lip again.

"No, the more I think about it the less I believe it would be the correct decision. You are right. Besides, that would go against his birth parents wishes to remain anonymous. We best just leave the paperwork where you have it stored, in the strong box in the closet."

William nodded at her, "That sounds like a good plan."

A smile crept across his face as he walked past Jean and back to the table. His posture had taken on an element of self-assuredness.

Jean looked at him in his equanimity and smiled.

Yeah, you are in control, you strong man you.

As she left the kitchen Jean gave him a smug smile, exiting the front door to work on her garden in preparation for the following spring.

William poured himself half a cup of coffee and sat at the table looking out the window to where Drew relaxed on the porch. He reflected upon the conversation which had just taken place and how easily Jean gave into his way of thinking and the smile she presented him as she left the house. And suddenly his victory seemed inconsequential.

God damn it, what the fuck is she up to?

William's hands curled into fists and he slammed them on the table causing the dishes to jump and rattle in surprise.

After several minutes he got up from the table, leaving his coffee unfinished, and went upstairs to his bedroom. Taking the key from his drawer, he went to the closet and removed the strong box, placing it on the bed.

William returned to the main floor carrying a large manila envelope. Putting on his jacket, he slipped the envelope inside it and left the house through the front door, shaking his head disappointingly as he passed Jean, before he got into his car and drove away.

Drew had been on the back porch for almost an hour before re-entering the house, feeling a renewed sense of purpose. He put William's coffee mug in the sink then poured himself a coffee and walked into the living room. Looking out the front window he saw his mother pulling dead plants from the garden in preparation for her spring masterpiece. She waved and gave him a broad smile. He observed that there was something different about her bearing as she looked at him, but he was not able put words to it. Then he noticed that his father's car was not in the driveway. For that he was not ungrateful.

Sitting at the computer desk he took a sip of coffee and looked at the blank screen for several moments. He stood back up and paced around the living room for a few minutes before he went to the chest where the CDs were kept – after they were brought up from a box in the basement – and grabbed *Genesis Live.* He placed the CD in the disc drive of the computer and chose the fifth song. Sitting back in his chair he waited for it to start, his heart pounding.

Knife.

Knife.

The Knife.

Finally, with the crowd cheering and the initial driving notes blaring out of the speakers, after all his procrastinating, and with a hint of trepidation, Drew opened up the internet search engine to begin the journey of unearthing his history. Slowly he typed in the words:

'Finding Birth Parents.'

CHAPTER EIGHT

For two months following his introduction to the *Barn Brigade* – a name coined by Mickey - Drew spent a majority of his time hanging out with his new friends. He and Mickey had dropped out of school and, with Muscles, idled away most of their days crashed out at the barn in a drug or alcohol influenced state. The dynamics of the group had become routine, the oligarchy rigid; Muscles was in control, collecting the bounties from their petty crimes and making all the decisions for the group, leaving no opportunity for others to voice their ideas. Any attempt to deviate from the norm was countered with swift censure. While the others seemed comfortable with it, Drew found it disconcerting.

Muscles had cold, dead eyes behind which there seemed to be a hidden agenda. His comportment could change in an instant, from a sneering misanthrope to an effervescent fraternizer. He wouldn't pay any attention to the others unless he wanted something; then he would gregariously chat up whomever he needed to until he got what he wanted. Just as he was with the others, Muscles didn't pay much attention to Kat other than when he was looking to have sex with her, and, more often than not, that was when she was drunk. As a consequence, Drew was even more leery of Muscles than the night he was first introduced to the group.

Mickey was just Mickey: the quintessential imp; stirring things up wherever he could and having fun doing it. He was the main reason for the fights they became involved in and had a mean streak that made him, pound for pound, the toughest guy in the group. Drew often suggested the moniker 'Wolverine' was better suited than

'Mickey'. Of everyone in the group, Mickey was the only one who seemed able to penetrate Muscles' aloofness, doing it with ease and élan.

Lorne unfortunately, was a complete outcast. He wasn't bright enough to hang out with the brainy crowd and was too much of a geek to hang out with the cool crowd. Just as regrettably, he still sought Muscles' approval and acted like a puppy, always at his heels. Everything he did, he did to impress Muscles. Much to Lorne's consternation, Muscles continued to treat him with cruel indifference, more spiteful than he was to the others in the group.

The conversations within the group were mundane, generally, and Drew found himself often gravitating to Kat, whom he discovered to be a bit of an enigma. She was intelligent with a quick wit and had a self-confidence that wasn't boastful or overbearing, yet had a timid smile and allowed herself to be dominated by Muscles.

There was the dichotomy: the cerebral girl who could urbanely discuss any number of subjects when she wasn't drinking, and the girl who all too often seemed to drink excessively, unable to stand up let alone put any intelligible thoughts forward.

When it was time for Kat to go home, Drew would walk with her until she turned onto the street where her house was located. Drew found that he had become fond of Kat and wanted to watch over her like a brother does his little sister.

Most nights had found the guys breaking into vehicles in order to get the money to pay Lorne's brother, Doug, who provided the soporifics. Recently, though, they had become more brazen and moved to breaking into homes and businesses, finding the rewards much greater. With further help from Doug, they dealt with a fence who gave reasonable payment for the spoils. Outside of participating in thefts and break-ins they would be found hanging around in the barn enjoying their spoils.

A late-October Indian summer of brilliantly, sunny days, warm temperatures and gentle breezes, hemorrhaged into a tormented November and December. For weeks, hostile, low-lying Cimmerian clouds entrenched themselves in the skies above, thwarting the sun's attempts to penetrate and warm the deficient earth below. With the clouds came plummeting temperatures and raging winds that howled like wolves on a winter night. Acrimonious rainfall vacillated between cold, watery droplets and frozen pellets, which hit the face with the sharpness of bee stings.

With the barn offering no defence from the harsh, unrelenting conditions, Drew, Mickey and Muscles stole a tarp from a local lumber yard to set up a makeshift roof in an attempt to keep them dry, if not warm.

One particularly dispiriting, December afternoon, the temperature was just above freezing and the falling sleet landed heavily, coercing the tree branches to bend, submissive to the weight. The strong wind had the tarp waving convulsively, making for low thudding and high snapping sounds.

Muscles appeared at the barn, drenched, with steam rising from his brow and breath, but wearing a self-satisfied grin on his face. He pulled a sealed envelope from his coat's front pocket and meticulously opened the flap so as not to tear the paper. From within the envelope he withdrew a single key and held it out for the gang to see. The others gathered around, faces inquisitive.

"Guys, we're moving. So get your shit together because we're going upscale. See this key, here? I got it from my parents' bedroom. It is the key to a guest house my parents own across the street." He pointed over his shoulder with a nod of his head to the southwest corner of the intersection, across from the mansion. "I'm going to get a new key cut before they realize theirs is missing so we can use the guesthouse as our new hang out instead of this shit-hole here. Today we will try out the new digs and I will have the key by tomorrow."

There was a collective sigh of relief from the rest of the group. Lorne and Mickey hastily removed the tarp from the barn roof and the five of them used it as a shield against the sleety blizzard as they made their way over to the guesthouse.

While nowhere near the grandiosity of the main mansion, the two-storey house was still large, though plain from the outside. A wrought iron gated driveway led up to a double-car garage on the house's south side. A cedar wood deck wrapped from the front of the house and along its north-side wall. Entering the house, Drew's mouth opened agape with bewilderment. He had never been inside a residence this large or pretentious and could only assume the interior of the main house would be even more profligate.

With dark hardwood floors and burnished brass accents throughout, Drew thought the inside looked more like a movie star's residence than one belonging to a family from Drury.

As he explored, each room offered its own surprise: just inside and to the left of the front door stood a large sunken living room with a floor to ceiling fireplace; double French doors with golden etched panels led to an office; the cathedral ceiling of the dining room shone with an enormous crystal laden chandelier which seemed to draw in and refract the modicum of light from outside before splaying it throughout the room. A spiral staircase rose from the front foyer to the second floor where another monumental chandelier hung from the high ceiling of the upper hallway to a point level with the top of the stairwell. The upstairs hallway was faintly illuminated by the dampened light leaching through a large skylight window in the roof. On the second floor were four large bedrooms, completely and extravagantly furnished, including big screen, wall-mounted televisions.

When he returned to the main floor, Drew found the others already had the hearth ablaze and were sitting around it drinking their beers and listening to music on the stereo. He removed his wallet and placed it on the mantle above the fireplace before he joined them, finding a place to sit close to the fire where he could warm up and dry off. Drew was too cold to drink beer, choosing instead to relax and gaze at the firewood as it crackled and hissed;

throwing bright embers up the chimney like the sparks from a forged sword on an anvil being struck by a hammer.

As the afternoon wore on the weather outside retreated, allowing Drew a chance to head home. Lorne and Mickey decided to leave as well, but Kat was drunk and in no condition to stand let alone walk through the ice and slush of the streets and sidewalks.

"Don't worry about Kat, I'll take her home after she has sobered up a little," Muscles reassured the others.

Outside, Mickey, Lorne and Drew said their good-byes before separating. Drew and Lorne headed back to Drury. They were halfway to town when Drew came to a sudden stop.

"Damn, I forgot my wallet on the fireplace mantle. I have to go back to get it. You keep going and I will catch up to you later. If I don't, I will see you tomorrow."

Lorne nodded and continued on. Drew turned on his heels and ran back toward the house, fighting to maintain his balance on the icy surfaces and his breathing in the cold weather.

By the time he arrived at the guesthouse, Drew was exhausted. Bent over on the front deck with his hands on his knees, catching his breath, he looked through the door's sidelight window and could see Muscles leaning over a sofa in the living room. He was moving his hands in an odd way but Drew couldn't make out what he was doing.

Curious, Drew quietly opened the door and made his way inside. With the music still playing, Muscles didn't hear Drew enter the house. Standing in the foyer Drew could clearly see what was happening. Kat was lying, unconscious and face down on the sofa, her pelvis on the armrest and her toes curled downward against the floor. Muscles had her pants and underwear off and her shirt unbuttoned. Oblivious to Drew standing just a few feet away, he was brutally penetrating Kat with the handle of the fireplace poker.

Drew stood there, too shocked to react, unable to take his eyes off what was unfolding before him.

Muscles leaned over Kat and grabbed her hair, pulling her head up from the sofa.

"You like that, don't you, you fucking bitch."

Kat garbled a few incomprehensible words before Muscles released her hair, her head falling limp, back to the sofa.

Drew regained his composure and rushed Muscles, knocking him away from Kat and to the floor before he had a chance to use the poker again. Drew removed his jacket and placed it over Kat's exposed buttocks before turning back to Muscles.

"What are you, a fucking animal? First I find the skinned carcasses around the barn and now this? You are a sick fuck; man you need help." Pointing at Kat, Drew continued. "And this is what you do with Kat when you are alone with her? You asshole, she isn't even conscious. Jesus Christ, you're fucking demented."

Muscles got up from the floor and casually straightened his shirt and brushed off his pants.

"Hey, she is my girlfriend, Drew, and this is none of your business. I can do whatever I want with her. Besides, I've never heard her complain about it."

He crossed his arms and had an arrogant smile embossed on his face.

Drew remembered back to the first night he met all of them. Those were the same words spoken by Mickey as they walked home.

"Girlfriend? Sounds like she is your fucking bitch. And what makes you think you can do whatever you want with her. I don't think Kat would be agreeable to getting that...that...Jesus." Drew raked his fingers through his hair, disgusted. "Or is that why you wait for her to get drunk, so she can't put up any resistance?" He was now yelling, his face wild with rage.

"Wait for her to get drunk?" Muscles replied contemptuously. "If I waited for her to get drunk, I'd never get an opportunity to fuck her."

Muscles took a pill box from his shirt pocket. Opening it he produced a small tablet. He extended his arm so Drew could see what he was holding. Then he placed the tablet back in the box and set the box on the table.

Drew squinted to look at it. "What is it?"

"What *is* it? You fucking idiot, this is my fast track solution to Kat's tea-totaling. I drop one of these puppies in her beer and it doesn't matter if she has only had one drink, within a few minutes she is as wasted as if she had ten."

"Then…?"

"Then she lets me or the other guys have our way with her. The next day she doesn't remember a thing. No harm, no foul."

"No harm? Are you fucking kidding me? Fuck, man, you were sticking her with this poker." Drew had picked the tool up and held it out, pointing it towards Muscles.

"With the handle you just happen to be holding. You'll probably be licking your palm all the way home, boy."

Boy!

Drew dropped the poker and charged Muscles. The two crashed across the table and grappled about the room. Every punch Drew attempted, every move he made, Muscles was able to block or avoid, countering with a quick jab to Drew's abdomen or a light slap in the face. Being much stronger, Muscles toyed with Drew, tossing him aside then allowing him to attack again. The entire time a smile of superiority creased Muscles' face. After several minutes Muscles had had enough. As Drew swung at Muscles, his arm was twisted up behind his back and he was thrust face down on the floor. Though he tried, Drew was unable to get out of Muscles' powerful grip.

"I thought you were going home. What are you doing back here?"

"My wallet," replied Drew, the pain coming through in his voice. "I forgot it on the mantle of the fireplace and came back to get it."

"Then I suggest you get it and get the fuck out of here before I use the poker on you. Got it?"

Drew nodded and Muscles released him. When he got up from the floor Drew took his wallet from the mantle and walked towards the exit, dejected.

"Hey," Muscles called, "you forgot something."

As Drew turned Muscles was tossing the jacket which had been on Kat. With a depraved smile, Muscles slid his hand between Kat's legs and winked at Drew. Catching the jacket and, defeated in every way, Drew left the guesthouse.

Walking towards town, Drew knew he had to talk to Kat, to make her aware of what was happening. He couldn't let it continue. Nor could he carry on overlooking the guilt that was weighing on his conscience from all the crimes they had committed. Drew realized that what he was involved in couldn't continue. He could no longer hang out with Muscles and Lorne, though he still enjoyed being with Kat and Mickey.

Nearing the town limits, he found Lorne waiting for him near the 'Welcome to Drury' sign. A new sleety snowfall started, muffling the sounds of his approach in its wetness.

"What took you so long?"

"Nothing. I don't want to talk about it." Drew's mood had not improved. "Why'd you wait? I told you to go ahead. You should be home by now."

"I was going home when I saw a car pull out of that house over there." Lorne pointed to a residence opposite to where they were on the street. "There hasn't been any movement since; no lights, no nothing. You think Muscles would like it if I brought in some booty tomorrow?"

Drew looked at him apprehensively. In previous attempts to impress Muscles, Lorne had made some rash decisions that had jeopardized others in the group.

“No, I think we should just go home. Besides, Muscles isn’t necessarily someone whom you need to impress. And what happens if people are there and you just didn’t see them? This is a small town and the chances are you would be recognized.”

“Oh, I’ll have an answer for them,” Lorne responded, his eyes blinking even more than usual.

Drew looked at Lorne quizzically.

“And what would that answer be...?”

Lorne reached around to the back waistband of his pants and produced a handgun, waving it around and pointing it at Drew.

“With this Glock 9, semi-automatic gun,” he smiled smugly. “And you guys didn’t believe I had one.”

“What the hell, Lorne, put that away, it might go off. Where did you get that?”

“Does it matter? The question is would I use it; and the answer is yes.” Lorne stood caressing the cold, metallic barrel as he spoke.

“Fits my hand nicely, don’t you think?”

Drew didn’t answer but continued to stare at Lorne, astonished by the cavalier attitude he was showing. It made Drew nervous.

“Take it easy, Lorne, it could go off.”

“Hey, don't worry,” Lorne reassured, “I checked the magazine and there aren’t any bullets in it right now. But if someone caught me I would just stick it in their face and, believe me, they would forget what I looked like.”

“No, this isn’t a game Lorne, let’s just go home. Breaking into someone’s house is one thing, using a gun, whether loaded or not, is another. Besides, it’s getting late and whoever went out may be coming home soon. We can do it another time, just not here; not in Drury.”

Drew put his arm around Lorne's shoulders and started to direct him away from the house but Lorne spun away and turned back towards it, a determined pace as he marched across the road. Drew tried to stop him again but Lorne brushed his hand away. In the middle of the road, Lorne spun around, facing Drew.

"Look, you may be too afraid to do this but I'm not. So go on home, little boy, and let the men do what needs to be done."

Boy!

As Lorne turned and walked toward the house, Drew felt the defeat he had experienced at Muscles' hands surge inside him again. He couldn't let it go. He ran up to Lorne and grabbing him by the arm, jerked him around. The two stared resolutely at each other, scowls scoring each face. Drew's hands curled into clenched fists his arms rigid. After several seconds he recognized that Lorne was set on his decision and all the arguments Drew presented had fallen on deaf ears. Contrary to his better judgement, Drew acquiesced.

"Fine, one last time," he said, almost as if he were speaking to himself. Drew's shoulders drooped and his muscles slackened, releasing all the pent up tension.

"But we get in, check the usual spots for cash or jewellery, and then we get the hell out as fast as we can. Agreed?"

"Agreed!"

The triumphant tone to Lorne's voice penetrated Drew's conscience, immediately causing him to regret his decision.

They made their way up to the house, checking in all directions as they approached to ensure no one saw them. Scanning through the main floor and basement windows, they searched for any sign that someone may be inside. After checking the front and back windows they determined the best entry point would be a basement window in the shadows. Once inside, Lorne would act as lookout while Drew searched through the house.

Using his elbow, Drew broke the basement window. They looked around to determine whether any of the neighbours had been disturbed by the sound before they climbed through and into the basement. Quietly they made their way up the stairs to the main floor, listening for any sound of movement. The only sound was the faint ticking of a clock in the living room. Drew looked back at Lorne who, now, didn't seem so sure of himself. On the main floor, Drew motioned for Lorne to go to the living room then made his way to a back bedroom. Lorne knelt in the living room looking outside in case the homeowners returned. The late afternoon light was quickly fading as the sun set in the west behind the overcast sky.

Lorne jumped, yelping, when the timer clicked to activate the light in the living room behind him. Drew, hearing the sound from the living room, ran from the bedroom to find out what was going on. When he entered, Lorne was standing near the window, paler than usual, with the gun in his shaking hand pointing back into the room. Drew walked over to him and slowly pushed the gun down to his side.

"Should we check the weight of your underwear?" Drew said with a smirk. The two started to laugh a nervous laugh and, giving each other a tacit look, agreed it was time to go home.

"If it is all clear," Drew whispered, "we can go out the front door."

Lorne took another quick look outside to ensure that the way was clear, and, satisfied, turned towards Drew. Immediately his eyes widened and his mouth dropped open as he peered over Drew's left shoulder. There was complete silence except for the clock in the living room which maintained its steady metered ticking. Drew slowly looked back to see a woman standing in the room behind him. He recognized her as Mrs. Aldred, one of his counsellors from the high school. She was a gentle woman who was more like a mother figure to the students than a teacher.

Drew looked back at Lorne who was still holding the gun in his hand.

"Let's get out of here," he murmured.

But Lorne stood there, frozen in Mrs. Aldred's gaze, his eyes were not blinking.

"Andrew? Lorne?" she said, startled.

"Let's get out of here," Drew yelled in Lorne's face before he ran out the door and down to the sidewalk. Looking back at the house he could see Lorne was still standing in the front room. He hadn't moved. It appeared as though Mrs. Aldred was talking to him, her hands stretched out as if asking Lorne to give her the gun. Drew yelled again but the snow's large, wet flakes acted like insulation, deadening the sound of his voice. Quickly, Lorne raised the pistol. Drew recoiled, falling to the ground as the sound of a gun blast from within the house exploded through the heaviness of the snowfall, striking him like a shockwave. Looking back at the house, Drew could see Mrs. Aldred had slumped to the floor, her face a bloody mess.

Moments of dead silence passed before Lorne ran from the house. He reached the sidewalk just as Drew was getting up from the ground. The two ran towards their homes, caring nothing of the attention they drew.

"I thought you said the mag was empty. Jesus Christ, are you sure the mag was empty?"

"It was; I'm positive. I took all the bullets out of it myself."

"Did you check the chamber, too?"

Lorne's look gave the answer Drew didn't want to hear.

"Fuck, Lorne, what have you done?"

The two didn't stop running until they made it to their houses. When Drew arrived, it was almost six thirty. He kicked off his wet shoes as he entered the house and went directly up to his room, closed and locked the door and climbed into bed.

He did not leave the room until the next morning when he heard the muffled voices of the police on the main floor speaking with his parents.

Suddenly Jean let out a high-pitched scream.

"No, it cannot be my baby. Not Andrew. Please, God, not my baby."

As Drew walked into the living room, he saw his father cradling his mother who had collapsed upon receiving the news. Two police officers stood near them eying Drew.

CHAPTER NINE

Sitting in the Department of Family and Social Services offices, Drew was anxious and excited. His search for his birth parents had led him here, and now he hoped he would get some insight into who they were. The hospital was unable to help with the search as they couldn't find any baby with the surname, given him by his mother, born on his birthday. Further, privacy laws prevented them from disclosing answers to other questions Drew asked. Drew also discovered that the guardian and adoption documents had all been sealed as part of the court agreement. This Department would be his last resort. He hoped that his biological parents had agreed to have their details added to the adoption registry and that a quick search would uncover who they were.

It was one-fifteen in the afternoon; only fifteen minutes past the appointment's scheduled time, but it felt like hours. Drew kept glancing up at the clock which drummed every passing second into his ears. Opening his wallet, he took out the picture one more time.

"Come on," he spoke while looking at the photo, "make this easy and be on the registry. Let me know who I am and where I come from."

Then he held the photograph to his forehead and squeezed his eyes shut as if willing the information to be there.

The door to the office opened and a young woman exited to meet him. Drew looked at her cautiously.

She can't be much older than me, he thought as he stood.

He put the picture in his shirt pocket and wiped his sweaty palms on the front legs of his pants.

"Hello, Andrew, sorry for the delay, my name is Francine Little, but you can call me Fran. I will be your case worker," she said extending her hand to Drew.

"Hello, Francine, I mean Fran, I'm Drew, sorry, Andrew, umm, Andrew Parsons. Well, Parsons is my adoptive name. I hope you can help me find my original surname and parents. And one more thing, please call me Drew, only my mother calls me Andrew."

The entire time Drew vigorously shook her hand.

Francine smiled and glanced down at their hands as Drew continued. He caught the meaning behind her look and stopped shaking her hand.

"Sorry, I am a bit nervous."

"That is completely understandable. Try to calm down, though; I will make this as painless as possible." She flashed a quick smile. "In fact once the door is closed we can loosen our ties and have a relaxed conversation; I promise. Shall we?"

Francine motioned her arm towards the office. Drew nodded and entered with Francine following. She pointed him to the chair in front of her desk as she closed the door.

"Would you care for a coffee? I brewed it just after lunch."

"Yes, thank you."

Drew observed Francine as she moved about the room. She was a tall, attractive woman. Though not stunning or gorgeous by societal standards, she had a beauty which came from her gentleness and a gracefulness to her movements. As though she was conscious of his stare, Francine would periodically glance over at Drew and give an effortless smile. Her face was bright and honest which allowed him to relax.

Having tended to the coffees, she sat down, opening a folder.

"Now, before we get to the casual I must tend to some formalities, Drew. It won't even take a minute." Again, her smile put him at ease. "I will look after your application but must warn you that, unless your biological parents agreed to the dissemination of their personal data, there will be some roadblocks that will impact your search. In such a case, I can find and provide you with certain details about them but not a complete background. For instance, I can give you their general descriptions, religious beliefs and the reasons why you were given up for adoption but not their names or address. Also, remember, this information may have been provided when you were adopted and is no longer relevant. Unfortunately for many people looking for their adoptive parents, this is the end result. Are you prepared for that possibility?"

Drew nodded.

"Good," she continued, "I also must advise you that the process could take anywhere from six months to one year before it produces any tangible results."

Again, Drew nodded.

"Okay, then, let's get started. I'll get some preliminary information from you regarding your date of birth, hospital, adoptive parents' full names, you know, that sort of information. Once I have what's needed, I'll begin looking into records, registries and court documents to try to find as much information, and hopefully enough information, to discover who your birth parents are."

Francine began with asking the basic questions. Drew answered the questions to the best of his ability, given the limited background he had received. Francine's manner was relaxed, and the conversation would alternate between fact finding and general discussions.

"Well, that wraps it up. Do you have any other questions about anything at all?"

"Not at this time."

Francine stood up from her chair and walked with Drew from her office.

"In that case, this is good bye for now. Take care, Drew, it was very nice meeting you. I'll be in touch with you once I have assembled all that I can. If you come into more information that you believe would help your search, don't hesitate to call me. I'll also be in touch if I come across something that needs clarification. Here is my business card. Again, if you need to talk to me, my work and cell phone numbers are there."

Drew shook her hand again, careful not to shake too hard.

"Thank you, Fran; it was nice meeting you as well, and I appreciate any help you can give me."

As he waited for the elevator, Drew looked back to see Francine still standing at her office door, a delicate smile on her face. The doors opened and he gave a quick wave before entering.

The entire trip home, Drew couldn't stop thinking about Fran. Several times he removed her business card from his wallet and stared at her name. He felt invigorated and more positive about the search than he had before and anticipated the findings he was sure were to come.

Drew arrived home just as the meal was starting. After changing he returned to the kitchen where he sat down at the table. His parents had already begun to eat.

"How was your day, Andrew?" his mother asked.

"Great, thanks; got some things taken care of."

His father gave a derisive laugh as he butted out his cigarette then withdrew another one and lit it.

Drew looked at him with raised eyebrows, his forehead corrugated.

"What was that scoff for, dad?"

"What did you accomplish today, son? Did you find a job? Did you even look for a job? You do realize that it has been almost a month since you came home from the penitentiary and you still don't have a job. Remember what I said to you the first night you were back, this isn't a free ride, you have to get a job."

"Yes, dad, you have made your wishes quite obvious and I do plan on getting work, not only to pay my room and board but also to start saving for enrolment in some university night courses. I would like to get a degree within the next few years."

A slight curl appeared on his father's lips.

"That's good to hear, son."

"That *is* good to hear, Andrew. What is it you were studying? I just cannot seem to remember."

"Art history and architecture." Drew replied.

"And what do you suppose that is going to do for you?" his father said dismissively, his smile replaced by smirk. "A job as a...a...Christ, I have no clue what that would do for you. Seems like a waste of money and time if you ask me."

"But that's just the thing, dad, I don't recall asking you. Nor do I feel your opinion is relevant to me or my interests now or going forward."

William glared at Drew who looked back at him indifferently before turning his attention to his mother, noticing how troubled she was becoming with the conversation he was having with his father.

"So mom, how was your day?"

"It was fine; busy so the day goes by quickly."

"You may not think my opinion matters, boy," William interrupted, "but seeing as I am the one who is working to put this food on the table, I have the right to express it."

"*Boy*? *Boy*? Who do you think you are calling boy?" Drew could feel the heat filling his cheeks. "I'm a grown man and don't you forget..."

"Ha!" William snapped. "A grown man is accountable and responsible. A grown man doesn't leech off his parents. A grown man gets himself out there and works. And you, you bastard, are no grown man; you are a disrespectful boy. "

"I can't believe you. That's your idea of a grown man: education doesn't matter; improving oneself doesn't count for anything. Then you certainly fit that mould. And who the hell are you to talk about accountability and responsibility? Am I talking to the man who beat a child mercilessly, or abused his wife? Or is this the man who squanders more time at a bar, preferring to drink with this friends over spending it with his family? What type of grown man are you, William? I think I am the one speaking to the boy!"

William exploded with apoplectic rage, knocking his chair over as he stood and pounding the table.

"Who the fuck do you think you are?" he yelled, pointing at Drew, the veins bulging from his neck. "Get out of my house, you son-of-a-bitch, get the hell out of my house before I throw you out."

Jean slammed her hands down on the table and stood up, moving towards Drew.

"Enough!" she shrieked. "William, Andrew is not getting out of this house. You do not have the only say around here. This is my house as well and I say he can stay. This has gone on far too long and it ends tonight. If anyone leaves this house, it will be you. Go to the bar and commiserate with your friends. Then find out if they will take you in and for how long they will tolerate your behaviour. Your anger is a disease that afflicts all who are around you and I will not stand for it any more. We do not need your money and we certainly do not need you vitriol. Leave Andrew and me alone. Get out."

As she turned to Drew her facial expression changed. Looking up at him reassuringly, her voice calmed.

"You see, Andrew, we will survive. We have survived with his evil; we can certainly survive without it. A mother and her son have the wherewithal to take on whatever challenges life throws at them."

A seething scowl tainted William's face. Drew stepped toward him as William raised his hand to point at Jean.

"You must be joking. Who the hell do you think you are talking to, woman? I am your husband, and you will show me the respect I deserve."

"I think she has, William, and given the little respect you do deserve, mom has given you beyond your entitlement."

"I've had enough of your insolence, you bastard."

William rushed him, but Drew was prepared. Taking advantage of William's momentum, he stepped aside and knocked him to the floor. As William attempted to get up, Drew put him in a stranglehold restraint. William struggled to get free but Drew held on, too strong for him to overcome. Jean looked into William's eyes and saw the complete and utter fear that had overtaken him.

"Drew, please, let him go. You've made your point."

After William agreed to calm down, Drew released him. As William got up off the floor Drew returned to the kitchen table and sat. William walked out of the kitchen, rubbing his neck, dejected and defeated. Gathering his jacket and keys, he put on his shoes left the house.

Jean followed William and watched from the front window as he backed out of the driveway and drove off. When the car was out of sight she continued to stare into the void, unfocused.

"I cannot stay here. I have to leave tonight, before he comes home. There is no telling what he will be like after he has had a night of drinking, but whatever it is it will not be good."

Drew walked up behind his mother placing his hands on her shoulders. Jean closed her eyes, bringing her hands and placing them on his, soothed by his touch.

"We can have you packed within the hour. Do you have a friend you can stay with for the night? Tomorrow we can arrange for you to find a more permanent place to stay."

"I will not burden anyone tonight. I can stay at the motel on the other side of town. We will see what tomorrow brings. You are going to stay with me tonight, right?"

"No, I can't. I will help you get ready but there are some things I need to take care of and I have to do them from here."

Jean turned and gave him a concerned look.

"Are you sure? It would be no problem if you were to stay with me tonight."

"It's okay, mom, I will be fine here. I will avoid William if he comes home. And, if things do start to become heated, I can make my way to the motel."

An hour later, Jean was on her way to the motel for the night. Drew ate his dinner and cleaned up the kitchen, after which he sat down in the living room, turned on the television and waited.

It was just before eleven o'clock when William entered the house to find Drew still sitting in front of the television. Drew turned it off and stood up as William removed his shoes and jacket, placing them in the front closet.

"Hello, William." Drew maintained a calm voice in order to keep the situation peaceful. William didn't answer, instead walking through the living room and up stairs to his bedroom. Drew waited. A few moments passed before he heard the footsteps of his father exit his bedroom and return back down to the main floor.

"Where is she? Where's your mother?"

"She has gone to stay with a friend tonight. I didn't ask her who that person was because I didn't want to have to lie to you if you asked for the name."

With a sigh and a sorrowful nod, William accepted what Drew had said as the truth. He sat down on the sofa in the living room and brought his hands to his face.

Then William began to cry.

Drew had never seen his father cry and, seeing him now, he felt nothing for him – neither sympathy nor anger – simply that he was responsible for his own misfortune.

"Why couldn't she accept the situation? It wasn't the end of the world, we could have survived. Don't you understand? It didn't have to be me or you. She didn't have to choose."

Not wanting to listen to William's tedious griping about what had happened earlier in the evening, Drew sat on the chair facing him.

"I think we should talk about what will happen going forward."

William removed his hands from his face. There was both dismay and anger in his expression.

"What do we have to talk about? I don't want you in this house anymore. As far as I'm concerned your presence has been a plague on this house since you were a child. With your return from jail our lives have been hell. While you were gone, your mother and I had a great relationship. And now she has left."

"If mom has the will, and my hope is she does, she won't be coming back, but that will be her decision. As for me, I'll be moving out within the next day or two, once I am convinced mom is okay. Living arrangements were offered to me for when I got out of jail but I wanted to return home first to try and make amends for my past. To a degree that has been achieved. I am proud of who I have become despite the environment in which you raised me. My attempts to reconcile with you have been met with nothing but resistance and hostility.

"I have helped mom see you in a clear light, to understand that she needs to take care of herself. And if that means getting away from you, so be it. But now it is time. I just wanted to speak with you while mom was not around. And you had better listen carefully to me because, going forward, I don't anticipate speaking to you ever again about it. If we do, it will mean that you have not listened to or heeded my warning."

Drew leaned forward, a steeled look on his face, and lowered his voice. William didn't move.

"This is not an issue for discussion. You will listen and only listen. If mom chooses to return, you will never lay another finger on her. Nor will you ever degrade her verbally, physically or sexually. You will treat her with the respect that she deserves. If she chooses not to return you will respect that decision and never try to coerce or persuade her in any way to return to you. If word gets to me that you have acted contrary to what has been said here tonight, understand that my retribution will be swift and absolute. You are not dealing with the boy you beat and humiliated, William; I am a man who is resolute in his conviction and decisive in his actions; as I showed you earlier tonight. Do you understand all that I have just said, William?"

The fear he tried to conceal came through in his eyes and his voice, "Yes, I understand."

"Good, then we are finished here. As I said before, I do not expect to be here by the end of the weekend. I'll start to pack my belongings and, as soon as mom informs me of her intentions, I will be gone, not just from this house but from this town."

Drew went to his bedroom and closed his door.

William sat silent for several minutes before he rose from the chair shaking and wearily climbed the stairs to his bedroom.

The following morning Jean returned home before William was awake. Drew was there waiting for her when she arrived.

"How did the night go? Did your father come home? Were there any problems?"

"Yes, he came home and no, there were no problems. We spoke for a bit, just to clear the air, and have come to an understanding. What needs to be done next is for you to find a place to live."

Jean placed her hand on Drew's cheek.

"You are such a good son; my son. I have already been speaking to a co-worker of mine. She and her husband have a basement apartment and it will be coming available at the end of next month. I asked if they could hold it for me until the school Christmas break and they said they will. I also told them that there is a possibility you will come to live with me. They were okay with that."

"I am happy for you, mom. It's nice of them to hold it for you. But you can let them know you'll be moving there on your own. I was offered a place to stay when released from prison and am going to move there. It is a place in Westwood, the family of that guy I told you about in prison."

Jean looked at Drew with an obvious sense of disappointment.

"Westwood? That is so far away. I thought you would stay with me until you were on your feet."

"Mom, it's time for me to move on. Truth-be-told, I knew within a short time of my release from prison that Drury was not where my life was or could be. And after three weeks it's time. But I don't have to leave until you have moved out, if that is what you want."

With resignation in her voice, Jean replied, "No, I will be fine here. You need your space, I know. And your relationship with your father is, for all intents and purposes, over. You are right; Drury is not the place for you."

Drew felt a pang of guilt. "Are you sure?"

"Yes, Andrew, Jean sighed, I guess you cannot be expected to stay with your mother forever."

Drew studied his mother for several moments before he turned and walked to his bedroom to finish packing his suitcase, still feeling a slight stitch of guilt. When he was done, he took the piece of paper from his wallet and picked up the phone. After three rings the line was answered.

"Hello?"

"Hello, is this Alicia Warren?"

"Yes, who am I speaking to?"

"Alicia, this is Drew Parsons, a friend of John. He told me to contact you after I was released from jail. Do you have time to talk?"

CHAPTER TEN

The Juvenile Detention Centre was run more like a recreation centre, encouraging co-operation and betterment. The dorm rooms were built like an idea chart with the separate pods connected to small common areas which, themselves, were attached to a larger, central common area.

On the morning of his transfer from the detention facility to the penitentiary, Drew had finished cleaning up his room and walked down the short hall to the naturally illuminated common area. Staring out a floor-to-ceiling window he was able to see the activity of the counsellors in the larger common area just down another hall. The night before he had said his good-byes to the staff at the small gathering they had organized as a form of send off; a gathering Lorne Jacoby did not attend.

Sitting on the recliner in the lounge, he noticed that the lingering harsh smell of the newly painted walls overwhelmed the rich fragrance of the potted plants which were just beginning to bloom.

Maisha Ndereba, one of his counsellors, entered the lounge and sat in the chair across from him, placing her briefcase on the floor beside her.

"Good morning, Drew," she said in her heavy Kenyan accent, "there will be a short delay in your transport to the penitentiary. Have you made sure you collected up all your things from your room?"

Drew nodded.

"Good. Drew, I know you didn't participate very much in the group counselling sessions or classes which were offered to you over the past two years, but I was hoping you could tell me, one on one, how you feel about your transfer."

Drew looked at her coolly for a few moments.

"No big deal; it'll be like moving from one hotel to another." He paused looking around. "Actually, the change of scenery will be refreshing."

Maisha looked at him with concern.

"The change of scenery, you so casually talk of, will be nothing like this," she warned, "Are you aware of what life in the penitentiary system is like?"

Drew shrugged his shoulders but said nothing.

No one bothers me here anymore and no one will bother me there either.

Maisha removed a book from her briefcase and offered it to Drew.

"Here, I hope you will accept this; I believe it will be of help to you."

Drew gave a passing glance at the book then at Maisha, but made no move to accept it. After several seconds elapsed Maisha placed it back in her briefcase.

"Well, Drew, I won't bother you any longer. As the people from my village say, 'Basu mungu nyayo kusababisha njia yako' – Let God's footprints lead your path."

Again, Drew didn't respond.

Maisha placed her hand on his knee and looked at him with benevolence in her eyes before getting up from the chair, smiling and walking away.

As Maisha left the lounge, a prison guard, one of the many who Drew didn't know, or care to know, entered.

Drew stood up from the recliner and walked towards the door.

"Well, let's go," he said while passing the guard.

The guard stopped Drew with a palm to the chest.

"Not so fast, Drew, we aren't going for a walk in the park, you know. I have some jewellery for you to wear."

It was then that Drew noticed the cuffs and chains the guard was holding in his left hand.

The ride from juvenile detention to the penitentiary was a long, quiet trip. Drew's wrists and ankles were shackled with a chain linking them together. While not uncomfortable, it constrained him and made any movement in the vehicle difficult. The guard escorting Drew sat stone faced and rigid beside him in the back seat of the prisoner transport vehicle. During the entire three hour drive between the facilities, he stared straight ahead through mirrored sunglasses. Drew wasn't sure he even blinked. The time in the vehicle gave Drew a chance to think about the past two years and look ahead to the next five.

The trial result was never in doubt; the evidence against Lorne and Drew was strong and, in fact, irrefutable. A gun was recovered during a search of the Jacoby household and ballistic test results established it was the weapon Lorne had fired the night of the break-in. The bullet striations were the same as those on the bullet which passed through Mrs. Aldred before becoming embedded in a sofa. Witnesses from neighbouring homes and along the street saw Lorne and Drew as they left the scene of the shooting. Most conclusive, though, was that Mrs. Aldred knew both of the boys from the high school and was able to identify them. It was fortunate that Mrs. Aldred had survived the gunshot wound to her head; however, the resulting damage would leave her rehabilitating for several years and with a permanent disability.

The fact Drew was not in the residence when Lorne shot Mrs. Aldred and that he pleaded guilty at the earliest court date worked to his advantage in the Judge's decision to impose a shorter sentence than the maximum prescribed by law.

Drew was convicted and sentenced to seven years for his part in the break and enter, while Lorne was convicted of break and enter and attempted murder and sentenced to a jail term of fifteen years, running concurrent.

The early months of his two years in juvenile detention had been tumultuous for Drew. He had found himself in a number of altercations with other inmates for not respecting the recognized territories established by the gangs.

As he recalled one of the confrontations in which his attacker was armed with a home-made shiv, manufactured from a toothbrush, Drew reached up and touched his chest. Though he was able to fight off the attack, Drew did so at a cost; receiving a stab wound to his chest which punctured his lung and left him in the infirmary for three weeks.

As time passed, though, the incidents he was involved in became more infrequent as he had proven his mettle and was no longer challenged by other inmates.

Drew was visited for the first time by one of his friends four months after his incarceration. Kat drove out one morning with his mother, and visited with him at the juvenile facility for their half hour allotment. Drew was surprised and thrilled to see her as she entered the visitation area, a bright, innocent smile on her face. After hugging his mother, Drew turned to Kat, noticing tears balancing on the edge of her eye-lids, her chin quivering.

"Don't you start, young lady, or you'll have me going and I would never hear the end of it," he warned her, pointing and shaking his finger. Then he gave her a long hug before the three of them sat down to talk.

Fifteen minutes later, Jean excused herself. "I will leave you two alone to visit. Just come out to the car when you leave, Kat."

Drew saw his mother to the door and gave her a kiss good-bye before he returned to Kat.

"I'm really happy you came to visit, Kat. How are you doing? How are the others?"

"Things are good. After your trial, or whatever it was, ended, everyone sorta went their own ways. On the positive side, my school grades have been improving. I haven't seen Mickey for about three months and Muscles and I decided to cool things down as well. Actually, I got a call from Muscles the other day and we are planning to go to a party next weekend."

Drew immediately flashed back to the day of the break-in and the events leading up to it. He glanced away from Kat, a look of concern present on his face. Kat noticed the change in his expression.

"What's wrong, Drew?" she asked, placing her hands over his where they rested on the table.

"No contact!" boomed a voice through the speaker system. Kat pulled her hands away.

"Kat, I don't want you to go to the party with Muscles. In fact, I don't think you should see him anymore. He is no good for you. I had wanted to talk to you the day of the break-in but things went all wrong."

Kat gave him a suspicious look.

"Why? Why shouldn't I see him? Just because we cooled things a bit doesn't mean we aren't still going out, you know. I know you never really liked him but he is my boyfriend."

Drew stared at this hands, not sure what to say next. After several moments of silence, he concluded that she needed to be warned about Muscles, about the dead animals, about how Muscles shared her with the other guys, even if that meant revealing what he had seen that day in the guest house. He looked long and intently into her eyes and Kat felt a surge of apprehension.

When Drew finished telling her about the abuses Muscles had laid upon her, including the day in the guest house, Kat sat dazed, unable to digest the account Drew had related. Her face became even more pallid as he stared at her. Her breathing became shallow and hesitant and her eyes rolled back. Drew could see that Kat was going to faint. "Kat!" He reached for her, before summoning a guard to help. They laid her down on the floor and attended to her with a cold compress then, after she revived, a glass of water. Despite the staff's insistence that she attend the hospital, Kat assured them that she was well enough to continue visiting. She and Drew were left alone, but only to say their good-byes.

As they stood at the exit, Kat looked at Drew with another tear in her eye, but it was apparent this one was for a much different reason.

"I want you to know that, as upset as I am, I appreciate what you told me, Drew. I'm sorry what happened to you that day and want you to know that I will always remember how you tried to protect me." She looked down at her hands then back up at him, her beautiful green eyes still misty. "I will come back to see you soon, maybe a month or two."

Drew smiled and gave an affirmative nod to her before stepping back. She turned to the exit doors. As she waved one more time and left the facility, Drew knew it was the last time he would see Kat.

As the transport vehicle neared the penitentiary Drew's heart began to beat a little faster and harder, his palms began to sweat and his mouth dried. The overconfidence he carried in juvenile detention started to evaporate with each passing minute. Drew understood he would be the new blood and was troubled by the prospect of the stories he had heard - the rapes and murders, the gangs and the lifers - and began to realize he was no longer the toughest guy and intimidator he had been in juvenile detention, but was going to be at the bottom of the food chain. He calloused himself against his growing concerns and decided the best defence would be to stand his ground and not back down from anyone.

Pulling up to the facility, Drew first observed the armed guards, standing in the towers along the high walls surrounding the grounds, carrying high powered rifles. With a shudder, he admitted to himself that his time in the penitentiary was going to be far more severe than his previous incarceration; that this wasn't going to be like 'moving from one hotel to another.'

When the transport vehicle stopped at the prison's front gate, the large, barbed barrier gate screeched in protest as it inched open in a process which seemed to take several minutes to resolve. Once the gate had completed the task the vehicle passed through and waited. When the first gate closed a second gate, also barbed, opened unbearably slowly as well. Once inside the grounds, the vehicle was parked and Drew escorted by the two officers to a heavy metal door, his chains rattled with every shuffling step. For the first time Drew heard his silent attendant speak, his heavy voice boomed into an intercom.

"Andrew David Parsons for intake."

A caliginous, ephemeral voice from the box responded, spitting out a command, before the door opened, its wheels grinding in their tracks. As with the gates to the compound, the initial door led to a second door which opened only after the first had closed behind them. The echoing crash of metal on metal vibrated through Drew and hinted at an element of ominous fate. The guards removed their weapons and handed them to an anonymous figure standing behind a two way mirrored screen. When the second door grumbled open, Drew looked in to see a line of fettered men standing against the wall to his right. They looked malevolent, most wearing scowls that were toxic with loathing. Drew quickly looked down and away, fearful of making eye contact with any of them.

Down the hallway straight ahead about thirty paces from where Drew was, was a counter behind which two guards stood speaking to prisoners and viewing their files. Further along was a second counter where prisoners spoke to other guards, taking account of their valuables, before heading off to a nearby room. Still other prisoners left the same room, through a different door further down, wearing orange prison garb and were escorted to the end of the hall and out through another heavy metal door. The entire scene reminded Drew of a manufacturing factory with the prisoners moving along a conveyor belt.

A group of police officers and transport guards stood off to the side in a small antechamber talking while waiting for their detainees to be attended to so they could return to their regular duties.

The transport guards led Drew to the back of the prisoner line where he was tethered at the ankle to the prisoner in front of him, before heading down to the room where the other guards were.

Forty-five minutes passed before it was Drew's time to go to the counter. There stood a massive guard whose sheer size intimidated Drew. As he approached the desk, his escort handed a file to the guard behind the counter and then removed the cuffs from Drew. As he stood back up after taking the manacles from around Drew's ankles, he looked at Drew, his face appearing softer than earlier.

"Good luck, Drew, and stay out of trouble. This is a different animal than what you were used to in juvenile detention and it can eat you up in a heartbeat."

Looking at the officers name tag for the first time, Drew nodded and gave a cautious smile.

"Thank you Officer Worthington," he whispered as his escort walked away. When Drew looked back towards the counter, the guard stood there with a wide grin pasted on his face.

"Okay, Andrew, I am going to tell you the process from here..."

"Excuse me, sir," Drew meekly interrupted. "Can you call me Drew, please? Only my mother calls me Andrew."

The grin faded from the guard's face.

"Okay, *Andrew*, I am going to tell you the process from here. To start off with, you'll be sent inside the room just down the hall to be stripped down and searched; that includes a cavity searched. After that you will be given the opportunity to shower, and then issued an orange prison jumpsuit and sandals. From there you will be taken to a holding area where all prisoners are kept until the next stage of the process. Got it?" The guard paused to allow the information to sink in before continuing. "Listen for your name to be called and go to the guard who will take you to get photographed for your prisoner identification card followed by a short interview to determine if you have any medication or special needs, gang affiliations, or medical conditions. After that you'll go to another processing area where you'll receive the property you brought with you from juvenile detention after a determination has been made as to what you can and cannot keep with you. That which you can't or don't want to keep will be held until you are released."

Again he paused, searching Drew's face for any signs of confusion.

"Once it is decided what block you will be housed at you'll go to the 'bullpen' where you will wait to be taken to your cell. When your name is called again, you'll receive your sheets and more clothing along with your housing assignment. You will then be escorted to your cell. Do you understand everything I have explained to you, Andrew?"

Drew nodded.

"I'm sorry, I didn't hear you."

"Yes, sir, I understand."

"Good, now take this file down to that officer at the next counter, he will get the ball rolling."

"Thank you Officer…Officer…"

"Officer Vincent will do."

"Thank you Officer Vincent." Drew said with a diffident voice.

The process went as Officer Vincent had said it would; however, Drew was held in the bullpen cell overnight.

Except for a dim light above, the windowless room was dark. Despite this, Drew was unable to sleep that night. Between the butterflies raging war in his stomach and the dread he felt with every cough or snore that broke the silence, he spent the night sitting on the floor in the corner, his knees pulled up under his chin, his eyes darted about the room at the collection of bodies bundled together inside the overcrowded space.

When morning finally arrived, he was tired and cramping and had difficulty getting to his feet. Though he hadn't eaten in almost a day, when the morning breakfast was served Drew couldn't bring himself to try it. He spent the morning waiting as different inmates were called out and new prisoners entered the cell.

By the lunch serving he was ravenous and looking forward to the meal, no matter what was being offered. Drew's stomach let out a conspicuous growl as he removed his ration from its bag. Setting his drink on the floor before him, Drew noticed a pair of slippered feet immediately in front pointing in his direction. Looking up he saw a cellmate standing before him. His orange jumpsuit had been removed at the shoulders, its sleeves tied around his waist. His muscular build was swaddled in tattoos, many depicting gang colors and emblems, his long hair and eyes had a daunting wildness about them.

Without saying a word, he extended his hand, palm up, and repeatedly waved his fingers. Drew didn't bother to ask, simply handing over his meal. The inmate, menacingly, knelt down until he was near to level with Drew, slowly eating the food he had confiscated and moaning with pleasure in a tormenting manner. Rather than swallowing, though, he let the chewed pieces fall from his mouth to the floor. Standing again, he threw the remaining scraps of the lunch, hitting Drew in the head, before he knocked over Drew's drink and walked away laughing.

Much to his relief, Drew's name was called half an hour after the incident. As he approached the cell door, he heard a chafed voice hiss his name. He didn't look back, knowing it was his tattooed tormentor.

Again in handcuffs, Drew was taken on a tour through the corridors which drove home the differences between this and the previous facility. The penitentiary was a closed in and dark place, austere and savage, made of metal bars and cinderblock walls. Dim lighting faintly illuminated the interior and there was no suggestion of an outside. The dining hall tables were cemented into the floor and made from stainless steel. Eventually, Drew was led to cellblock “C” and shown to cell number twenty-three.

Drew’s new cell was entered through a solid metal door with a small plexiglass window and a tiny access slot which barely allowed for hands to fit through. The six foot by eight foot room contained a bunk bed, stainless steel toilet and sink, a shower and a small table with an attached chair. A fluorescent light shone from the ceiling.

Sitting on the top bunk was an inmate who appeared to be in his twenties. His head was shaved bald and he had blue, dim eyes. His crabbed smile displayed brown, rotting teeth. When he jumped down from the top bunk, Drew saw that he was diminutive with a slight build. He spoke in short choppy sentences and his voice was elfish sounding. Below his rolled up sleeve the inmate had a swastika tattoo on his left forearm as well as one on each side of his neck.

The guard introduced them.

“Andrew Parsons, this is Peter Hughes. You two will want to get to know each other; you’re gonna be cellmates for quite a while.”

Drew entered the cell, gazing around the confined space he would, henceforth, call home.

“You have any questions, Drew?” the guard asked.

Still preoccupied by his surroundings Drew gave a perfunctory shake of his head, only to be brought out of his stupor by the sound of the door slamming closed and the lock being bolted. The finality of the clamor plunged Drew into a sadness he had never before experienced. Drew faced the door, his shoulders drooping. The slot opened and he was instructed to slide his hands through so the shackles could be removed.

When the slot closed, Peter’s deportment changed.

“So, this is your first time in The Pen, huh?” he said as Drew turned away from the cell door.

“Yeah, but I spent two years in juvie.”

“Well, this isn’t juvie, boy. You’ll hang around with me and if you do just as I say, everything’ll be fine. I’m in with a gang of guys and no one bothers us. There are rules in here you hav'ta follow. If you don't you could get fucked up by some of the other gangs. I'll tell you who to avoid and how to stay out of trouble."

Peter paused and looked carefully at Drew.

"First things first; we don't hang out with the niggers or spics or Jews or anyone else who ain't pure whitey, got that?"

Peter's words were more a warning than a question.

Drew stood there too dumbfounded to respond.

Peter peered at him.

"You look like a little bit of a dirty darky yourself, what's your background?"

"My parents are white, been in this country for many, many generations."

"Your mom fuck a Injun? Cuz you sure don't look like white bread."

"No, she didn't fuck an Indian. And remember, even white bread has a darker crust."

Peter snorted a derisive laugh as cold tension filled the cell. The two cellmates stared at each other for several seconds, each sizing the other up. Sucking air through his tight lips, Drew broke the silence.

"Look, I want you to understand right away that I am a loner. I didn't affiliate with any gangs, or anyone for that matter, in juvenile. I'm just going to put my time in here and get the fuck out as soon as possible. You're in a gang that has set ideas, and that is your thing, I get that. But it is not my thing."

Peter continued to eye Drew up and down.

"What are you in for?"

"Another guy and I broke into a house and he shot the homeowner. How about you?"

"Attackin' some Spics. Me and some friends swarmed the fuckers at a bus stop. One of them was stabbed. Worst thing about it was that we got caught and he didn't die."

There was a pause as Drew measured Peter's words.

"And what do you do in here? Of course that's when not hanging out with your skinhead friends."

Peter gave Drew a petulant look.

"Like I said, Drew, this ain't juvie."

Drew discerned the threat behind the words.

"Sorry."

Peter sneered for several seconds before he appeared to accept the apology.

"I work in the janitorial department from eight in the morning until four-thirty in the afternoon. We get a thirty minute lunch at noon. When we're not working, inmates have the option to spend the time in their cells, in the recreation hall - playing cards or watching television - or going out to the yard. Or you can take part in various programs, such as AA or religious study. But if you aren't on a work detail or taking programs during the day, you have to remain in your cell until the others have returned from their details."

They had talked for a while when their conversation was interrupted by the sound of the five o'clock alarm activating to indicate dinner.

"Well, you ain't got no other friends in here, so you better tread carefully in the mess," Peter pointed out to Drew. "You'll wanna remember what I'm about to tell ya. It's hard to make and keep friends here but easy to make and keep enemies. So choose smart."

Drew thought about the situation he was in and the words of Officer Worthington, *'This is a different animal than what you were used to in juvenile detention and it can eat you up in a heartbeat.'*

He knew he already had one adversary; he didn't need a whole gang of them by the end of his first day.

"I guess I don't have much of a choice. I would love to have dinner with you and your buddies." he said with subtle contempt that Peter didn't pick up on.

After roll call, the door to their cell opened and Peter and Drew entered the confluence of hundreds of other inmates who exited their cells as part of a regimented flow that moved like traffic on a freeway cloverleaf, descending on the mess hall.

Drew received his ration of meat gravy, mashed potatoes, broccoli and creamed corn before following Peter to the table. The entire time Drew kept his face pointing towards the floor for fear of making eye contact with any of the other prisoners. As Drew crossed the floor he was distracted by a voice that hissed his name. Looking to his right, Drew saw the inmate from the bullpen who had taken his lunch earlier that day. A spiteful smile disfigured his face as he pulled his index finger across his throat in a slicing manner. Drew looked away and continued to where Peter led him.

Peter's introduction of Drew to the gang at their table was met with a lukewarm response, which was fine with Drew. There was an edge to the babble in the mess hall. Bouts of laughter periodically erupted; however, there was an underlying aggression in the conversations around the tables in the vicinity of Peter and Drew which left him feeling uptight. Though they weren't overtly antagonistic, Drew sensed the hostility in the eyes of Peter's gang members as they watched him.

Time passed painstakingly slowly. The anxiety Drew felt churned in his stomach. Eating became difficult and he feared he would throw up the food with each swallow. Drew had finished just over half his dinner when the bell mercifully rang indicating the end of the meal. They returned to their cell to brush their teeth and clean up before attending the recreation hall.

Drew joined Peter but, once they were in the recreation hall, Peter met up with some other gang members and started playing pool. Drew chose to watch television.

For ten minutes Drew had been sitting by himself at the end of a large couch when three men entered the room. After milling around for a bit they moved to the couch taking a seat beside him. As the one closest to him, who appeared to be in his late thirties, sat, Drew got up to leave.

"It's okay, kid, I don't bite," he said, his voice commanding, yet with a welcoming tone. "Sit down and enjoy the program. You don't get much freedom in here so you may as well take whatever pleasure you can from it."

Drew thanked him and sat down timidly; stiffly leaning toward the armrest. The three men, paying no attention to him, talked casually and laughed easily about their day. Listening to them calmed Drew and he could feel himself unwinding, his body relaxing as he felt more at ease. From their conversation he reasoned that they were on the crew which worked outside the prison on road and ditch detail. Suddenly and surprisingly the man beside him turned to Drew.

"You're new here, aren't you, kid?"

Drew gave a shallow, uncertain nod.

"What's your name?"

Drew stammered to answer. "Andrew, I mean, Drew Parsons, sir."

The man let out a thunderous laugh, slapping his hand onto Drew's shoulder.

"That's a good one. You hear that, guys...*sir.*" He turned to face Drew again, still laughing. "You can call me John. John D-C 0-7-2-0-6-2."

Drew looked at John, perplexed. "John D-C 0-7-2-0...? I don't understand."

John continued smiling.

"Consider this your first lesson in here. Drew, in jail your life is numbers; your Department of Corrections number, the penal code you were charged with, the length of your sentence. Nothing else matters. Not the names of days or months, not your cellmate's name, not the guards in here, nothing. That's because, eventually, everything takes a back seat to one numeric series. I have no idea, nor do I care, what day of the week it is or, for that matter, what month it is. I was given fifteen years, have served five and still have ten remaining. That's sixty-two months or eighteen-hundred and sixteen days spent here. You count the days you've been in for the first half of your sentence and days you have left over the second half of your sentence. See? That series of numbers is the only thing that really matters. Don't ever give your last name to anyone else only your Department of Corrections number. They are not your friends and don't need to know that information."

John asked Drew for his Department of Corrections number.

"Drew D-C 1-9-0-9-9-0 is how you will refer to yourself from now on, do you understand?"

Drew hesitantly nodded.

"No, I don't think you do."

Looking around the room, John observed and pointed towards four muscular inmates, playing cards.

"See that guy with his back to us playing crib? He is in here for shooting three people in a botched home invasion. Do you want that guy knowing anything about you or your family?" he asked rhetorically. "He is no friend, he is a criminal and criminals can't be trusted. In here guys would cut you for a pack of smokes. If he knows your last name or any other important information about you, it could come back to haunt you."

Again he examined Drew. "You're a fair size. You were the big man at juvie hall, weren't you, Drew?"

"Yeah, I carried my own," Drew responded, not intending to sound as arrogant as he had. "But I know that I am nothing here. A small fish in a big piranha filled pond."

John let out another hearty laugh.

"You got that right, Drew D-C 1-9-0-9-9-0. You aren't a simpleton, I can tell. What are you in for?"

Drew wanted to give the penal code number but couldn't recall it. He sat there for several moments trying to remember, all the time staring at John with his eyes wide open. Then he recalled.

"Four sixty-nine. I have spent two years of a seven year sentence in juvie but I hope to be able to get out of here in three for good behavior. So that's twenty-four months..."

"Lesson two: do the full ticket," John broke in. "Parole is a pain in the ass with all the conditions. You finish your sentence and you leave a free man, ready to start a new life, not a puppet on some parole officer's string."

Though he was wracked with fatigue, Drew experienced an awakening as he and John D-C 0-7-2-0-6-2 sat in the recreation hall talking. He listened intently while John gave erudite advice on many of the prison's unwritten rules. Unlike earlier, time now seemed to pass by quickly and, taking Drew by surprise, the alarm rang indicating it was time for the inmates to return to their cells.

"You're new here so this one gets a pass, but you was spending a lot of time talkin' to that darky," Peter chided after they had returned to their cell.

"I was kinda cornered. Besides, where else could I go? It isn't like the rec hall is very big."

"Like I said, you get one pass."

Soon after, the lights were turned out. That night Drew slept a deep, undisturbed sleep.

The next morning the daily routine started at six-fifteen with the wake up alarm. Prisoners had forty-five minutes to clean their cells, shower and prepare for the day. At seven, after roll call, the doors opened and the regimented procession to the mess hall started again, as it would for every day of every year spent in the penitentiary. Drew followed Peter down to the cafeteria. In the mess hall, John saw Drew and waved him over to sit with him and his friends. As he neared the table, Drew heard the now familiar voice hissing his name. He refused to react, instead staring straight ahead to where John sat.

Over breakfast Drew sat quietly, listening as John and his pals sat talking. Finally, John turned to Drew.

"Have they talked to you about what you want to do? You know, work project or school courses?"

Drew shook his head. "Not yet, I think they intend to speak to me today at some point."

"What are you planning to ask for, Drew?"

"I was listening to you guys last night and working the road crew sounded fun."

"*Fun*? No, it is laborious and proletarian."

Drew looked at John, confused, "Proletarian?"

"Yeah, proletarian, as in 'not sophisticated; working-class.' Anyway, how long have you been in jail now? Did you say two years?" Again, without allowing Drew to answer he continued. "You probably have limited education, I'm guessing. You shouldn't work in prison, Drew, and certainly not in a mundane job like a road crew. You are young. Here is another lesson; educate yourself in prison so you can get a job, a good job, once you are released. Get your high school diploma and take university correspondence courses. Give yourself a chance once you leave this hole. Like I said last night, I can see you are no idiot, so don't make stupid decisions."

Drew was somewhat offended but did not show it. He sensed that John said everything with a purpose in mind. And, though he had known him for a very short time, there was something about the way John spoke and treated Drew that made him want to conciliate John and, in fact, to make him proud.

As John rose from the table at the end of breakfast, Drew was surprised by the stature of the man. He hadn't noticed it the previous night, likely because he was so tired. John stood well over six feet tall and had a lean body which wasn't tremendously muscular but well defined. He had a dark, tanned complexion, with long black hair extending between his shoulder blades and a full beard which hung to his mid-chest and was braided and beaded at the end. His eyes were dark brown and piercing. His nose appeared to have been broken often and carried several crooks along it as a reminder. His arms, chest and neck were capriciously tattooed. As he walked away he carried himself with an air of confidence that suggested he was in charge of his situation.

When breakfast was completed and Drew had had the opportunity to clean himself afterwards, he was summoned to the staff sergeant's office. Arriving, he was directed to a chair. Drew nervously sat for several minutes before the Staff Sergeant entered and took his seat across from Drew, a slight smile on his face.

"Hello Andrew, I'm Staff Sergeant Jackson. How have things been going so far? Do you have any problems or concerns? Now is a good time to voice them," he said with a full, reverent voice.

Drew offered a sheepish smile. "Good morning, Staff Sergeant Jackson. Things are fine, thank you. But, and I mean no disrespect, could you call me Drew, only my mother calls me Andrew."

"I can do that, Drew. I know the transition from juvenile detention to the penitentiary is not an easy one. Understand, though, we are here to help you any way we can. However, we can't help those who are unwilling or uncooperative. So, the choice will be yours: put forth your best effort and leave here a better person than the one who arrived or fail to improve yourself and finish your time here no better off than when you entered."

Recalling the words John spoke that morning, Drew took in a deep breath.

"Yes, sir, I want to improve myself and I have been giving it a lot of thought."

"That is good to hear, Andrew. Sorry, Drew. There are many options available to you while you're here. You will find that keeping yourself occupied makes your stay easier and that time passes quickly. What is it that you decided you'd like to do?"

"Yes, sir," he said unnecessarily, "I would like to complete my high school education and, if I have the time, take some university courses."

"That's a wise choice, Drew. Starting immediately we will get you enrolled in courses with that end in mind. What grade have you completed?"

"Nine." His face blushed with embarrassment.

CHAPTER ELEVEN

As Drew stood on the porch, knocking on the front door, an overpowering sense of uneasiness gripped him with the clutch of a boa constrictor. His breathing became difficult as his throat tightened and, despite wearing a heavy overcoat and winter hat, Drew was shivering. Though he needed to escape the miserable confines of his parents' house, suddenly Drew wasn't sure this would be the appropriate refuge. This was John's house; she, John's wife; and they, John's children. Despite his concerns Drew felt he had nowhere else to turn. The friends he had hung out with were still living a life he no longer wanted, or had moved away. The only other option was his mother's suggestion that he live with her when she moved out of the house in a month. For Drew, that was not an alternative. Not only did he need to get out on his own but the location she had found was still in Drury and it was imperative that he escape from there nearly as much as he needed to flee his parents' house.

When the door opened, Drew was met by a stunningly tall, beautiful woman with straight brown hair, striking blue-green eyes and a slender, curvaceous body. She was wearing tight, hip-hugger blue jeans and a tank top that fit her like an extra skin, the combination accentuating her firm breasts and slim legs. From what he had been told by John, Drew knew Alicia was in her mid-thirties and had been married to John for thirteen years. Though they had children, her body revealed no suggestion of being pregnant once, let alone three times. Beside her stood their two children, Zoë, twelve and Benjamin, nine. John had told Drew that their first child had died when he was one, though he never disclosed the circumstances behind the death.

With a brilliant smile, displaying white teeth as straight and perfect as a line of soldiers standing at attention, she offered her hand in welcome.

"Hello Drew, I'm Alicia. Pleased to finally meet you. John told me so much about you I feel like I have known you for years."

"Hi Alicia, I feel the same way," he laughed, gently shaking her hand. "I'm glad to be able to finally put a face to the person he talked so lovingly about."

They stood gazing at each other for several moments before Alicia broke the silence.

"How rude of me, please come on in. Benjamin, help Mr. Parsons with his things and take them to the room that we prepared for him." She looked back at Drew. "And before you say anything, Drew, this is what we do for our guests."

Drew grinned, nodded his head slightly in acceptance, and, after she had hung his coat in the front closet, walked with Alicia as she led him into the house and showed him around. The residence was a bungalow with an L-shaped living room/dining room immediately to the right of the front entrance and an eat-in kitchen straight ahead, where the front hall ended. Running to the left of the front hall where it met the kitchen, a second hall led to the washroom and three bedrooms. The basement, where Drew would be staying, housed a bedroom with an ensuite bathroom, the laundry room and a large television room, which was used as a storage area.

After the house tour, they sat at the kitchen table. Alicia poured both of them a coffee.

"I work at a restaurant in town. It isn't a great job but the owners are very flexible with the hours knowing that I am a single mother. I started working there just after John entered the penitentiary," she paused, slowly stirring her coffee. "Your moving in will go a long way towards helping me with the monthly expenses."

"I hope it does. My intention is to get a job as soon as possible; it'll be something menial at first but as time goes by my objective is to look for something more along the lines of a career. Regarding rent, how much do you want? My mother gave me some money to cover the first month's rent, but we should discuss all the costs involved."

"I think three-hundred fifty dollars each month will be enough. That will include utilities. If there is a crazy jump in any of the costs, like water or electricity, we can revisit it.

"Just so we're clear, Drew, you will be treated like an adult with no expectations regarding the hours you keep and the people you are friends with as long as you treat me and the children with respect."

Drew nodded his head.

"Fair enough, and so you are aware, I'm looking at this is a temporary situation; once a decent full-time job is found, a permanent place to live will be required. There will be no problems from me, but if things do fall apart and become untenable, I'll move out immediately, whether I have a job or not."

Alicia got up from the table and grabbed the coffee pot to refill their cups.

"During my last meeting with John, we firmed up our plans for offering our assistance. He recommended that you be introduced to an old friend, Jessica Dean." She only poured another half cup for Drew at his request. "She owns a successful art store and gallery in the city and John hoped that she could find you a job, given your interest in art history. I talked to her when John asked me to but couldn't tell her when or if you would be in contact." She poured herself another cup. "She's very nice; very down to earth. But that doesn't mean she is a push-over. You don't become as successful in business as she has become without the necessary drive. Jessica was hesitant at first but eventually said she would be open to the possibility of giving you an interview. She made no promises, though, which is all we can ask. But, even if she can't give you a job, I'm hoping she may be able to put you in touch with someone who can."

Drew was astonished; he was completely unaware of John and Alicia's plans. As she spoke about the job potential he became cautiously excited by the prospect.

"That sounds promising. The only difficulty," he observed, "is transportation. While this is a lot closer to the city than Drury, Westwood is still a fair distance away from it. Does the transit system extend this far?"

"Not quite, the last stop's about a half hour walk from here, but we can make arrangements to get you into the city for work until you get your license. I can drive you in on my way to my job or drop you at the nearest bus stop when not working. But, whether you get the job or not, you will need to get your license."

The excitement began to overtake Drew. "Oh my God, this is awesome. What's Jessica's phone number? I should call her."

"No, the store is closed and won't be open until Tuesday. They are open Tuesday through Saturday and are closed Sundays and Mondays.

In the meantime, Drew, is there anyone you need to notify about your address change? I know you served your full sentence but do you still need to contact parole?"

"No, not parole, but I do need to contact the Department of Family and Social Services."

Alicia narrowed her eyes giving him an apprehensive stare. "Why? Is there something you should be telling me?"

Drew laughed. "No, it's nothing like that. I'm in the process of finding my biological parents and have been in touch with the Department to assist in the search. My case worker, Francine Little, will be calling when she finds the information or may need to contact me before then for clarification."

Smiling again, Alicia mockingly brushed her forehead and flicked the imaginary sweat from her hand.

"Phew! So when did you start looking for them? My God, this must be an exciting few months you have been experiencing. It is funny; John talked about you with a certain amount of adoration which I'd never heard him speak before. He often said you come across as a great deal older than your years. And you do, both in your maturity and physical appearance."

Drew blushed and focused on his coffee cup, not knowing what to say. He had a great respect for John and now, with their magnanimous offer to allow him to live there and learning about Jessica Dean and their plans, his admiration deepened. When he looked up he found Alicia gazing at him, almost quixotically, deepening his discomfort.

"You remind me of him," she said, aware of his uneasiness. "He could never take a compliment, either."

They both laughed: hers heartily; his nervously.

Wanting to change the subject, Drew directed the conversation back to Alicia and John.

"How did you and John meet?"

"This may make you laugh, but I met John in university. He may not have looked the part when you met him but when I first did, he was clean shaven and had short, beautiful, wavy hair. He was studying English Literature at night school. You may have noticed he was well spoken. He came from a well-to-do family and was successful in school but couldn't stay out of trouble. It's too bad, really, because he had always envisioned himself as a teacher. That was what his mother did; his father had an engineering company. John would have been a good teacher, too. Unfortunately, I believe he felt pressure of living up to his parents' standards and he crumbled under those expectations. It almost seemed like he would commit some crime as an act of rebellion when things got too intense for him. Most of the crimes were petty; shoplifting, vandalism and theft. But the last one, the robbery, was just stupid. I just thank God that no one was hurt."

Drew smiled, "How long have you lived here?"

"Thirteen years, I moved in when we got married, but this has been John's house since he was a child. When his parents decided they wanted to move permanently into a condo they owned in Florida, they kept this house for him; an early inheritance, so to speak. They thought this would help him settle down. It was very generous of them, especially given all the trouble John had been in over the years, but they've always been very good to him."

Drew sensed something in the way she spoke. "And you? How are they with you? If you don't mind me asking."

Alicia gave a faint smile, staring at her half finished coffee before looking back at Drew.

"I'm the mother of their grandchildren. They'll offer help but let me know that I'm beholden to them."

"That's unfortunate; nothing was ever said by John?"

"I never told him. There are things best left unsaid."

After they had finished talking, Drew made his way down to the basement. He found his suitcase on the bed in the completely furnished room and proceeded to remove his belongings, filling the dresser. He placed the pictures of his adoptive mother and his biological father holding him, on the side table and Francine's business card beside them. Once he finished and put the suitcase away he lay down on the bed and took a short nap.

After dinner, Drew played with Zoë and Benjamin until their bedtime. Once Alicia had put them to bed and changed into her sleep apparel the two returned to the living room.

"Would you like a drink, Drew? I like to finish the day off with a relaxing beverage."

"No, I'm good, thanks. It has been a long day and I would prefer just vegetating in front of the television for a bit before heading off to bed."

Alicia gave him an inviting stare. "Are you sure?"

Drew smiled, "Ok, you twisted my rubber arm; a beer would be fine, if you have one. But I do need to get some sleep."

"That's fine," Alicia replied, "I'll be staying up a bit longer tonight. There are some things to take care of but I will try to keep the noise to a minimum. Some friends may be dropping by later, they have to work late and need to get something to me. My shift doesn't begin until eleven tomorrow morning; it's the lunch and dinner shift which has me working until after seven."

At ten o'clock, Drew made his way to bed. He and Alicia had had a great conversation and he felt comfortable with his decision to take John up on his offer. Settling into bed, he thought about the events of the day, about John, but mostly about Alicia, who not only was, possibly, the most beautiful woman he had ever met, but also a warm, compassionate and intelligent person. With those thoughts still in his mind, the blackness of sleep cradled him.

Drew woke up to find Alicia standing directly over him. He knew it was still night but a peculiar light shone through the window.

"Drew, I need you to help me with something," she breathed, her voice spectral.

"Sure, what is it? Is there a problem?"

"Follow me," Alicia whispered as she fluidly glided away toward the door with the gracefulness of a sylph, the light seeming to direct her movement.

Without thinking, Drew got up from the bed and followed, oblivious to the fact he was wearing only his underwear. Exiting his bedroom, he looked out into the darkness but Alicia was nowhere to be seen.

"Drew, I'm up here," her voice lingered in the shadows, suspended in its clarity.

Not confident where she could be, he walked slowly towards the top of the stairs guided by the last resonating syllables of her words.

"Alicia, I can't see you," he called in a hushed voice.

As he inched upwards, there were no sounds, no discernible shapes. The house was analogous to being in a vacuum.

Once at the top of the stairs, he noticed the light shining through the front windows, though its source seemed to be coming from within the house. Drew used his hand to shield his eyes from the brightness as he cautiously approached the living room. Looking around the room for a sign of Alicia, he became aware of a presencc behind him. Drawn by it, he turned to find her standing there. For all the light behind him, she remained in a cloak of darkness. As Alicia's body became imbued by the light, he realized that she was wearing only a bra and panties. A salacious smile conveyed her intentions as Alicia gazed deeply into Drew's eyes.

They embraced, kissing passionately, their tongues searching the other's mouth. Drew's entire body tingled in the exhilaration of the moment. Slowly they lowered to the floor where Alicia cradled Drew back, before resting her full weight on him. As they continued to kiss, Drew's hands began to stroke her back, moving down towards its arch. Alicia pushed herself upright and straddled his hips; a nefarious look adorned her face. Rhythmically she began to grind her pelvis forward and back over Drew's erection. The air was fragrant with the scent of her sex, her warm wetness seeped through her panties and his briefs.

"Does that feel good, Drew?"

Drew struggled to respond finding he was breathless and unable to speak.

Alicia's smile widened.

As he reached up to touch her breasts, Alicia removed her bra, offering them to his caress, sighing as his hands cupped them. Leaning forward she positioned her hands to either side of his head and lowered herself to allow his mouth to suckle her nipples while she continued to slowly move her hips. Amatory moans escaped her lips as Drew licked and softly bit the areola.

Moving away, Alicia began to kiss Drew's chest, circling each of his nipples with her tongue. Breathing in deeply to relish his masculine aroma, she slowly manoeuvred herself down his rippled stomach. As she did, she removed his underwear to expose his virility. Drew lay there allowing her to take him in; Alicia wrapping her mouth around his erection. He shuddered as Alicia's mouth moved up and down and her hand lightly massaged the base. With her free hand, Alicia began to scratch down from Drew's chest. Drew could feel the rigidity of his body as his muscles tensed and surged towards orgasm.

Suddenly her finger nails felt like claws ripping into his stomach. As Drew looked down, Alicia released his erection. She raised her head, giving a tilted look.

"After all I did for you, you fuck around with my wife the first chance you get?" The voice was John's.

Alicia's smile vanished and her teeth turned to fangs. She bit Drew's erection, tearing it off at the base.

With a gasp, Drew woke to find himself wrapped up in the bed covers, sweating profusely. Throwing off the sheets he checked his stomach and inside his underwear to ensure it was only a dream. He lay there in the black stillness, the only sounds being the blood coursing through his ears as his heart pounded, and his laboured breathing. The remainder of the night was spent in restless sleep, Drew too anxious to allow the possibility of another dream.

As the sun rose above the horizon Drew got out of bed to prepare for the day ahead. Stepping from the shower he could hear the sounds of Zoë and Benjamin moving around as they got up and ready for school. Drew looked at the clock; seven-thirty. He made his way upstairs. Nearing the top step he heard Alicia exiting her bedroom and walking down the hall to the kitchen. He froze, unsure what to do. Taking a deep breath through his nose and expelling it from his mouth, Drew calmed himself before continuing up to the main floor. Silently he admonished himself for being so ridiculous.

Entering the kitchen he was confronted with Alicia's back as she stood speaking to the children at the table, the sun shining through the window, silhouetting her body through the thin, short kimono, her long shapely legs gracefully flowing below it to the floor. Drew found himself gazing at her as the children greeted him with waves. Alicia turned around to meet his eyes with hers, unaware of the effect the sun was having on her kimono and him. Drew looked down at the floor, embarrassed and feeling guilt-ridden from his dream of the previous night.

"Good morning Drew, did you have a good sleep?"

"Good morning. Yes, it was fine, thank you."

He still hadn't looked at her, scanning around the kitchen pretending to look for something.

"Is there something you need?"

Drew glanced at her, looking at the kimono rather than her face before, again, looking away. Alicia grasped the situation and began laughing to herself.

"Sorry I embarrassed you, Drew; it slipped my mind that you were here. I will go change right away and will try to remember from now on." Alicia winced, "You weren't made too uncomfortable, were you?"

"No, I'm not uncomfortable," he replied, completely unconvincingly, "just sorry you have to change your routine because of me."

As Alicia passed him she patted him on the shoulder. "I don't *have* to," she whispered, before waltzing down the hall to her room, laughing.

After the children were on the school bus, Alicia returned to the house to find Drew sitting at the kitchen table with a bowl of cereal. He looked up at her, his eyes sad.

"What is wrong, Drew? Is something bothering you? Something you want to talk about?"

Drew wanted to talk about the strong bond he had with John, but couldn't bring himself to do it.

"No, nothing is wrong; I just didn't get as good a sleep as I thought. Moving around will get me feeling better; maybe I will go for a walk after breakfast just to wake myself up."

When breakfast was completed and the kitchen cleaned, Drew went for the walk, strolling around the town of Westwood to become more familiar with it. The morning was sunny but brisk with a light breeze from the northwest. It was edging past the middle of November and the trees were barren, having lost their leaves to the cold and blustery early part of the month. Drew kept bundled up; the low lying sun remained concealed behind the buildings, casting shadows across the sidewalk as he strode along the main street. Similar to many small towns Westwood's main street was where most of the stores and other businesses were located. Like Drury, Westwood was nondescript in its appearance, though being larger had a bustling vitality to it. After walking for a few hours, Drew returned to the house.

By the time he got back Alicia was gone; Drew was relieved. Entering the house he paused in the front hall and drank in the silence. In the kitchen Drew found a note from Alicia advising him that she had been in touch with Jessica who was expecting him the following morning for an interview. He went to his bedroom and returned, soon after, with Francine's card in his hand and dialed the number.

"Department of Family and Social Services, Francine Little speaking, may I help you?"

"Hello, Francine, it's Drew Parsons, do you have time to talk?"

"Sure Drew, how can I help you?"

"I am going to be in the city and was wondering if you could meet for lunch? There is some info to discuss with you and a picture I forgot to give you when we saw each other the first time."

Fissures

Drew met Francine at a small Thai fusion restaurant just around the corner from Francine's office.

"I have written down my new address." he said, producing a piece of paper. "Also, here is a picture of what my biological father looked like about twenty-two years ago. That cute baby on his lap is me."

Francine smiled as she took the picture and the paper.

"Would it be okay for me to take a photocopy of the picture and mail the photo back to you?"

Drew nodded his head. "So, you don't look that much older than me, how old are you? What is your background?"

"I hope that isn't a problem for you, Drew."

Drew shook his head reassuringly.

"I'm twenty-six. I have my degree in sociology but am working towards my PhD. I've been here, with the Department, for slightly less than two years and love the work. And what about you? The other day you mentioned something about being with the Government Forces. In what capacity did you work for the government?"

Drew knew he couldn't continue with the façade.

"Fran, I have to make something clear."

Drew's tone sounded portentous. She looked at him a little concerned.

"My past seven years have been spent in the penitentiary. The expression 'Government forces' is used so people won't prejudge who I am."

Francine looked at him with a furrowed stare as she processed the information. Drew looked back wincing. After several moments of silence, he spoke again.

"Would you like me to leave?"

"No, that isn't necessary. Admittedly, I'm a bit stunned by the news, but in social services one deals with all types of individuals with all types of history. I only wish you had told me up front; been more honest."

"I'm sorry, you are right. From this point forward you will get nothing but the truth."

Several more moments of silence passed.

"Seven years seems like a long time for a simple break and enter, did you already have a criminal record?"

"No. It's not that we weren't involved in petty criminal activity, we were, but never got caught. But there was violence involved with the crime. The homeowner caught us in the house. I ran out but the other guy, Lorne was his name, shot her in the head. He didn't realize there was a bullet in the gun. The irony of it was that I had decided earlier that day that I was no longer going to hang out with that group of friends and was on my way home when I met up with Lorne."

"That's really unfortunate. Can I ask you something?"

"Sure, what would you like to know?"

"Can you tell me about your upbringing, your parents? We talked about you biological parents, but what about your adoptive parents?"

Except for asking for certain points of clarification, Fran sat, silently listening. She looked at him with wonderment in her eyes as Drew told her matter-of-factly about his upbringing. After he had finished Fran continued staring for several moments before she finally spoke.

"That was incredible. I have to admit I'm surprised that you didn't become more involved in crime given the violent, intolerant environment you grew up in. And to think, in all those years you never raised a hand to him? You are a very strong individual, Drew. That must have taken great restraint."

Drew shook his head to wave off the compliment.

"Don't sell yourself short," she said. "It was very fortunate you always had your mom to turn to for protection. She was never far away. It seems to me that if she wasn't there the story could have been much worse.

All your father's drinking, alone, and the arguments it caused."

"Yeah, I remember we went to Florida one year. Though I don't recall much, my dad got really drunk and my mother and he had this incredible agreement; probably the biggest I ever heard them have. She came to my room later. She told me she was afraid my dad would attack one of us in his drunken rage."

"My goodness, were the police or social services never involved?"

"No. You know, thinking about it, that's the funny thing. For all the problems, all the abuses she and I tolerated, my mom never called either. She would just tend to me; protect me herself."

"That seems strange. You would think she would have done something like that. I guess things were different back then."

Drew didn't respond to Fran's comment for several moments but his eyes remained fixed on her.

"Fran, we have only talked for a few hours, between Friday and today, but I was wondering if you might like to go out with me sometime."

Fran's eyes flinched and moved from Drew and out the window of the restaurant to the traffic passing along the street, a look of uneasiness on her face. Drew knew what was going to come next.

"Drew, I find you fascinating and really do enjoy your company..."

"But..." he led her on.

"But I cannot become involved with a person whose case I'm working on. Emotions would get involved and conflict could occur."

"What conflict? I don't understand."

"There would be a pressure, whether real or perceived, for me to work a little harder than normal, maybe to do a little extra. And the pressure would be for me to complete a successful investigation. If it isn't, what would happen? This is for your protection and mine."

"You are right, that was very self-centered of me to put you in that position. I am sorry."

"No, please, don't apologize. I'm flattered that you would want to see me."

Drew smiled and nodded.

After walking Fran back to her office, where she took a copy of the picture, Drew wandered around the city for the next several hours. When he got back to Alicia's house it was after nine and the children were in bed. Alicia was watching television in the living room wearing a bath robe, her hair wrapped in a towel. She turned smiling at him as he entered the room. Drew returned the smile, sitting on the couch across from her.

"How was your day?" she asked.

"Good, thanks. I met with the woman from the Family and Social Services Department and gave her some information, then walked around the city and shopped for clothes for my interview with Jessica. If I get the job I will have to go out to buy more, I don't think my current assortment of apparel will cut it. Oh, I dropped in to the Department of Motor Vehicles and set a date for a driving test. Fortunately, it won't be for a few weeks. Do you think I can get some practice in during that time? How was your day, busy?"

"Yes, very, but the busier the more tips; so I'm not going to complain. Today alone, I made over two hundred dollars in tips." She held up some cash that was sitting on the table beside her. "I need all the money I can get; it isn't easy trying to keep up with the bills.

"But some patrons make life difficult. I have to tell you what happened with this one guy today.

"I take his order and, as with all diners, I read it back to him to ensure it's correct. Well, when the meal's brought out he tells me it took too long to arrive. I look at him like he has two freakin' heads," she laughed, "I mean, it was about 10 minutes. Then this piece of shit tells me the meal isn't what he ordered, saying he wanted his steak done medium and that what was brought to him was well done. He obviously doesn't have a clue what medium is because when he explained what he wanted, he described rare. What a dick. Of course, being the stellar server I am, I offer to take it back and have a new one brought out. Still grumbling, he says that he will eat what was served. After talking to the owner and explaining the situation we offer this guy twenty percent off the price of his meal; which is more than he deserves. Begrudgingly he accepts it without even thanking me. So he gets the bill and he signs off on it, then asks me for another glass of water. I bring it to him and walk over to tend to another table. I just happen to look over at him as he is reaching into his wallet. You know what the prick does? He takes out twenty-five cents: five pennies, two nickels and a dime, and drops them into the glass. Then he seals the top of the glass with a piece of paper and quickly turns the glass upside down so that none of the water spills out. What an asshole. Next he pulls the paper out fast, you know, like people who rip table cloths off tables without making the dishes fall. Well, I've had enough of this guy's bullshit and march up to him and say loud enough for everyone in the place to hear, 'thank you for the twenty-five cent tip, sir, it was very generous of you.' While he is still sitting there going red with embarrassment I pick up the glass and remove the change. Of course the water spills all over the table and pours onto the lap of his fine suit. He jumps out of the booth and storms out of the place. It was outstanding. Other patrons at the restaurant started applauding. Even the manager thought it was funny. Man, don't screw with me."

As she finished the story Alicia was laughing so hard she had tears running down her cheek. After several moments she regained her composure, though she continued to giggle.

"Anyway, I was going to say, call next time you need to be picked up."

"I'll remember that next time; I was starting to feel the cold on the walk from the bus stop. Also remind me to never short change you with a tip."

They both shared another laugh.

"As for practicing your driving, sure, we can go out and get you behind the wheel.

"Also, just give me your new shirt; I will iron it and leave it out for you for tomorrow."

Just like the previous night, Drew found himself falling asleep as he sat watching television with Alicia and, before long, he excused himself and went to bed. He looked forward to the day ahead of him and wanted to be well rested for when he spoke to Jessica.

In the bedroom he set out his jacket and pants along with the tie he had purchased that day. As he was looking everything over it dawned on him that he had forgotten to buy shoes. Frantically he rushed up to the main floor.

"Can you drive me to the store? I can't believe it but I forgot to get dress shoes." Drew said with a voice strained from anxiety.

Alicia shook her head. "Sorry, but the stores closed over half an hour ago. But there are some of John's shoes in my bedroom that may fit you, I doubt John will need them."

Alicia left the living room and returned a few minutes later with three pair of dress shoes. Drew tried them on and each pair fit. He elected to go with the black loafers. With a relieved, appreciative smile, Drew went back to his bedroom. Anxious about the interview in the morning and fearful of another dream like the previous night, his sleep that night was fitful.

CHAPTER TWELVE

It was visitation day and Drew looked forward to seeing his mother. It had been a couple of months since her last visit and he missed catching up with her. After more than four years in the penitentiary system he had virtually no contact with the outside world other than her visits. In juvenile detention he had visits from both family and friends on a regular basis, but over time and because of the distance to the penitentiary, the number of people visiting dwindled until it was only his mother who came to see him. In the beginning, even though Drew never asked, Jean made excuses for why his father hadn't attended. By the time she would finish, anger would be rising in Drew. Finally he had had enough and told her he didn't want to hear any more reasons for William's absences.

On this occasion, visitation took place on a Saturday, not that Drew was aware of it. Just as John had advised, days, weeks and months had ceased to have names or meaning. He only knew that it was his seven-hundred and eighty-eighth day in The Pen. Almost eight-hundred days inside and he had settled in with little drama. Drew's classes were going well and he had just begun his final year towards completing his high school diploma. He had discovered an interest and aptitude for ancient art and had already decided to pursue his university degree in that area.

The only conflicts he ever encountered were with the wild-eyed antagonizer he had met while in the bull pen when he had first arrived.

Skewer was a gang member who earned his moniker due to his proclivity for using a knife. He was in jail for a carjacking during which he stabbed the victim in the face, causing the woman to lose her left eye.

Drew tried to steer clear of Skewer but periodically their paths crossed. When they did, inevitably Skewer would cause trouble. Though most of the altercations were verbal, when the opportunity presented itself, Skewer had attacked. On those few occasions, Drew found he was alone and outnumbered. He would be swarmed and pinned down while Skewer delivered body blows. During one incident Drew was assailed in the yard with a shank. Fortunately the guards were quick to react but Skewer handed the weapon off to one of his minions before the guards arrived. Drew, however, kept the confrontations quiet, never letting on to anyone what was happening.

Earlier in the day, Drew had eaten breakfast with John, his mentor and the closest thing to a friend. They were going to play a game of basketball in the yard at ten o'clock, as part of the pick-up league for the prisoners, before their families arrived. The two teams met for a friendly game: John, Drew and John's buddies against another team, most of whom Drew had never seen, let alone met. Though the games were mainly for exercise, often the play would turn competitive and, once in a while, emotions would boil over. John always reminded Drew to keep his focus on the game as well as the crowds which would gather to watch.

The day was sunny and warm and the game robust. It wasn't long before both teams were stripping off their shirts. The game was played competitively yet in an enjoyable, sportsmanly manner. When it ended both groups headed to the shadow of the prison walls to cool off.

As they sat in the shade Drew took notice of the names tattooed on John's chest: Zoë on his right pec and Benjamin on the left. Across his stomach just below his navel, in a concave design, was the name David.

"Are those the names of your kids?" Drew asked.

"Yeah, Zoë is my daughter, she is nine. Benjamin is my son, he is six. I got his name tattooed just before coming to prison, about six months before he was born.

We knew it was going to be a boy and had decided the name."

"What about the one on your stomach: David?"

John looked down at the name.

"David was my first son, he was a cute kid. Unfortunately he was taken away from us when he was one," John looked at Drew but was lost to some distant memory.

"Hey, David is my middle name," Drew revealed.

"Yeah, well it is a pretty common name. Probably twenty percent of the guys in here have the name David as their first or second name," John replied flatly.

Drew could tell that the loss of his son still troubled John.

When wouldn't the death of a baby ever be difficult to deal with? Drew reasoned.

When the teams dispersed, Drew and John stood and began walking back to the building.

Recognizing John's discomfort with the issue, Drew changed the subject.

"I'm looking forward to a visit from my mother today. We haven't visited in a couple of months. Will your wife be visiting today?

"Absolutely!" John answered, a vibrant smile stretching his face wide. "Alicia never misses a visitation day; especially when they are conjugal." He winked, nudging Drew with his elbow. "I just wish we had more of those."

The two men laughed as they neared the doors. Then John's face took on a serious tone. He stopped. Taking Drew by the arm, he moved close, his eyes staring with an intensity that made Drew uncomfortable. Lowering his voice, John spoke deliberately to Drew.

"Lesson twenty-one: don't do this to people you love."

John gestured at the building and prison yard surrounding them.

"You deprive them of a complete life. People love you and you are part of them; physically, emotionally and spiritually. To deprive them of who you are is to deprive them of an element of who they are. I know my wonderful wife struggles every day without me and my kids miss their dad. I'm not just speaking of my physical presence, but also of the spiritual connection she and I have, the emotional support we give each other; being there to lift her spirits when she is angry or depressed. And, honestly, the fact is Benjamin has never had a father in his life, only some guy he occasionally visits in an ascetic building far from his home where a hundred other guys wearing the same orange prison jumpsuit also congregate. And that eats me up.

"The kids and I are lucky that Alicia is such a strong person in our lives. She keeps the ship sailing straight, but that still doesn't make it right or fair.

"Just as unfortunate you deprive yourself of life's treasures, of family. And sometimes those lost things can weigh on a person more that you can imagine. This place can take away your humanity, your will and your life."

John paused as Drew looked down at a spot on the ground he had been kicking.

"Drew," he said bringing Drew's attention back to him.

"I'm sure this hasn't been easy on your parents, either. When you get out of here, it is imperative that you attempt to reconcile with your mother and father. You have injured them, left a hole in their lives and that needs to be tended to."

Drew nodded. He realized that, despite all the disagreements they had had over the years, William had still raised him. And like anyone else, deserved a second chance.

After the two parted, Drew went to his cell to shower, thinking about the advice he had received from John.

As Drew was readying to leave his cell for the visitation room, Peter walked in with another, larger, skin head, stopping just inside the cell door.

"Me and my buddy, Hank here, have had enough of you hanging out with that big nigger. I told you the first day and many other times that there are rules." Peter's voice was cold.

"Not that it matters but he ain't a black guy. And even if he was, I told you the first day that I wasn't going to be joining your gang. I'll decide who I will and won't hang with; not you."

"Drew, I don't think you understand. You're wrong. You don't make the decision; you get told."

Drew looked at the two as they stood blocking the door. He pointed his chin toward Hank.

"Is Hank here as your muscle?"

Peter gave a sardonic laugh.

Hank portrayed a menacing grin while opening and closing his fist. His eyes remained fixated on Drew.

Drew stood silent, sizing up the situation.

"Well guys, I don't think *you* understand," his voice lampooning Peter's, "I'm not asking you, but telling you, the both of you, to fuck off."

"What is it with new guys, that they think they are different than everyone else and don't have to do what they are told?" Peter said, looking at Drew but speaking to Hank.

With a slight nod of Peter's head, Hank charged Drew. Seeing that Hank had left himself exposed, Drew reacted quickly. With precision he delivered a roundhouse kick that caught Hank mid-way up his left thigh, paralyzing the leg. As Hank dropped to the floor, Drew moved back in front of him and punched him in the face followed by another punch to the throat. A second roundhouse kick caught Hank across the right ear sending him tumbling. Hank lay on the floor ineffective, his mouth spewing a bloody discharge.

Peter tried to escape but Drew caught him before he could make it out the cell. Spinning him back into the room, Drew cracked Peter's head off the bunk bed before slamming his body against the wall. Coiling Peter's arm behind his back, Drew forced him up on his toes. Drew then leaned in and whispered with a low, calculated voice.

"We're stuck in this fucking cell with each other, Peter, we have no choice. So, from my vantage point, we have to make the best of a bad situation."

Drew paused for a moment, wrenching Peter's arm further up his back. Peter grimaced in pain.

"If you ever threaten me again, I will kill you. If any of your maggot Arian gang member friends ever threatens me, I will kill *you*. You and your kind are a fucking pestilence; bugs that need to be squashed and I'll do just that. You think you're bad ass in your gang with your shaved head and swastika tattoos? You don't know the fucking meaning of bad ass. But that lesson will be taught to you if you ever cross me again."

Drew jerked Peter around, grabbed him around the jaw and the back of his head and forced him to look at Hank.

"See Hank there? That was easy for me; I could just as easily have killed him, but chose to only hurt him. And hurt he is. You'll have to help him back to his cell once I'm gone. Remember that image next time you think about fucking with me."

Snapping Peter's face away from the groaning mass on the floor, Drew brought his face close.

"Have I made myself clear, Peter? This living arrangement can work if you are willing, but I will kill you if need be. You know the consequence, you decide the action."

With blood trickling down his forehead, Peter looked wide-eyed at Drew, petrified, as he paroxysmally nodded his head.

Releasing Peter and stepping over Hank, Drew left the cell and walked towards the visitation area. Finding a community washroom he slipped in and vomited for several minutes.

After cleaning himself up, Drew continued down to the visitation area where he restlessly waited for his mother's arrival, his nerves still prickling.

As he sat at a table, he observed John enter the room and take a seat on the opposite side from him. Drew had hoped John would sit closer. He wanted to introduce John to his mother, but whenever they had corresponding appointment times, John always sat far away.

The visitation room was open concept, but Spartan. Unlike the visitation rooms which house a row of seats, separated by panels on either side of plexiglass windows where the inmates speak to the visitors via telephone, this room was filled with thirty-five stainless steel tables divided over seven rows. Each table had four metal seats: one for the prisoner and three for visitors, who sat across from him. All tables and seats were secured to the floor. The guards sat at desks located behind partitions with tinted plexiglass windows, giving the inmates and their families a sense of privacy and to reduce the feeling of constraint. Each visitor had to sign in and go through a search before entering the facility. With so few tables in such a large facility, the visits were short and allotted based on a rotating schedule. If, for whatever reason, an inmate did not receive visitors on the assigned date and time, he had to wait through the rotation until his name came up again. Jean had missed the previous visitation day.

When his mother arrived, Drew rose from his seat and greeted her with a long, warm hug. Sitting, she gave Drew a rundown of the events which had occurred during the previous two months. Just having his mother there was a good remedy for the tedium of jail; Drew could have sat in silence in the comfort of her presence. Jean told the same stories Drew had heard for the previous twenty visits but, fluff or serious, he couldn't get enough of them: Mrs. Peterson's escaping cats; their own dogs making mischief with her gardens; or Mr. Phillips, who suffered from dementia, wandering around the neighbourhood in a heartbreaking attempt to find his childhood home.

As Jean spoke, Drew periodically surveyed the room, looking to where John was sitting in hopes of getting his attention. Unfortunately the ebb and flow of the inmates and their families obfuscated both John and his wife, Alicia, whom Drew had never had the opportunity to meet. When the visit ended, Jean got up from the table and gave Drew another long, comforting hug before promising that she would not miss the next visit. As they walked towards the exit, Drew, again, glanced to where John had been seated but the table was occupied by another prisoner with his wife and children.

What Drew hadn't realizing was that John and Alicia were now sitting at the table nearest the doors.

When Alicia arrived, John found an empty table near the entrance door and directed Alicia to it.

"How are the kids?" a child-like enthusiasm crackled in his voice.

"They are doing great. Zoë had her first test and scored very well. Benjamin is having lots of fun in grade one. They want me to give you a big hug and kiss, of course. How are things going in here?"

"No complaints. Working like a sonofabitch, but it keeps me fit and I have been helping Drew with his studies and giving him sage advice," a smirk crept across John's face.

"How are you holding up these days? Are you making enough each month? If you are having difficulty you can call my parents, they would be willing to help."

Alicia moved her eyes from John and down to the table where she scratched at an imaginary speck on the surface. She despised asking his parents for money or any type of assistance, for that matter. Though John wasn't aware of it, Alicia felt that whenever she had asked for their support in the past, they would lord it over her, bringing it up at every opportunity, and the indebtedness she carried was like a stone yoke around her neck.

"It's hard, but I do what needs be done to meet the bills every month." She paused momentarily. "I've been thinking; what if we get a boarder? The basement could be rented and the extra money that brings in would allow me to…" Her voice trailed off, her gaze even more intent on the imaginary speck.

"Allow you to what?" John asked, his eyes narrowing as he turned his face slightly to the left, examining Alicia.

"Allow me to spend less time at the waitressing job and more time with the children. I sometimes think the kids are the ones who are suffering the most."

John shook his head.

"I'm not comfortable with that idea. I know this is not easy for you or the kids, but I also have faith in you; that you can overcome this."

"But John, it is really tough making ends meet. Every month I feel like the walls are closing in, I'm becoming almost claustrophobic. And your parents shouldn't be depended upon. It just brings stress into our relationship and that isn't fair to them or me and the children."

John felt the guilt take a chokehold on him as he listened to Alicia's plea, knowing that he wasn't at home to deal with all the stresses of meeting bill obligations, of working long hours and being a parent to their children. He thought about it a little longer. Reaching across the table, he took Alicia by the hands and gave her a compassionate look.

"If you would be willing to hold on for a while, I think there may have an arrangement that satisfies your concerns and mine. Actually it was something I have been considering for a while but was going to speak to you about it at a later time. Would you be open to that?"

Alicia nodded.

"I can try; it depends on what you are proposing."

"That's my baby. Okay, here is what I am thinking: Drew is a great kid who has grown up in a shitty situation, one that he shouldn't go back to when he is released in a few years. He is currently working at getting his grade twelve diploma by the end of this year and has done very well, from what I understand. If you can last for another two and a half years, he can live in the basement and pay rent. I know that seems like a long time but it will go by quickly. And he is a guy I trust, absolutely."

Alicia thought about what John had planned and agreed to wait, on the condition that Drew was willing to get a job in a relatively short period of time after his release and pay rent. However, she felt guilty for not being honest with him. The bills had been piling up for quite some time and she couldn't meet them given the income she was making as a waitress. Even working double shifts didn't bring in enough.

Without his knowledge or approval she had already been renting out the basement bedroom for the past several months to John's long time friend, Richard. She was charging him three-hundred and fifty dollars each month. While there was nothing inappropriate about their personal relationship, she had given her consent allowing him to sell drugs out of the house and, as a result, Richard had been paying her extra from the money he was making from the trafficking. Between the rent and the profits, she could pay all the bills and have a bit of money left over at the end of each month.

By accepting John's proposal, she knew that she would have to put an end to the basement rental arrangement prior to Drew's release to ensure that Richard was not discovered. That wouldn't be for about two and a half more years, though, and would give her time to squirrel away some of the profits.

As their visitation time drew to an end, Alicia stood and gave John one more kiss and a hug from the kids before she left the room. John watched her until she disappeared through the exit doors.

When Drew sat with John for the dinner meal, he looked somewhat downcast.

"What's wrong, Drew? Something eating at you?"

Drew didn't look at John, choosing instead to concentrate on the food he was idly playing with.

"No, nothing really, it's just that I keep hoping to introduce you to my mother. Every time we have the same visitation time, you sit at the furthest spot in the room from where we sit. Do you do that on purpose?"

"Well, yeah, actually I do."

Drew looked at him bewildered.

"I don't want to meet your mother. Don't take it as an affront; you should keep your life in here separate from your life out there. Your mother doesn't need to be introduced to a shaggy, tattooed shit like me. The result could be devastating for her. It would likely make her more worried about you than simply allowing herself to think that the populace in here is no different than that in the outside world. It is easy for people to protect themselves from reality when not confronted by it. In the same vein, there is no need for you to meet my wife and children. It just makes things complicated. This place is too transient; prisoners come and go and trying to explain it to my kids can be very difficult for them, emotionally."

"I get you not wanting your kids to meet me. But my mother isn't a child. She sees what this place is every time she comes here. If you gave it a chance, you would like her and she would like you, too."

"Drew, I appreciate what you are saying, but I'm not interested in meeting your mother. Period. You may think she is aware, but she comes here monthly and visits with you. And I guarantee, she is aware of the other prisoners here but she isn't *conscious* to what they are. You have to trust me on this one, Drew; she doesn't want to meet anyone else in this hell-hole except for her little Andrew."

At the conclusion of the meal, Drew began to make his way back to his cell still on edge, both from what he felt was John's snub of his mother and the earlier confrontation with Peter and Hank.

As the crowd milled about he heard the hissing voice of Skewer calling his name behind him. Reactively,

Drew spun about and approached Skewer with purpose in his stride. Coming face to face with Skewer, he hadn't noticed the other gang members had moved towards the two of them.

"I don't know what your problem with me is, you fucking shit stain, but let's see if you are as tough without all your fuck-buddies around you or a shiv in your hand. You're probably just some lame-ass pussy."

As Skewer moved closer Drew realized other gang members had surrounded the two of them. He had let himself get into circumstances contrary to what John had often warned him about.

Lesson twelve: Never allow yourself to be in the middle of a hostile situation.

Drew knew he was in real danger, not just from the surrounding crowd but the nearness of Skewer and not knowing whether he had a shank. Still, as Skewer stepped closer, Drew refused to back down.

"You want to see how tough I am, you motherfucker? I'm gonna beat you down and corn-hole you. Then I'm gonna stick my dick in your mouth and make you suck it clean. You will be my bitch not that old man's you're always blowing."

Jesus Christ, twice in one day. Fuck, Drew.

Drew let out a short burst of air, "Okay..."

Like a snake strike, he lashed out, punching Skewer in the face, feeling the crush of Skewer's nose as it shattered under the force of his fist. Staggering back, Skewer fell to the floor. By the time he got back to his feet, a thick, clotting flow of blood seeped from his nose down his chin and onto his clothing. Pinching the bridge of his nose, Skewer blew out a large gob of blood which splattered on the mess hall floor. Focusing back on Drew and with a crazed look in his eyes, Skewer charged and threw a flailing punch. Drew ducked under the oncoming fist and delivered a sledgehammer-like blow just below Skewer's rib cage, sending his diaphragm into spasm. With Skewer doubled over unable to breathe, Drew brought his knee up quickly, striking him, again, in the face. The spray of blood, now from his mouth and nose, arched into the air above them as Skewer's head pitched back and his body followed.

Before he could move toward Skewer, Drew felt the weight of several bodies and was driven into the floor. The crowd swarmed with loud shouts of attack and moans of anguish booming off the cafeteria walls. Drew suffered the pain of being battered, repeatedly kicked from unknown assailants. With his arms pinned underneath his body, he was unable to defend himself against the onslaught. Then he heard a loud yell and felt the weight on him lessen before a hand grabbed him by the back of his jump suit and lifted him from the floor.

"What the fuck are you doing?" John demanded, exasperation evident in his voice. "Get the hell away from the middle of all this; step back like you are watching, before the guards get here."

Drew backed into the crowd, away from where the fighting was taking place. He watched as John turned back towards the mêlée and pushed his way through the swarm before grabbing Skewer by the scalp. In quick succession he kneed and punched Skewer before tossing him to the floor, unconscious, his nose mashed, his teeth broken and his face crimson. John continued walking away and toward the opposite wall as if he were going for a stroll. Drew estimated there were nearly thirty prisoners involved in the fight now and over one hundred gathered to watch.

As he continued to back into the crowd Drew sensed a sharp pain between his shoulder blades radiating like fire into his neck, shoulders and lower back. His eyes opened wide with the shock. Slowly he dropped to his knees as colours flashed before his eyes and his head began to spin. He felt the sharpness being withdrawn before it plunged in again, slightly lower than the first stab. His breathing became laboured and shallow. Drew frantically reached behind him to try and remove the object from his back but was unsuccessful, feeling instead, the wetness of the blood as it streamed down his back. When the weapon was withdrawn again, he recognized a rapid laughing voice behind him but couldn't make out who the person was as the sound was washed away by a strange, high-pierced ringing in his ears. His vision began pulsing white rings which encircled his view, before his eyes rolled back. He thought he heard John's yells above the din of the fight, just before there was darkness. Drew felt nothing of his defenceless face striking the floor, the hard surface splitting his forehead.

CHAPTER THIRTEEN

The morning of his interview, Drew rose early to make sure he was ready to meet Jessica. The jacket, pants and tie were just where he left them and the ironed shirt sat on a coat hanger hanging from the doorframe. He showered and dressed for breakfast, wearing jeans and a T-shirt; worried he would spill something on his new suit. At breakfast Drew had difficulty eating; his nerves were stretched to capacity, and eventually he gave up on the idea.

"I'm so nervous; I have never formally applied for a job let alone interviewed for one," Drew said, as he paced about the kitchen. Alicia and the children watched him, amused.

"Drew, it'll be fine. Just be enthusiastic and talk about what you want and what you know. Even if you aren't the right fit for what Jessica is looking for, she said she'd be willing to help you get work somewhere else. And remember what I said to you the other night, she's very down to earth, very approachable."

"I'm not so sure about this."

"Oh, come on, I think she will like you and you her. You'll do fine. Come here and sit back down. You shouldn't be so worried; it will only undermine your resolve."

In spite of her reassuring words, Drew's anxiety didn't diminish. In vain he tried to coax himself into believing everything would be fine.

Drew sat back down, placing his elbows on the table and clasped his hands. He leaned his forehead against his intertwined fingers. Alicia walked behind him. She began massaging his shoulders. Drew closed his eyes and again tried to relax. As she continued massaging, she spoke with a soft, mollifying voice.

"Drew, you are an articulate, intelligent, polite man; a great guy. If you talk to her with the confidence you have shown me over the past few days, there will be no issues. Just stay within yourself and know that you can do it."

Drew stood up and turned to her. Smiling uncertainly, he nodded his head slightly. Alicia cupped his face in her hands; her eyes were reaffirming and supportive, and restored a degree of Drew's confidence.

"You'll knock her dead." Alicia said with an enthusiastic smile, punching his shoulder.

When Drew had finished getting ready, Alicia gave him a ride to Jessica's gallery.

'The Art of the City' was a posh art shop and gallery partial to new and unknown artists while still maintaining classical art styles, and had a penchant for enticing high end clientele. The shop was shouldered in amongst trendy antique brokers, upscale furniture stores and fashion houses.

Alicia dropped Drew off at the corner a half hour early, wishing him luck before she drove away. He made his way to the store to look at the front windows display before navigating through traffic to a coffee shop across the street. Taking a window seat he observed the comings and goings of the coffee shop patrons while paying attention to the store on the other side of the road and the activity of the area.

Just before nine o'clock a grey Audi pulled into the parking lot and a woman wearing blue jeans and a three quarter length coat stepped out. Drew watched her closely. Rather than walking to the store, she made her way over to the coffee shop. Standing in line, she kept looking back at the car nervously.

Disregarding her, Drew turned his attention back to the shop. A second vehicle, a red Mercedes, pulled into the lot and, again, a woman stepped out. Drew could see she wore a dress and high heeled shoes. She walked with a confident elegance as she approached the front of the store and, drawing a set of keys from her purse, proceeded to open the front door and enter.

Leaving his coffee behind, Drew rose from the bench table and made his way out of the coffee shop and crossed the street to the gallery.

Entering 'The Art of the City', he observed it was much larger than it appeared from the outside. A mix of prints from familiar paintings of gothic, renaissance and baroque to neo-classical, surrealism and abstract expressionism were displayed in different sections of the store, juxtaposing diverse exhibits of modern artists' works along with sculptures and some video and photographic presentations. Drew wandered about marvelling at the beauty of not only the art but also the design of the store itself. The flow of the displays led the eye of the observer along the contiguous movement from one section to the next. Drew began to walk up the set of stairs to the second floor.

"May I help you?" The woman's voice pulled Drew from the magnificent distraction.

As he turned, his eyes met those of the woman he had seen open the front door. Unbeknownst to Drew she had come from the back office. She was of average height, with short, black hair and brown eyes behind a pair of rectangular glasses. Her voice had an accent which Drew guessed to be British. Appearing to be in her mid-thirties, she wore a slight, arrogant look of superiority as she gazed at him with her left eyebrow raised.

"Hello," he replied, extending his hand in greeting as he walked back down the stairs. "I'm Drew Parsons."

The woman didn't accept his proffered hand; instead she continued to look at him, arms crossed, giving no indication of acknowledgement.

"A friend of John and Alicia...," he continued unaware of the door opening behind him. "Alicia said she contacted you yesterday about me coming."

"I believe it is me you are looking for, Andrew."

The voice gave Drew a start. He turned and immediately recognized the woman from the coffee shop.

"Jessica? Jessica Dean?"

She flashed a quick smile and walked toward him holding her hand out in greeting. Drew took it, making sure to gently shake it, his face beaming with excitement and relief.

"Hello, Andrew, it is very nice to meet you."

"The pleasure is mine. And, please, you can call me Drew, if you don't mind. Only my mother calls me Andrew."

"Okay, Drew. I see you already met Kimberley. Please follow me to the back where we can talk."

Jessica led him to the back office where she removed her coat and scarf, placing them on a coat rack standing in the corner. She was slightly taller than Kimberley with an average build, wavy, shoulder-length fawn coloured hair, soft blue eyes and dimpled cheeks. Her high cheek bones and a dark birthmark on her neck were her most distinguishing features. Her appearance was appealing, her smile wide, and, as Alicia said, Jessica's manner was casual and approachable. She sat behind a desk and offered Drew the chair across from her.

"Let me start by saying that Alicia gave me a glowing introduction to you when we spoke several months ago and again yesterday when she contacted me. I understand you are studying art history at university. What year are you in?"

"That's correct; I am currently going into my third year. I have put it on hold for a bit while looking for a job but will be taking night courses through York University once I am able to afford it again."

"That's good to hear. And how have you done to this point? How are your grades? What exactly have you studied and what are your areas of interest?"

"My marks are good; I completed my second year with a three point seven grade point average. The area I'm most interested in is the art and architecture of the Gothic through to Rococo eras. But I also have interest in how art of antiquity evolved and how it has impacted or influenced subsequent styles right up to today."

"And you believe that art from the Renaissance, for example, has relevance even today? Is there an example you can give me?"

"Sure, I would say Masaccio's 'Holy Trinity' is an intellectually complex and sublime piece of systematic linear perspective painting from the High Renaissance. Throughout the art world since then, you can see his influence. But there are many, many more - Leonardo; I don't think I need mentioned anyone else." Drew gave a quick smile which Jessica reciprocated.

They continued talking for the next thirty minutes. Finally, Jessica had Drew critique and discuss some of the works she had on display. She listened, intrigued, as he explained with great ease, clarity and passion, both the positive and negative aspects he saw in each piece of art. His knowledge was far more intrinsic than learned. He didn't look at the art, he experienced it; it fed him.

They returned to the office for the final few points of discussion. When they were finished, Jessica sat back in her chair; a broad smile brightened her face.

"Drew, I would like to hire you but have to figure out how exactly to utilize your talent. Can you give me a couple of days to make a decision? Even if I can't find anything for you here, I would be more than happy to refer you to one of my colleagues. To be honest, though, my first choice is to have you come to work for me. Now, before we finish, do you have any questions?"

"Yes, just one; the other woman, Kimberley; is she always that...that..."

"Snooty?" Jessica said with a chuckle. "Yes, Kimberley is a perfect yin to my yang; I am in the world of jeans, she is haute couture. She is exactly the person needed to deal with many of our clients; to be the face when people come into the store. I'm more of a behind the scenes person, determining the direction the gallery is going, dealing with importers and other dealers and keeping an eye out for new opportunities. And her natural cautious nature offsets my higher energy aggressive style."

"Fair enough."

Jessica smiled and got up from his chair. Drew stood as well and again shook her hand before they walked from the office to the front of the store. After saying their good-byes, Jessica reiterated she would be in touch by the week's end.

When he left the shop, Drew walked down to the corner and turned it before letting loose an ecstatic holler, jumping around and dancing to the joyous music in his head.

Since he was in the city, Drew decided to drop in on Fran to see if she would be available for lunch. He showed up at her office just prior to noon.

The receptionist received him and called through to Fran before she directed Drew to the chairs in the waiting area. Drew sat and waited. A few minutes later Fran emerged from her office, appearing surprised.

"Hi, Drew, what brings you here?"

"I had a job interview this morning at an art store not far from here. That's as long as you consider the other side of the city not too far," he quipped. "Sorry for not calling ahead; I just hoped you would be available to go for lunch."

"That's amazing; I was just going to call you. Some information was uncovered that is pretty important and will go a long way in determining the approach we take in the search for your birth parents."

Drew was thrilled. A wide grin crept across his face.

"Great! So can we talk it over during lunch?"

"Sure, but be aware, I don't have as much time for lunch as I did yesterday," Fran smiled.

Once Fran had her coat they left for a Chinese restaurant nearby. Having settled in to a table for four and ordering their food, Fran pulled Drew's file from her bag and opened it. From it she took an official document and laid it out so both could look at it.

"This is the document from the adoption agency. Your biological parents didn't agree to have their personal information released but there is enough other information to help further the investigation. That being said, the fact they didn't consent will pose a significant obstacle though it doesn't mean the end of the trail. I know you already spoke to them, but can your parents not assist us in any way?"

"I think my mother was honest with her information given the degree of her involvement in the process. It was William who wouldn't give me any insight into the matter. I can try again but, with the situation so strained between my mom and William, it may be too much to expect. I will look into it as soon as possible but unfortunately it may be a spell. I should find out about the job by the end of the week and have three weeks to learn how to drive. So it'll likely be sometime next month before, or if, anything is looked into."

"That's fine, surprisingly, yours isn't the only file I'm working on," she smiled, "I will wait for the information from you to arrive."

They finished lunch and Drew walked Fran back to her office. With her promise that she would keep him apprised of anything she discovered, Drew left and headed for home.

When he arrived back at the house, Drew grabbed a pen and paper and began to write out a list of items he would need if he were to get the job. At the top of the list was a cell phone. He had spoken with his mother and she agreed that she would co-sign, if need be, to help him get one.

While he was still writing out the list, Alicia arrived home from work. As she entered the front door Drew met her and before she could ask him how things went he picked her up with a hug around her waist and spun her, laughing.

"I don't know how to thank you. The interview went amazing. She was amazing. Today was amazing. You are amazing."

Alicia laughed as Drew continued to spin. Suddenly he became aware of what he was doing and stopped, setting her back down on her feet. He looked around trying not to make eye contact.

"Umm, yeah, thanks. I...I should get back to the list I was writing."

As he walked toward the kitchen, Alicia followed, looking at him pityingly.

"Drew, don't be embarrassed," she said with a slight laugh, "you needed to let that out. Why don't you finish the list you are working on and then you can tell me about the interview. In the meantime, I'm going to get changed out of these work clothes."

Drew nodded and walked back into the kitchen flustered by what had just happened. It felt like he had crossed a line and the guilt bothered him to the point that he couldn't concentrate on the list. Several minutes later, Alicia reappeared at the kitchen entrance, wearing tight jeans and a buttoned shirt. She walked to where Drew was sitting at the table and began lightly stroking the back of his head.

"Come on, Drew, you did nothing wrong. It was just the excitement of how the day went. When was the last time you felt that invigorated or that thrilled, by anything? Things have been building up and release was needed, that's all. Think nothing more of it."

Drew looked up at Alicia and offered a weak smile before going back to the list. She walked into the living room to pour herself a drink. As she looked out the window, the school bus arrived and Zoë and Benjamin got off. True to their daily routine, they raced each other up to the front door with the winner getting the first hug.

The meal that night was spent listening to Drew recount the interview. The kids showed as much interest in his story as Alicia, thinking it quite funny when he told them about mistaking Kimberly for Jessica.

When they finished and cleared the table, Drew assisted Zoë with an assignment which needed to be completed by the next morning while Alicia helped Benjamin with his reading. By eight-thirty both children were bathed and into bed. When Alicia finished tucking them in she returned to the living room where she found Drew sitting on the couch.

"Would you like a drink, Drew?"

"You know what? That's a great idea. Do you have whiskey?"

"Yeah, how would you like it?"

"On the rocks, please."

Alicia poured two glasses of whiskey from the liquor trolley and handed one to Drew. Sitting on the chair near him, they toasted his successful interview. One drink was followed by another as the conversation moved from one topic to the next. The discussions had been easy and Alicia gave her total attention to him and showed genuine interest in what he had to say. Drew was fascinated as he learned more about Alicia.

"After getting my B.A. in administrative studies I worked at the corporate headquarters of Centurion Industries; they produce equipment for work in the oil fields. The job was enjoyable and I worked there the year before Zoë was born and between the births of the two children. It came to an end about six months before Benjamin was born."

"What made you leave?"

Alicia sat quietly for some time. Drew waited for her response.

"Sometimes it is just time to move on."

As Drew poured the third drink he knew he would be getting into dangerous territory if he wasn't careful. He determined that the drink he was pouring would be his last.

"I'm so glad that John told me to come see you after my released from prison," he said handing a drink to Alicia. "The fact that the both of you would be so willing, so generous as to help me out, well, it's still difficult to comprehend. Especially given that John isn't here and all. John gave me a chance to survive on the inside and prepared me for my release and you have given me the support to continue that on the outside. But, I still don't understand why. Have you ever helped out any other ex-con? If not, why me?"

"Nope, we've never done this before, but when John first brought it up he essentially said that he trusted you implicitly. He felt that you coming to live here would be of benefit for both of us in that your rent would help me with the bills and you wouldn't have to go back to live with your parents. He told me your adoptive father was a terrible man but didn't go into details."

Drew raised his eyebrows. Alicia continued.

"The last time I visited John, he said he was going to mail me a letter giving more details about you but wanted to wait until he heard what Jessica's decision was. But it hadn't arrived and then, when you called and showed up here, it didn't matter. The first night we sat in this room, as we talked, I knew he had made the right decision. You said you would leave once you were established in a job and could afford a place to stay, but, if you want, you can continue living here. The children've really taken to you and, I must admit, it's clear why John spoke so highly of you. And it is because of the circumstances that I am glad you decided to come here."

As Alicia looked at Drew, the smile on her lips couldn't hide the sorrow of John not being there in her eyes.

Just before two o'clock, Drew stood and took the empty glasses into the kitchen and placed them in the sink. When he returned to the living room, Alicia was standing, her head bowed. Drew placed his finger under her chin and raised her head until she was looking up at him. Tears were glistening in her eyes and her lips quivered. Slowly he moved his face closer to hers. Alicia didn't pull away. With great tenderness, Drew kissed her; a long, passionate, delicate kiss. As her breathing began to tremble Alicia drew him closer, her left hand cupping the nape of his neck, her right gently running through his hair. When their mouths parted, Alicia slid her hand down Drew's left arm and took his hand. Together they walked down the hall to her bedroom. She closed the door and began to unbutton her shirt. Drew placed his hand over hers.

"Are you sure this is what you want?"

Alicia didn't speak but continued unbuttoning. After removing her shirt she stepped towards Drew and took his hands in hers, placing them on her breasts. She kissed him again and angled him towards the bed where she undid his pants. Drew moved his hands around to Alicia's back and guided her onto the bed. Lying on top of her, he kissed her neck and shoulders before moving towards her breasts. He raised himself up and removed her jeans and panties along with his clothes. While his hands rubbed the wet warmth between her legs, he continued to lick and lightly bite her nipples then slowly nibbled and kissed her as he worked down past her abdomen to her moistness. There he remained for several minutes licking, rubbing and entering her with his tongue and fingers. His hands moved up to cup and squceze her breasts. As Drew's tongue continued to caress her clitoris and canal, Alicia's back arched and she released a throaty moan, her hands reaching down to clutch his hair guiding his head up and down as his tongue glided over her vulva. Pulling Drew up towards her, Alicia again reached down and began to stroke his phallus before guiding it into her. As each stared libidinously into the other's eyes, Drew began deliberate, rhythmic thrusts each time driving a little harder and a little faster; Alicia could feel her entire body tingle each time Drew plunged inside her. Her fingers moved to and began rubbing her clit. As she reached orgasm, Alicia tightened around Drew's erection, inducing his climax.

They had lay on the bed in silence for several minutes, their bodies still joined, Drew holding her close, when Alicia began to quietly weep. She moved so that Drew withdrew from her, and rolled away from him, hugging herself. Drew placed his hand on her upper arm, rubbing it slowly, but Alicia did not respond. After a several moments, he rose from the bed, guilt assailing him, and collected his clothes.

"Sorry," he whispered before exiting the room. Alicia didn't acknowledge him but quietly continued sobbing.

Lying in his bed, Drew disparaged himself until sleep finally released him from his self-loathing.

CHAPTER FOURTEEN

Two years had passed since the fight in the cafeteria and Drew still felt the pain from the stab wounds. The split forehead had left no obvious disfigurement but the puncture wounds and ensuing operations to repair the injuries caused considerable scarring on his back. Whether phantom or real, the pain could be extremely uncomfortable and difficult to deal with at times. Unfortunately, follow up visits with the doctors discovered no physical causation for his discomfort.

The investigation into the stabbing hadn't turned up any suspects though Drew was positive it was one of Skewer's gang members who had done it. Despite the ongoing investigation, it was unlikely that the case would ever be solved.

Skewer had only been seen a few times since that day and the damage done to him remained on his face as a souvenir of the punishment he took. Still, Drew knew that retribution was possible, if not from Skewer then from another gang member. He often recalled the words spoken by Peter the first day they met; *'It's hard to make and keep friends here but easy to make and keep enemies.'* Heeding that warning, he was always circumspect in large group situations. Whenever he found himself in one he made a point of keeping his back to a wall. Outside of meals, the periodic basketball games were the only place where he allowed himself to be in an open area among large crowds. During those times, however, the knowledge that he had teammates there to assist if anything happened, gave Drew the sense of security.

Following the altercation, Drew had stayed out of trouble and bore down on his studies. After completing his grade twelve diploma he had started a correspondence course through York University and had enjoyed great success at it. He had requested and been accepted to a job in the library, which afforded him the opportunity to spend many hours there studying. Often, he and John could be found together at the library as John helped with Drew's schoolwork and studying. Drew sensed that John carried guilt with him and could only assume it was over the attack in the cafeteria, though Drew asserted that John was, in no way, to blame for the events of that day.

During this time, his relationship with John had strengthened and Drew had more insight into his life with his parents, particularly his father, and told him about the events leading up to the day of the shooting.

John also spoke of his life growing up.

"I can't complain about my upbringing," John confessed one day. "My father was a successful businessman, both here and in India, where he met my mother. Dad brought mom back here to get married. He was born and raised here and my mom was born and raised in India. They met while my dad was doing volunteer work in Mumbai; actually its name was Bombay at the time. My mom was from a mixed marriage as well; her father was British and her mother Pakistani. Each generation has become progressively lighter in complexion; you should see my kids, their complexion is closer to yours than mine. I have an older sister, Samantha, who took over my father's business, an engineering firm, and has been running it for about ten years now. My mother taught high school English, which always seemed funny to me.

"My parents were more than tolerant of my behaviour as a kid and for that matter, into my adulthood. I never wanted for anything and my relationship with them was good, considering all the grief I caused. Unfortunately a lot of stupid mistakes were made by me that have hurt them over the years. It took me until my arrival here to realize how foolish I had been; not only regarding my parents but Alicia and the kids. It'll be the last time this guy ends up in prison. Let me tell you," he smiled. "A mundane existence where you return home to a loving family is infinitely better than a mundane existence where you return to your prison cell. Look at my life, Drew, look at what I've done to my opportunities, and ask yourself if this is where you want to be in twenty years."

Drew knew the answer.

As a result of the fight in the cafeteria, Drew understood why John wouldn't sit near or interact with them when Jean came to the family visits. He no longer looked for John during those visitation days they shared. Each would visit their respective family and meet after.

Jean continued to visit on a regular basis, still with the same stories. But during her most recent visit she seemed unhappy and distracted, finding it difficult to remember any of the events that had happened in Drury during the previous month and constantly wringing her hands.

"Mom, what's wrong? You seem a little distant today. Is there something you want to talk about?

"Everything is fine," she replied, offering a distracted smile. "Andrew, my schedule is so busy these days that I cannot seem to stay focused on any one thing. Between work and the ladies auxiliary, I seem to be running around like a chicken with its head cut off."

"Well, what about the neighbourhood cats? Is anything new happening at work? How are Sasha and Spartacus? Still digging up your garden? What are your plans for the garden this year? Come on mom, there must be something you can tell me."

"Nothing is new, really. Like I said, I am just very busy these days, with the ladies auxiliary; we are starting to prepare for the annual spring sale..." her soft voice trailed off as she looked away. Jean wrestled with the news she hadn't disclosed.

The remainder of the visit was spent in virtual silence; only a few words were spoken. As they said their good-byes, Jean gave Drew a longer hug than usual.

When she released him, tears brimmed in her eyes. She turned quickly and left the hall not having told him about the deaths of both Sasha and Spartacus.

When Alicia visited with John that same day, he was ready to start preparing for Drew to live with her. Though John knew there was no guarantee Drew would follow through, he wanted Alicia to be prepared should he decide to make the move. He had already spoken to Drew about the living arrangements, and given him the phone number where he could contact Alicia.

As she entered the room, John met her with a kiss and a hug before walking her to a table. After a short discussion and update on the kids' progress he began to lay out his plan.

"I have given Drew the phone number to our house. He has told me he wants to make amends with his parents before he decides whether to contact you. But, based on what he has told me about his adoptive father, it's unlikely he will last there very long."

Alicia's brow creased with concern.

"What about his father, is there anything I should know? Remember, John, we have two young children at home."

"No, there is nothing for you to worry about. His adoptive father physically and emotionally abused Drew as a child. There are deep scars Drew has suffered as a result. I have been trying to build up his sense of self-worth over the years and there is an inner strength in him that wasn't there when he arrived."

"John, I don't understand why you have taken such an interest in Drew. Don't get me wrong, from what you have told me he is a very decent, very mature person, but…" Her voice fell silent as she searched his face for the answer.

John sat for several moments and reflected on what he wanted to tell her.

"My entire life was completely self-centred. Because of that, mistake after mistake was made which have hurt loved ones. Why? Because, when it came down to it, I didn't give a shit about anyone else. When I first met Drew and we talked, taking him under wing and helping him was the only option. He was making the same mistakes; his attitude had been moulded by his upbringing but he was still young enough to change who he would become. He came here from juvenile detention full of piss and vinegar but there was a scared child behind his eyes.

"It was like the fates had intended for us to meet here. That he'd been let down and abandoned as a child and I was given a second chance to help; and it was to teach Drew to grow up, to make the right choices, to be a man, not only in the penitentiary but give him hope once he left; to be his guardian, if you will. With my guidance he has a chance to make good of himself."

"So that's why you want to do this, to somehow make amends for your failures in life?" The irritation was evident in her voice. "You're right; you *have* made a lot of mistakes; some of them terrible mistakes. But if you're so concerned with balancing everything out, how about you start with helping your own family? Will helping Drew relieve your guilt? Because, really, this isn't about Drew, it's about you. There's nothing altruistic about your motives, no fate involved. It's about you trying to rid yourself of some guilt you carry."

"My actions cost me a child when I was younger. This is a chance for me to save Dav... I mean Drew. We have both been given a second chance."

Realizing how important this was to John, that he felt an obligation to Drew, Alicia calmed herself.

"John," she reached across the table and held his hands; her voice soft. "I know you want to help Drew, and respect you for that. But you have two children at home. They need their father. Saving Drew won't bring David back to you. Don't you understand? Drew can't be your surrogate son."

John looked down at the table, losing the fight to hold the tears back. "Maybe...," he whispered. When he looked back up at Alicia, his face was stamped with torment.

"I don't look at him as a surrogate son. But there's more to this story than you know. I don't feel comfortable talking to you about this here. There're too many ears and too many emotions involved. I'll put everything down in a letter and send it to you, explaining the situation in detail, but you have to trust me about this. Can you do that?"

"I guess so," Alicia sighed.

"Thank you. There is something else that needs to be done. Again, I'll explain it more fully in the letter."

Alicia stared at him, confused.

"More? Can you at least give me a heads up?"

John blew out a long breath.

"You remember Jessica Dean? She has been a friend of mine since we were young." When Alicia nodded, John continued. "Well, as you may also recall, she runs a successful art gallery in the city. I'd like you to get in touch with her and tell her about Drew. She may be able to give him a job. I'll give you more details later but if you could give her a call and ask her if she would consider the possibility. As I think about it, a letter to her'll also be put in the envelope if she does agree to speak with him."

"How'll I get in contact with her? Do you have her number?"

John shook his head.

"No, but I believe the name of the store is 'In the Art of the City' or something like that. You should be able to find it in the telephone book or online."

"And what should I tell her?"

"Tell her everything I've told you about Drew. Tell her I need this favour. Tell her what you need to, to get Drew an opportunity to get in front of her. She will like what she sees. There'll be more information in the letter.

But make contact with her as soon as you can so the letters can get to you and Jessica, if necessary."

"I will speak to her, but you have to give me time. I'm really busy at work trying to get as many hours as I can in. We are short a server and the overtime is non-stop."

"That's fine, we have time. Get to it when you can but let me know when you have spoken to Jessica and what her answer is."

When visiting time was up, Alicia gave John a kiss and long hug from the children and a promise to contact Jessica.

That evening John penned his letters to Alicia and Jessica. When he finished he set them aside to be mailed once he heard back from Alicia.

Two weeks passed and John still hadn't heard anything. During that time he continued to work with Drew on his university studies. With each success, John felt like another hurdle was overcome and Drew carried himself with more confidence. He didn't show any signs of arrogance just an assuredness that spoke of his maturation. That morning in the library Drew confided in John about something that was on his mind.

"John, do you remember the day when you told me that not being part of a loved one's life deprives them of an element of who they are and robs me as well?

"Sure, how could I forget that day?" he replied with a wry smile.

"I have been thinking a great deal about my background and in particular about people who aren't in my life; my biological parents. When I get out of here it'll be one of my missions to find out who they are. So much has changed during my years here and I feel that I need to know about them. Without that knowledge there is incompleteness, an element, a part of me that's missing and it needs to be found."

John stared at him for several moments, a look of astonishment on his face.

"Wow. Do you have any idea who they are? Their names? Where they live? Anything at all? I mean, where do you start something like that?"

"I'm not sure, but I'll have to talk to my parents about it. They should be able to shed some light on my background. I just hope they are receptive to it."

"What about you, are you sure you would be ready to find out who they are?

Drew snickered.

"To be honest, no, and I won't know until I do. If luck is on my side they will be filthy rich and feel guilty for having abandoned me."

John smiled, "Yeah, and who knows, maybe your birth parents are looking for you as well. Maybe there is a guilt that needs to be appeased. Stranger things have happened. I hope you are successful in your search."

Drew nodded his head thoughtfully.

"Well, Drew, you will have to put that aside for now, it is time for us to clean up the area and head out to the courts."

While returning the books back to the shelves, Drew turned to John.

"I don't know if this has been said before but thank you for...for everything. You have guided me through myriad situations since my arrival here and now that I'm so close to leaving I realize my time here would never have been this successful without your direction. You are my *friend* and I will never forget that."

John blushed, a smile creasing his face.

"It has been my great pleasure. And you've made me very proud. Just remember, you're better than this place and you deserve more than what you have. You just need to keep working at it and keep improving yourself and believing in yourself. And when I'm released we will have to reconnect."

"When you are released? I plan on staying in touch with you until you are released."

The two looked at each other with admiration.

"Come on," John said, his face beaming. "Let's go before I kiss you. We have a basketball game to win."

They made their way out to the basketball courts where the rest of their team was waiting. Drew was surprised, and a bit apprehensive to see that the assembled opponents consisted of his cellmate, Peter, along with Hank and a number of other skin heads.

Drew and Peter continued to share their cell but that was the extent of their interactions. Outside of the times they were confined to their cell, they spent no time together and few words were ever exchanged. Following the confrontation years earlier, Peter had stayed clear of Drew and there had been no retribution, no threats from the skinheads.

Peter had been involved in other incidences, however, and his parole, which was to have occurred the previous year, was delayed.

"Peter, I didn't know you boys liked to play pick up."

Peter's stare at Drew reeked of contempt.

"We're here to show you, you nigger-lover, how this game should be played."

"Now Peter," Drew spoke superciliously, "I hope that wasn't a threat I just heard."

Peter didn't respond.

While the exchange was going on, Hank glowered at Drew, his hands clenched into tight fists. Noticing the aggression, Drew winked at Hank.

The weather outside had been threatening all day but the rain had held off. In the distance blue skies could be seen slowly moving towards the penitentiary as rays of sunlight sliced across the landscape. Between them, however, sat dark fertile clouds. John wasn't sure they should play, but the other team insisted despite the potential rain. After a brief discussion both teams agreed to try to get the game in, at least, before the rains started.

As the game progressed, a number of inmates gathered around the court to cheer on the competitors. By the mid-point of the game there was an unusually large number of spectators; so many that they began to crowd the court. Drew looked at John, a note of concern on his face. John acknowledged Drew and signalled for him to try to calm down. Drew played the remainder of the game with a heightened sense of anxiety.

With the conclusion of the closely contested game nearing, Drew drove the basket for a lay-up and landed directly in front of the horde at the end of the court. John, standing at the top of the key, was distracted by a flash of movement in the crowd. Drew turned to run back to defence. At that moment it struck John what the movement was.

"Drew," he yelled, "behind you."

When Drew looked back, Skewer and other gang members emerged from the throngs and attacked. It seemed as though every one of them had some sort of edged weapon. John rushed forward and pulled Drew away with his left hand while punching one of the assailants in the face with his right. When the first attacker fell back a second appeared: Skewer. Before John could react Skewer drove a shank into his ribs just below his right armpit. John flinched and Skewer withdrew the weapon.

Drew rushed to John's aid but was jumped.

He and the other man fell to the court then separated as they got back up on their feet. Opposite Drew stood Hank, his face seething with hatred, a low growl emanating from this throat.

"Peter didn't finish the job with the shank in the cafeteria so this time you're mine," Hank blustered before he charged towards Drew.

Drew immediately noticed that Hank had, again, left himself exposed.

Swiftly, Drew kicked Hank between the legs before stepping back. Hank gasped for air as he doubled over and his knees buckled. His hands covered his crotch. This time Drew charged Hank, driving his fist into Hank's jaw, feeling it break and separating the mandible from the skull. As Hank looked on helplessly, his mouth drooped open and bloody, Drew pushed back his head, exposing his throat, then reared back and with his entire might, punched Hank, crushing his windpipe. Hank toppled to the ground unable to breathe.

Drew reeled about to help John, leaving Hank writhing, his face turning blue as he feverishly struggled against the death he could not escape.

Drew saw John's shoulders hunched forward and his body jerking up and down as each stab from Skewer's frenzied attack entered and withdrew from his body.

Other inmates in the crowd surged forward and smothered Skewer in a flurry of punches and kicks before pulling him into the swelling masses. The remaining gang members attempted to escape from the swarming multitude only to be chased down and beaten or stabbed with their own weapons.

As the clouds parted and the sun shone through, illuminating the prison yard, Drew rushed to John who had collapsed on the basketball court. Blood, escaping from the numerous stab wounds which penetrated John's stomach and chest, pooled on the court and glistened in the sunlight like black diamonds. Going to his knees, Drew placed John's head on his lap. Though he tried, Drew wasn't able to stop the bleeding from John's mutilated torso.

"John." Grief strained Drew's voice. "John, please hold on. You can't die, not like this. God damn it."

Tears flowed from Drew's eyes and mucus trickled from his nose as he looked up to the skies.

Unaware of the fighting going on around them, Drew frantically yelled, "God, please. Someone get some help!"

John's eyes flickered open and he looked up at Drew. With blood gurgling up from his throat he tried to speak. Reaching with a crimsoned hand he touched Drew's cheek.

“I’m sorry I couldn’t protect you the first time but I did this time.”

He coughed, blood spraying in Drew’s face.

“Yes, John, you protected me. You saved me.”

Drew held John’s head up and cradled it under his chin, his tears tracing lines through the blood on John’s face.

John coughed again.

As Drew lowered him back down, John’s eyes opened wider and a drawn, dark red smile alit his face. A tear fell. Drew could barely hear the words over the surrounding chaos as John spoke, his voice faint. “...y blood...” John reached up to touch Drew’s face again but his arm dropped, giving in to his failing body. Breath and blood gurgled up from his throat, his body went limp, and his eyelids narrowed as John succumbed to his wounds.

Drew continued holding John, rocking him for several moments before the guards arrived.

Officer Vincent was the first to appear. Moving John’s head from Drew’s lap, he set it gently on the ground.

“Drew, you have to get up, there is nothing you can do for him,” his voice was heartfelt.

With great care Vincent helped Drew, who was now in a state of shock, slowly get up from the court.

As the other guards arrived, the mob of inmates moved away from the court like a wave retreating from the beach. In their wake lay the bodies of three gang members who had attacked Drew and John. Skewer lay motionless, his face pulverized, his skull crushed, a shank protruding from his throat. Of the other gang members who attempted to escape, two were taken to hospital in critical condition and a third died before medical treatment could be administered. Hank’s corpse lay in the middle of the court, its hands still grasping at its throat, its eyes wide with panic. Peter was beaten but only suffered minor injuries and needed no medical attention.

Though he received no physical injury, Drew was taken to the infirmary where he was kept sedated and placed under watch for several days. By the time he was released from the infirmary, John's cell had been emptied and his belongings handed over to Alicia. He had been buried in a cemetery in Westwood.

The investigation into the murder uncovered evidence proving that the skinheads on the opposing basketball team had conspired with Skewer and his gang to commit the attack. Drew was unaware that during the fight each of his teammates had been assailed by members of the opposing team. Fortunately, none of them were seriously injured. The plan had been devised weeks prior and explained why Peter and his teammates were so insistent on playing the game that day.

The investigation further revealed that the deaths of the other gang members occurred when they were attacking and murdering another person. As a result, their deaths were deemed to be justified and no charges were filed.

The remaining members from both gangs involved in the attack were charged with premeditated murder and attempted murder along with numerous other charges. They were placed in segregation until their trial.

For the months leading into summer, Drew dedicated all his time to his studies. More so than ever, he wanted to make John proud. Outside of meals and lockdown, he seldom left the library.

Periodically he would be paralyzed by the realization that John wasn't there and never would be again. Sometimes it would be a picture, other times a thought. But there was always some trigger. Fortunately for Drew, as time passed, those moments became less frequent.

Every night in his cell, Drew would say a quiet thank you to John D-C 0-7-2-0-6-2 as he crossed another day off the countdown to his release.

When the school year had concluded, Drew received his final marks and envisaged himself in a lecture hall the next time he took a university course.

On a clear, cool October day, Drew said his good-byes during breakfast. At the end of the meal, as the other inmates went to their various details, he returned to his cell and gathered up the few personal belongings he had with him. Finally, Drew was escorted to an administrative area where he changed out of his prison jumpsuit and into his street clothing and prepared for his release. He had already received his Prison Discharge Slip and filled out some final forms before being escorted to the front counter to pick up his belongings which had been held since his arrival. At the counter he received and checked the manila envelope and talked with Vincent for a bit before leaving. After seven years, and with great relief, Drew exited the penitentiary system and walked into the waiting arms of his mother before taking the long drive home.

CHAPTER FIFTEEN

The days following their encounter, Drew and Alicia mostly avoided each other. Both felt guilt about their actions and awkward in the other's presence. Dinners were quiet and, in the morning, Drew wouldn't leave his room until Alicia and the children had left for the day. Adding to Drew's stress was waiting for Jessica to call. Each time the phone rang his heart would pound until it felt as if his chest was going to explode. And each time he was disappointed when he discovered the caller wasn't Jessica.

Finally, on Friday just after noon the call he had been hoping for arrived. Drew ran to it then paused a few moments to compose himself before picking it up.

"Hello? Drew speaking."

"Hello, Drew, this is Jessica Dean. How are you?"

"Great thanks, Jessica, and you?"

"Just fine, thanks. Drew, do you have a few moments to speak?"

"I think I can spare a few," he said with mocked inconvenience.

Jessica laughed.

"Drew, I would like to offer you a job as my assistant; if you are interested, that is."

Drew's heart jumped at the words. His face beamed. He didn't even try to calm himself with the news.

"Interested? Absolutely! This is fantastic. Thank you, Jessica. When can I start? Do you want me there today?

"Whoa, settle down there cowboy. We will have to go over the details first and then you will need to sign a contract. You can take it home with you and read it over carefully. The contract can be signed next Tuesday.

"Tomorrow, if it isn't too much of an inconvenience, I would like you to come into the shop so we can go over your duties and responsibilities. We can also discuss your wages and all the other necessary formalities. It will take a couple of hours to get that out of the way then we can start teaching you the ropes."

"Tomorrow will be fine; will nine in the morning work? I will need Alicia to drive me in."

"Nine is perfect. We'll have to work on your schedule so I will likely have to be in touch with Alicia to figure that out. And Drew, I look forward to our collaboration."

"So do I, Jessica. Thank you for giving me the opportunity, you won't be disappointed."

After his conversation with Jessica concluded, Drew immediately called his mother at work. She agreed to meet him in the city later that afternoon so they could go out and pick up a few items he would need. The rest of the day Drew spent trying to keep occupied in order to take his mind off the time. In the mid-afternoon he left to meet his mother.

Just after four-thirty, Jean arrived at the meeting spot. When Drew saw her exit the vehicle he rushed to the car and gave her a long hug.

"Thank you, so much, for helping me, mom. I promise to get the money back to you as quickly as possible. This job has me so pumped."

"Andrew," she said, her smile almost as radiant as his, "I could not be more proud of you than I have been in these last couple of months. And you do not have to worry about paying me back. While you were in prison I started putting money away each birthday and Christmas you were not home, knowing that when you were released you would need it to get yourself established. Today would be a good day to use the money. Consider today a gift for all the birthdays and Christmases you missed. If there is money left over when we are finished, I will give it to you. I am sure there are things we will have overlooked."

Drew didn't know what to say and simply gave his mother a hug in response.

The remainder of the afternoon and evening was spent buying things Drew would need for work. After those errands were taken care of, Drew and Jean went to a restaurant.

"How are things at home, mom?"

Jean gave a resigned sigh, staring at her meal for several seconds before looking up at Drew.

"Strained; when your father is home he avoids me but, the fact is, he is seldom home during the day time and leaves for work before I get home, then does not return home until after I have left in the morning. On the weekends, we avoid each other like the plague. That is made easier due to the fact he spends that time with friends and at the bar."

"So, you haven't had much interaction with him? Has he tried in any way to persuade you to stay with him?"

"There has been virtually no interaction between us. So, no, he has done nothing to try to influence me. I sleep in your room on the main floor and he knows not to enter there." Jean paused and took a sip of her coffee. "I was speaking to my friend whose basement I will be renting and she and her husband have agreed to allow me to start moving my belongings over this weekend. Your father will not be around, in all likelihood, and when the day comes for me to leave, I want to move out quickly."

"I understand." Drew paused to sip his coffee. "Mom, can you do me another favour? Can you get hold of the adoption paperwork you said he has? My case worker is running into a few roadblocks and believes the information contained in it might be of great benefit."

"I will see what I can do. But it could be difficult, the strong box is locked and I do not have the key. I will look in his side table, but I think he carries it on his keychain. But he told me he got rid of it years ago, though I do not necessarily believe him."

"If you can't find it, would it be possible to speak to William about it? I know it's a lot to ask, and if you aren't comfortable doing it that's fine, but I feel like that information will be the key to me finding out who they are."

Jean looked away from Drew, chewing on her bottom lip as she thought about what he was asking. Several moments passed.

"Okay, if the key cannot be located, or the information is not where I think it is, I will speak to him. However, it will not be done until after the weekend, as that is when my belongings will be moved to my friend's house. If time permits, I will look for the key but first have to prepare things for the move."

"Thanks mom, you don't know how much I appreciate what you are doing for me."

Jean reached across the table and held Drew's hand, "I know, and I would do much more for you; for us."

With their dinner finished, Jean drove Drew back to Alicia's and wished him good luck with the job. He entered the house quietly and made his way to his room. He could hear Alicia reading with Benjamin in his bedroom. Drew put away all his new clothes: five ties, five dress shirts, two casual jackets, two suits, three pairs of dress pants, two pairs of shoes and two belts. He then took his wallet out of his pocket and removed Fran's card from it. He called and left a message for her giving his new cell phone number. Once he had done all of that, he went back up stairs where he found Alicia sitting in the living room watching television. He sat in a chair and turned towards her, displaying an uncomfortable smile.

"Jessica called me today and offered me a job. I'll be her personal assistant, starting tomorrow morning at nine o'clock. If you could give me a ride to the bus stop it would appreciate it."

"Congratulations, I knew you could do it and knew she would want you working there, not at some other gallery. Of course I can drive you, not just to the bus stop but right into the city. Is that why you were gone all afternoon? Did you do some shopping? Did you remember to buy shoes?"

Drew laughed.

"Yes, thank you. I also picked up a cell phone. I'll write the new phone number down and stick it on the fridge."

This time it was Alicia's turn to laugh.

"Write it and put it on the fridge? Drew, it's time you learned about the digital age. You can text me the information, that way I can make a new contact and keep your number on my cell."

Drew knew about cell phones but, never having owned one, was bewildered by what they could do. After an hour of Alicia's guidance, Drew had a working understanding of his phone. He set up contacts with her, his mother, Fran and 'The Art of the City' and Jessica. After playing with it a bit longer, he set it aside. Alicia got up to go back into the living room.

"Wait," Drew said, lightly holding her forearm. Forcing himself to keep eye contact, he continued. "I need to talk to you about what happened the other night. It has been eating away at me and I feel so...so wrong for what I did."

Alicia sat back down, looking at him with a benevolent expression on her face and placed her hand on his, which remained on her arm.

"Drew, that isn't necessary. We're both adults, you even stopped and asked if it was what I wanted. The guilt is mine to bear, not yours. And I should've been the one to approach you, knowing it was bothering you and aware that you must have been stressing over the job. I was angry at myself but projected that anger onto you. I screwed up; it's as plain as that."

She paused for a long moment before continuing, her voice taking on an assertive tone, her eyes fixed on his.

“That being said, I will not apologize for what occurred that night and, in fact, am thankful that it happened. I needed comfort and you gave it. The past several months have been very difficult and there has been no one to turn to. You were tender and it was as if you sensed my needs.” She leaned forward, “Unfortunately, while you were holding me, I was reminded of John. He used to hold me tight to him whenever we finished making love. That’s why I cried, it wasn’t you. Sorry for what I put you through the past week.”

“Thank you. That means a lot to me.”

There was another long pause before Alicia spoke again in a cheerful voice.

“Now, about tomorrow; what time did you say you have to be there? Was it nine?”

Drew nodded, smiling.

“Okay, I’ll drop you off fifteen minutes beforehand. When you are coming home, text or call me and I will pick you up. Drew, I’m very happy for you.”

“Thanks. Well, I should be heading off to bed, tomorrow will be an exciting one for me and I want to be awake and alert when I start my first day.”

Drew stood up from the table, stretched and covered his mouth with the back of his hand in response to a yawn. He pushed in his chair and each wished the other a good night before Drew retired down to his bedroom. Despite his desire to, he couldn’t sleep. The nervousness settling in his stomach, felt like a thousand caterpillars trying to eat their way out.

As he lay in bed he heard a knock at the front door. He listened to the muffled voice of Alicia as she spoke to whoever had knocked and moments later closed the front door and appeared to go to bed. Thinking nothing more of it, Drew was able to slip off to sleep.

The following morning his alarm buzzed at seven o'clock. Drew got up to shower and, like the morning of his interview, he ate breakfast wearing a t-shirt and jeans before returning to his bedroom to get his suit on.

As planned, Alicia dropped him off fifteen minutes early. Drew dashed to the coffee shop and grabbed himself a latte then sat at a window and watched for Jessica or Kimberly. At eight fifty-five, Jessica's Audi pulled into the lot. By the time she was at the front door, Drew had crossed the street to meet her.

"Good morning Jessica."

"Good morning Drew, ready to get going?" She paused for a moment looking at him. "Darn, sorry, I was going to call you and tell you to wear something casual. After we are finished going over the formalities, which could take a couple of hours, I will take you back to Alicia's so you can change. In the afternoon, we will be doing some re-arranging in the shop, moving some displays and bringing out some new pieces. In fact, most of our days are going to be spent in blue jeans. Remember what I told you on Tuesday, that is how I work. Hope you didn't spend a lot on new clothes."

"No," Drew replied, "I didn't...my mother on the other hand..." He smiled. "Hopefully they'll take the suits back, but I'll keep one at least."

They walked to the back office and went over the contract. There would be a probationary period of three months at a lower wage. Once that period was complete, Drew would receive a raise. Jessica explained the duties he would be carrying out: he'd be responsible for the art displays and maintenance in the store, would travel with Jessica to shows, assist with the assessment and purchasing of new pieces and, in general, be her right-hand man. If things went well, he would be given more responsibilities with the potential of moving into purchasing and travelling to other countries to seek out different styles of art and new artists.

Once they had completed their discussions, Jessica took Drew out to the showroom and formally introduced him to Kimberley.

"Kimberley, this is Andrew Parsons."

Drew glanced at Jessica who met his questioning gaze. He was about to speak when Jessica shook her head slightly to quell any objection.

"Andrew is how you will be referred to when in the showroom or when we interact with other people in a business environment. When we are behind the scenes and it is just us, we will call you Drew."

Jessica refocused on Kimberley.

"He will start working here on Tuesday, officially. For the next hour or so, I would like you to show him around the store and give him a quick lesson on dealing with our clientele."

Jessica left the two of them and returned to the back office. Once she closed the door, Kimberley turned to Drew.

"Just to clarify, Andrew, whenever you speak to me, whether here or in private, you will use my proper and complete name - Kimberley. Do you understand?" Her voice was cold and had the same air of superiority that it had the first time they met.

"Yes, Kimberley, I understand completely. Now, what do I need to learn?"

"First, that I am the initial contact whenever anyone enters the store. My tenure here is over seven years and most of the clientele who enter are return customers. You will be there to assist me when necessary, or cover for me when I need time off or am sick, though Jessica usually does that."

"That sounds reasonable. I'll defer to you unless you advise me otherwise. Now, about the displays; Jessica said I'll be responsible for them, but it's obvious you are far more experienced in that area and, if it is okay with you, I would appreciate any and all input you may have with the creative process, if you don't mind."

Kimberley appeared to let a bit of her haughtiness ebb. She agreed, then proceeded to guide Drew through the store, explaining display layouts and giving some insight into the subtleties of dealing with clientele and business people in the art world.

Eventually, Jessica reappeared from the back office and, pointing at the clock, suggested it was a good time to go back to Alicia's house to get changed.

After returning from Alicia's, Jessica went over plans with Drew for a new display she was considering, showing him the sketches she had drawn and explaining the look of the display and desired response from clientele.

"If it's okay with you," he offered, "I would like to look these over during the weekend and get them back to you with any suggestions. It needs my full attention. The same can be said about the contract." Drew paused for a moment. "Though I'm sure the legalese will be fairly straight forward," he said with an ironic smile.

Jessica looked up at him with a thin smile. "Sure thing, but can I get your initial reaction?"

"Well, my gut tells me that I should look it over during the weekend."

"Fair enough, but understand I want you to be honest with me about it. And that goes for everything. It won't work if you aren't honest."

Drew bowed his head slightly. "Absolutely, I have no problem with that."

"There was something I had intended to ask you about when we spoke yesterday. Alicia mentioned that you were a friend of John's, is that correct?"

"Yes, I knew him for about five years. We were good friends. That's how I ended up living at Alicia's place and how I ended up here."

"Alicia mentioned that. Apparently there was supposed to be more information coming from John but I never received it before he was killed. Alicia had told me that you are intelligent and articulate, and came highly recommended by John. But how is it you know him?"

Drew looked at her, confused.

"Alicia didn't tell you? I was in the penitentiary with him. I was under the impression that she had told you pretty well everything about me and my circumstances."

Jessica took a step back.

"In prison? You were in prison? What for?" Her voice was strained.

"I was involved in a break and enter when I was fifteen. I spent the past seven years in Corrections; two years in juvenile and five years in the penitentiary."

There was a long pause as Jessica stared at Drew, a look of dismay on her face.

"This changes things. I didn't know you were an ex-con. Alicia just said you were away and had gone back to university to upgrade your education. I thought she meant you were away at university."

There was another pause. Then Jessica let out a short laugh.

"Shit, the subtlety of language, huh? Alicia is smart. Sometimes it's all in how you frame it. She probably knew that if she had told me you were in jail I wouldn't have even considered hiring you. And she was right. I have to say, that was a wise move on her part. Having the opportunity to speak with you allowed me to evaluate you with no preconceived ideas."

"So I'm not fired?" the perplexed look remained on Drew's face.

"Nope, how can I fire you when I haven't hired you?" Jessica laughed. "Drew, you have impressed me immensely in the little time we have spoken. What Alicia did tell me, she was bang on about. I've never met anyone who so inherently understands art and design. I've always had an appreciation for it, but you, well it's almost like it's in your DNA. You will be a great fit here. So, the offer still stands, if you want it."

Drew's smile beamed, indicating his desire to work for Jessica. But then the smile faded and a serious expression crossed his face.

"I will take the weekend to decide," he winked.

That evening at dinner, Drew spoke to Alicia about the day and brought up the act of omission she had perpetrated on Jessica. With a smile, Alicia accepted his thanks.

Over the course of the weekend, Drew poured over the contract and found nothing that concerned him. He also reviewed the store design Jessica was developing and made several notes which he would discuss with her the following Tuesday.

CHAPTER SIXTEEN

Early Saturday afternoon, Jean's co-worker, Karen Brown and her husband, Paul, showed up at Jean's house with their van and a small trailer. As they had planned, the larger belongings Jean intended on taking with her when she moved out were to be relocated early so to expedite the process on the day she left the house.

Just as Jean had predicted, William wasn't at the house when they arrived, he hadn't returned home after the previous night, she assumed, at the bar. It took them two trips to transport the belongings; however, the move went with few glitches. As the last of the items was moved into the Brown's basement Jean felt a sense of hope; hope that the years of unhappiness were finally over, hope for the life that lay ahead of her and Andrew. Andrew was safely living at Alicia's house which, upon reflection, wasn't that far away, and had found himself a job, and she no longer felt the weight of William's subjugation and abuse.

That morning had been a difficult one for Jean. While, logically, she knew the decision to leave William was the right one, the emotion of it was settling in and causing her to question her resolve.

In preparation for the move, she attended to some of the furniture – breaking down the bed, removing drawers from the dresser in Drew's upstairs bedroom and the cushions from a couch and chair which had been stored in the basement. The entire time anxiety hit her like waves against a break wall.

Once Jean had completed those tasks she went to William's – no longer *their* - bedroom and began searching for the key to the strong box which contained the adoption paperwork. She searched his dresser without success before turning her attention to his bedside set of drawers. Jean knew the top drawer of William's side table contained his handgun in its case along with the ammunition. After a quick look to ensure it was the only thing in that drawer, she searched the bottom drawer. As she rummaged through the various items she discovered a large envelope at the bottom of that drawer and, looking inside, saw it contained several letters. Dumping the contents of the envelope on the bed she picked up one of the letters and started reading. Her heart sank and tears began to trickle from her eyes. Feeling her legs begin to weaken, Jean sat on the bed holding the letter to her chest, lost.

Looking at the page again she began to read.

Jan. 1981

Dear Jean,

I now know what pain is. It is not a physical discomfort; it is the agony I feel in my heart of not having you near me. Spending the holidays without you to share them with has been unbearable. I have come to the realization, confirmed it really, that I am an empty, lost, shell of a person without your presence in my life. Your laugh is infectious and your beautiful, dimpled smile fills me with a special warmth no fire could compete with. Your wit and wisdom carry me forth, excited by the potential of what will come next. Each night I have gone to bed holding your picture, aching for the time I could hold you. I am so lucky you are mine. I prayed that Christmas morning you would be my present under the tree (knowing it couldn't come true) and have been counting down the days until we are together. I will be home in five days and long to see you, to touch you, again. I vow to you that my parents will never again come between us. An entire army would not be successful if it attempted to keep us apart. Know that my affection for you only grows daily.

I love you today and will love you always.

William.

Jean picked up a second, third and fourth letter, reading them all; each a snapshot of a time in their life together; each of William championing his undying love for her and promising that nothing would stop that devotion. And he had kept them, letters she had long thought lost. There must have been a dozen more, but none later than when Andrew entered their lives.

In the midst of the pile she found an envelope with her name on it which had not been opened. She sat on the bed deliberating whether to read it or not before deciding that her name on it meant the letter inside was hers. Apprehensively, she opened it and began to read. This time she felt a devastating shock of despair and a rush of anger as the words assaulted her.

March 1995

Jean,

I would like to say how sorry I am for what happened this morning when Drew went through the sliding door window. I would like to but I can't. I can't because he is still here tonight. The only thing I am sorry about was that the cut he suffered to his chin wasn't three inches lower. It would have been difficult to deal with his demise but I am sure you would eventually have overcome the devastation. To be honest, there have been many times over the past five years when I prayed fate or divine intervention or whatever you want to call it, would find a way of "ending" your relationship with him. Since his adoption I have become a second class citizen in this house. He's been a wedge in our marriage. You give him more attention and love than you've ever given me. It seemed too easy for you to forget me once his adoption was finalized. Even tonight you are sleeping with him rather than being here in our bed with me, where we could be a couple, husband and wife, lovers. I want you but you show through you actions that you don't need me. And, the reality is, I know things will not change for a long time. When, and if, the day comes where he is no longer part of our lives, it will be the day I can, again, rejoice. My only hope is that you are worth the wait.

The letter was left unsigned.

As Jean placed the letters back into the envelope all the anxiety, all the consternation she experienced about the decision to leave William were exorcized. She felt nothing for him.

He does not deserve me in his life; he does not deserve Andrew in his life. We will carry on together without him.

With newfound determination she continued searching the drawers. She discovered what appeared to be a snuff box and, opening it, found a small key, the key to the strong box. The excitement of the find blanketed her and a feeling of anticipation caused a physical shudder. She went to the closet and took the strong box down from the shelf, carrying it to the bed. Placing it down she took the key and slid it into the keyhole, slowly turning it until the latch released. Taking the box lid at its corners she lifted it, revealing a large manila envelope inside. Thrilled by her find, Jean removed the legal package. String bound the flap closed. She undid it, reversing the figure eight pattern and opened the lapel. Withdrawing the contents from within, her excitement evaporated as she discovered it was the mortgage papers.

Nothing else remained in the envelope or the box. Jean moved her hand around the inside and turned the container over to search the bottom looking for some hidden compartment. Resigned to the fact the information was not there, she placed the papers back into the strongbox and it back on the shelf in the closet.

My God, maybe he told the truth; maybe he did get rid of the adoption paperwork. But if he still has it, I must find it; I cannot let him give it to Drew. Not without seeing it first.

With near frantic devotion, she searched the entire room for the documents, checking inside and the underside of drawers, tossing clothing on the floor and sweeping the tops of the dressers clear of all articles which sat on them. The search proved fruitless and when she had finished the room looked like it had been through a hurricane. Jean cleaned it before the Browns arrived for fear that William would return while she was moving and discover what she had been doing.

It was late in the grey, discouraging December afternoon when Jean returned from the Browns' house. She, again, set about trying to find the adoption papers; positive she had completed a thorough search of the master bedroom. She thought hard as to where else the paperwork may be kept but the only places she came up with proved incorrect. Frustrated, she called Drew to tell him the news.

"Hi mom, have you moved your stuff yet? If so, how did the move go?"

"Yes, we moved the furniture earlier this afternoon and everything went smoothly. The reason I called though, is to let you know that I searched the house and was unable to find the adoption papers. I have been racking my brain trying to think of where they could possibly be."

"The strong box, were you able to check that?"

"Yes, I found the key but the only paperwork in that had to do with our mortgage. I turned your father's bedroom upside down looking. I am concerned. As I mentioned before, I do not even know if the paperwork exists anymore, your father may have disposed of it years ago, just like he said, I just do not know," Jean conceded.

Drew heard the pessimism in his mother's voice and understood she was upset about not being able to find the adoption paperwork to give him.

"That's okay, mom, thanks for trying. It was a slim hope, if any at all. Are you going to speak to William about it or would you rather not?"

"I will try to speak with him, though, as I told you before, we hardly communicate much anymore. If he comes home later, and is not stinking of alcohol, I will broach the subject with him."

"That's all I can ask. Thanks mom."

"You are welcome. If he is willing to give me the paperwork, I will text you and let you know so we can arrange to meet."

Jean paused.

"Drew, your father just pulled in the driveway. I will call you back after I have spoken to him. Good bye."

When William walked through the back door, Jean was sitting at the kitchen table. She stood, gazing at him, trying to determine whether she would talk to him.

"What are you looking at me for?" he sounded exhausted as he removed his shoes and overcoat.

"William, we have to talk. I know you are upset but can we have a civil conversation?"

William looked at her, no longer surprised by her incongruous comments and assertions.

"You're asking me to be civil with you? You, who has been bitter and aloof, malicious and controlling; you are asking me to be civil?"

"I am sorry you feel that way. But this is not about us, it is about Drew. Could you please give me the adoption papers to pass on to him so he can try to find his biological parents? Your relationship with him is over and there is no point in keeping the information from him any longer. Just hand it over to me and I will make sure he gets it. Even telling him it was your idea."

"Why? Why should I give it to him? We wouldn't want to ruin the image he has of us. That would completely destroy his comfortable, fucked up view of the world. No, we can't be truthful with that delicate child. We have our parts to play in this tragedy and I have no intention of straying from mine."

"But if you despise him so, why not just give me the paperwork. Why can you not give him what he wants and be done with it? I just cannot understand your rationale."

"Why should I despise him? No, it has nothing to do with despising him; it's just that I get enjoyment out of knowing I have the power. But I do find it interesting that you want to be civil with me, thinking that I have the paperwork and could hand it over to him at any time," he let out a short, sneering laugh. "If, and when, I'm ready, I'll be more than happy to hand the paperwork over to him directly. Until then it stays with me."

Jean looked at William horror-stricken.

"Jesus, don't give me that God damned self-righteous look; we are equally responsible for this situation. We are both guilty of relentless sabotage. But my motives have been straightforward; out of love, not fear."

Jean walked from her chair moving toward William, placing her hands on the lapel of his jacket. William looked down at them.

"William, please. He just wants..." Jean's voice silenced as William slowly looked back up at her, his baneful eyes seething with contempt, the convexity of his lips producing a snarl.

"Take your fucking paws off of me you bitch, and leave me alone. We have nothing else to talk about."

William stepped past Jean as she slouched back into her chair, astonished, and continued up the stairs to his bedroom.

He had never spoken to her with such words or such hatred. There was only one justification Jean could come up with for William's behaviour.

Just like a spoilt brat.

Twenty minutes later William returned; Jean still hadn't moved from the chair, her eyes were vacant as they stared off unfocused. He sat at the table and looked across at her. She did not meet his stare.

"Jean, I'd like to say I'm sorry for what just happened. I would like to but I can't."

Jean glanced up at him, alarmed.

"If you are going to search through my things, the least you could do is put it all back where you found it. I'm guessing you found the key to the strong box; boy that must have been a bitter disappointment." The corners of William's mouth curled slightly.

"Did you think I wouldn't figure out that you'd try to find it to give him? Just by your reaction the day he told us that he wanted to find his parents, it was obvious that you'd want to give the adoption paperwork to him and to somehow make it benefit you. The only thing I can't figure out is why? Why are you so set on me handing the paperwork over to Drew? What would you gain from giving that information to him?"

William shook his head as he considered the situation.

"Maybe I can't figure it out right now but believe me, Jean, given the time it'll come to me, and, rest assured, it *will* come. And one more thing; the file is nowhere in this house; at least not while you're still here. When I left that morning it came with me. Originally, I had intended on destroying it but thought I could use the paperwork as leverage at some point down the road. It appears that I was correct on that account."

With that, William stood and put his shoes and overcoat back on before he left the house.

CHAPTER SEVENTEEN

Drew worked hard over the next couple of weeks to learn as much as he could about his job. The days were long, with Drew often arriving home after dinner; followed by the evenings, consumed reviewing the notes he had taken at work. Added to that was the studying necessary for university; Drew had very little free time. The art component of the job came to him with great ease but the business side proved to be far more difficult. The bulk of his days were spent at Jessica's side, discussing strategy and talking with other dealers and importers. When alone, she would discuss business acumen but, almost always, the conversation would turn to discussions and debates about art and artists. Their relationship was professional yet untailored; they wore jean jackets and were more inclined to grab sausage from a street vendor than eat at a swank restaurant.

When time permitted, on his days off, Drew would practice his driving with Alicia's assistance and, on the day of his test, he had little difficulty passing.

The following Sunday, in celebration, Drew took Alicia and the children to the local zoo. While Zoë and Benjamin went to look at the giraffes, Alicia and Drew sat on a bench watching them.

"This is very generous of you, Drew. You didn't have to do it."

"You're right, I didn't. But I wanted to. It's my thanks for everything you and..." he looked down at his hands, his throat tightened, and grief welling up.

Alicia moved closer to him, rubbed his back and put her chin on his shoulder.

"Drew, you have to overcome what you are feeling. I know it isn't easy, believe me, but you have to confront your demons and find some form of closure." She paused and looked at him warmly.

"I remember the first night we spoke; you said you didn't want to know his last name until you were ready, but..."

"No," Drew blurted out, "Until I'm ready he will remain John D-C 0-7-2-0-6-2. And when I am ready, only then will I ask you for his last name."

Alicia looked at him for several moments.

"Drew, you haven't been to his grave since your release. Maybe you need to do that to get some peace. But in order to do that you need to know his last name."

"Alicia, I'm aware of that. But, again, I'm just not there yet. I need a bit more time."

"That's fine; I just wouldn't want you getting comfortable in your misery. The 'better the devil you know' attitude is a dangerous game and too often people have a tendency to shy away from things that aren't comfortable; usually to their own misfortune. Drew you are smarter than that, don't become a victim to your own fears."

Drew shook his head. There was a long silence as he continued to watch the children move between the various animal cages.

"I know what you are saying but I'm just not sure I'm ready for that, yet. The simple thought of him sends me spiralling. The funny thing is, he would slap me up the side of the head and tell me to 'get over it' if he were here." A slight smile surfaced. He moved his sad eyes away from the children and looked at Alicia.

"I'll give it some thought but need time. It's almost like, you know, when I was released my life got so busy with things that needed to be done that no thought was given to John. And now the hurt, and maybe the guilt, is really hitting me hard. Does that make any sense to you?"

Alicia moved her arm from Drew's back and tucked it under his arm, putting her head back on his shoulder.

"Who am I to say anything if that is how you feel? But, please, do consider my words."

The visit to the zoo was followed by a nice dinner at a restaurant in the city before they returned home. No more was spoken of John.

The children were being put to bed by Alicia when there was a knock at the front door. Drew opened the door and was met by two sordid looking men wearing black leather jackets. Both stared at him with surprise on their faces. The nearest one, tall and obese with long black hair under a bandana and a bushy, black beard, stepped forward.

"I'm looking for Alicia, is she here?" his voice was callous.

Drew scrutinized them for several moments, suspicious of who they were or their intentions.

"Who shall I tell her is calling?" he responded in an insolent voice.

The obese man's nostrils flared but before he could respond the second man stepped forward lightly grabbing his companions arm. Though just as tall, he was thin and had short cropped hair and was clean shaven.

He answered in a convivial manner. "Just tell her acquaintances from down in the city are here to see her. Please."

Alicia had heard the conversation and approached the door.

"It's alright, Drew, I will talk to them. Can you go make you and me a drink? This won't take long."

Drew hesitated but Alicia gave him a look that pleaded for him to do as she asked. As he walked away, Alicia walked out to the front porch.

"You God damn morons..." She closed the door behind her.

Drew tried to listen and, although he could no longer make out the words, recognized the tone in Alicia's voice indicating that she was quite upset with their unexpected and unannounced appearance. A few minutes later she re-entered the house alone going directly to her bedroom, only to emerge moments later. Drew was sitting on a chair in the living room watching television. Alicia sat in the other chair where her drink waited on the table beside it. Drew stared at her, inquisitively.

Alicia looked back, an apologetic disposition on her face.

"They are old friends of John. Occasionally they show up here unannounced. Most often it isn't an issue but I have repeatedly asked them to respect my wishes and call before dropping by. They are a bit thick so one can only assume it hasn't sunk in. Hopefully they didn't bother you, especially the fat one, Richard; he can come off a bit boorish."

"What did they want?"

"I don't mean to be rude, Drew, but it really is none of your business. As discussed the first day, I won't ask you about your friends. I hope you will respect me and not ask about mine, either."

Though Drew acknowledged her with a smile and indicated by slightly shaking his head that she didn't offend him, he remained apprehensive and concerned about the events of the evening. After finishing his drink he wished Alicia a good night and went to bed.

With the incident from earlier continuing to peck at him, Drew lay awake in bed, on his back with his hands interlaced behind his head. As he thought about the men at the front door, he heard Alicia get up from the living room chair and walk to her bedroom. Exiting it almost immediately, she made her way to the kitchen, directly above his bedroom. He could hear her shuffling about, moving things in the cupboards, then going to the table. She went back to the counter, foraging through the utensil drawer, before returning to the table, again. Then there was silence.

Curious, Drew got up from bed, dressed and made his way to the main floor. Like being drawn to a traffic accident, he didn't want to look but felt compelled. Entering the kitchen, he saw Alicia sitting at the table, her back to him. Over her shoulder he noticed small, resealable plastic bags strewn about the table and a food scale. On the scale sat a baggie partially filled with a white substance which Drew recognized as cocaine.

With the velocity and violence of a pin prick to a balloon, Drew's world fragmented.

As though she heard the crash behind her, Alicia swivelled on her chair.

Drew's head swam. He reeled back devastated, before stumbling towards the basement stairs.

Alicia raced to him, grabbing his hand.

"Drew, please."

He stared at her with clouded, distraught eyes. His mind was numb; he was numb, anaesthetized by what he had just witnessed and recognizing what all those late night visits meant. With his free hand he tore Alicia's grip from his hand before he turned and descended the stairs to his room, holding the railing in fear his legs would give out on him.

Alicia started to follow him but stopped, knowing the damage was done, and that nothing she could say or do would be enough to lessen the significance of what he had witnessed. She sat on the stairs, her elbows on her knees and her face in her hands as fierce lashes of guilt whipped at her.

"I'm so sorry. I'm so sorry," she whispered. "Please forgive me."

In his room, Drew sat on the bed, lost. The situation was too surreal for him to comprehend. He couldn't reconcile the woman he so respected and admired with the person he had just seen; the people with whom she associated.

Why would she risk her life, her children's lives? Had she learned nothing from John's actions? And for all she had talked about, how could she be so thoughtless, so self-centered, so disrespectful. And to put me into this position.

He pulled out his suitcase and removed his clothing from the drawers. As he began to pack his belongings, the magnitude of the situation struck him. The scenario was repeating itself: he had nowhere to go, no one to trust. He was the child who was abandoned, the child who was abused, the child who was imprisoned by his circumstances which he couldn't control and needed to escape. But to where? What would tomorrow bring? John and Alicia were there for him when he needed support. He had never felt a stronger bond to anyone else than he had with John, and Alicia picked up where John had left off, carrying on John's wishes and opening her doors to Drew. But now John was gone and Alicia...this was too much. She had put his freedom in a vulnerable position, had undermined everything he had believed about her.

Though he didn't sleep that night, Drew remained in his bedroom until after Alicia and the children had left for the day.

Finishing his breakfast, and knowing that his mother would be at work and unable to answer a phone call, Drew sent a text to her about the previous night's occurrence and his need for a ride to a motel for the night. Then Drew left the house and walked to the florist.

The radiant December day was in contrast to Drew's mood. The day was crisp but cloudless, and the sun shone diamond bright with its brilliance casting shadows like Japanese ink paintings on the ground where it passed through the leafless trees of the cemetery. Unfortunately, Drew didn't see the beauty; the world he saw was without colour, without texture.

"Good morning, may I help you?" The woman behind the counter of the cemetery office asked in a soft, comforting voice.

"Yes, good morning." Drew paused trying to determine his approach. "This may be an unusual request; I am looking for a friend's grave but, and here is where it gets weird, I don't know his last name."

The woman raised her eyebrow.

"It's sort of a long story but he would never tell me his last name only giving cryptic clues that I was never able to solve. Unfortunately, he died suddenly about seven months ago, before he got the chance to tell me."

She moved her chair towards the computer.

"You're right, that is an unusual request." She smiled, "What is his first name and date of burial? Is there anything else you can tell me about his burial?"

"His first name was John. I'm not sure of the exact date but it would have been mid-April of this year. I don't know if this will help but his wife's name is Alicia."

After several long moments of searching the woman took a map of the cemetery and, with a pen in hand, she stood up from her chair and, placing the map on the counter, marked two locations: the first was the office and the second the grave site. Then she drew a line following the laneway to the site. Drew thanked her for the assistance and left.

Minutes later he was approaching the grave site marked on the map. A foreboding nervousness leached into him, his stomach quivered and his heart pounded. Drew wanted to know who John was but still wasn't sure he was ready to confront the reality. He stopped along the laneway for several moments and took a number of deep breaths before continuing along to the grass area indicated on the map. Crossing the last few steps of the lawn revealed the inscription on the headstone:

John David Benjamin Musgrave

January 28, 1971 – April 19, 2012

In Loving Memory of a Father, Husband, Son.

Drew traced the lettering on the headstone with his finger before he placed his hand on top of it. Closing his eyes, tears fell and his chin trembled. He stood there, hushed, before walking to the foot of the grave and dropping to his knees, facing the headstone.

"John, help me, I don't know what to do. There is so much good in Alicia, yet to find out what she is doing makes this so difficult. I can't forget what she has done, yet if she told me she would stop...Please, John, I need your guidance, I need another lesson."

He remained kneeling at the foot of the grave for fifteen minutes.

Then Drew lay down on the ground over John's grave, in silence. His body set supine, his hands clasped over his stomach as if he were awaiting burial.

He prayed: *John Musgrave, talk to me, I am open to your words.*

Drew lay on the grave for nearly half an hour before he rose. Placing the flowers at the base of the headstone, he said good-bye to John before heading back to Alicia's house.

"Hello, Jessica speaking."

There was a pause at the other end.

"Hello? Is someone there?"

"Hi, Jessica, it's Drew, do you have some time to talk?"

Jessica could tell by the tone and manner of Drew's voice that something was wrong.

"Of course, Drew, what's the problem?"

"Jessica, I just wanted to let you know that I may have to take the next day or two off work. Alicia and I had a falling out last night and it doesn't look like the current arrangements will work going forward," Drew's tone was cheerless. "I've left a message for my mother to pick me up this afternoon to take me to a motel for the night. She will likely try to get me to live with her but Drury is too far away so I'll have to look for something to rent in or near the city. But if I can't, there may be no other choice but to stay with her until something becomes available. Hopefully, I can find a place nearby that is affordable."

"Drew, I have a large house, too large probably. If you need a place to stay until you find something more suitable, you are welcome here."

"That is very kind of you, Jessica, but I couldn't impose like that. I just wanted to let you know what was happening."

"Impose? If it were an imposition, I wouldn't have offered." She paused before giving a slight snicker. "Thinking about it, I could also pick your brain without having to pay for it."

Several moments passed in silence. Then Jessica heard the sound of muffled crying.

"Oh Drew, I'm sorry, I shouldn't have made light of the situation. I realize this must be hard, knowing how much both John and Alicia have meant to you. But the offer still remains. How about you talk to your mother and see what she thinks. If you want to take some time to think about it, that's fine. I won't be offended if you choose not to stay here. Don't worry about coming into work tomorrow. In fact, if you need more time to find a place that will be fine. Get the situation straightened out and then let me know your intentions."

Drew thanked her and agreed to advise her of the outcome of his decision.

At three-thirty, after a long, emotionally draining day at work, Alicia arrived home. Inside she found Drew sitting at the kitchen table, his packed suitcase on the floor behind his chair. Beleaguered by the previous night's episode and seeing the suitcase, Alicia could no longer defy her surmounting despondency. Slumping into a chair, she placed her forehead in her hand.

"I'm sorry, Drew. Please forgive me. I know it is wrong. Please, don't go," she begged through her tears.

"Alicia, I cannot stay here if you continue to deal in drugs." His voice was calm. "It jeopardizes my freedom and, more importantly, it endangers Zoë and Benjamin. If the cops ever caught you, and I was still living here, the shit would hit the fan."

He paused, thinking about the situation and considering a solution.

"If you promised me that you would stop dealing, immediately, then I would think about staying. I don't want to go, I love living here, but..."

"Drew, I don't want to be selling drugs. Jesus Christ, if I thought I had an alternative, I'd stop in a heartbeat. But I don't and, without the money it brings in, I just can't make ends meet."

"I can pay more for rent or cover some grocery costs or utility bills; wouldn't that take care of the money problem?"

"That's a kind offer but doubling your rent wouldn't be enough to keep us afloat in this house. I'm not proud of my involvement, but as much as I hate to admit it, selling drugs has helped me through so many tough times; it has paid as many bills as my pay cheques. I don't participate in the actual selling but I cut and bag it, not that that makes a big difference. I want to give it up but I could lose everything we have. Don't you understand?"

"No. While I do understand what you're saying, I *can't* understand your reasoning, the logic just doesn't fit. If you get caught you *will* lose everything; including your children. Haven't you thought of that; didn't John's actions teach you anything? You can't make me believe you have no other choice."

Alicia's face transformed from sorrowful to indignant as she stood back up.

"Don't you dare sit there all sanctimonious and lecture me about my situation as if you have any idea. You're just a kid who has no experience in the realities of life. Wait until you are forced into decisions out of circumstances you can't control. That is what life is, trying to make the best out of the shit it throws you." She pounded her index finger on the kitchen table. "And I'll tell you right here, right now; I'm a survivor. I fight the battles that are thrown at me and claw my way through it all, whatever it takes. I came from little and have built so much. I'm an educated woman who has to take a job as a waitress because big industry believes I should pay for the sins of my spouse. I've been raising my children alone for ten years and have sacrificed and slaved to feed, clothe and shelter them."

Alicia turned away from Drew and walked to the kitchen sink, placing her hands on the counter and leaning forward to look out the window. After several moments she turned to Drew, her voice quiet, almost exhausted.

"And to suggest you know what I should have learned from John. What he taught me was to somehow keep everything on track without him because he was never here, even when he wasn't in jail. You've no idea the pressure on me to appease him and his expectations. To make it appear that everything's smooth sailing; to always be the all-caring, all-compassionate, ever perfect wife and mother; and now landlord – a Stepford Wife. All because of the guilt he carries…carried. If he had ever learned of the truth, he would have been crushed under the weight of his shame. And that burden is borne upon me every day, every waking moment until I want to scream; even now, all these months after he died. It was up to me to maintain the image after you arrived because of what he had told you, how he built up my reputation: to be that venerated, perfect, gentle, saintly icon. Well you know what? I'm not, but I couldn't allow his picture of me, even up 'til now, to be tainted. So, no, there is no choice. I'll do whatever fucking-well needs be done to care for my babies; to keep them in this house. To keep this 'ship sailing straight' as John use to say."

"I'm sorry for all the misery John and his incarceration has caused you and that you believe this is necessary for your survival, but I have to think about my welfare and the risk your actions impose on me. I must protect my well being."

Alicia didn't respond.

"Then, Alicia," Drew said, his voice still composed, "I guess we have nothing more to talk about.

"My mother is coming to pick me up. Then I'll be out of here. I am truly sorry that it has come to this but I have no choice, and, apparently, neither do you. If it's alright with you, I'd like to stick around to say good-bye to the children."

Alicia turned her back and looked away, again out the kitchen window.

"In that case, I'll wait outside for my mother."

After Drew closed the front door, Alicia slammed her fist on the kitchen counter.

"God damn you, John! God damn you and your perfect wife!"

Just after four o'clock, Jean arrived. Drew looked back at the house before putting his suitcase in the trunk of the car and getting into the passenger side.

Alicia stood at the front window, tears coursing down her cheeks.

Jean backed the car out of the driveway and passed the oncoming school bus. Drew looked in the rear view mirror to the bus stop and saw Zoë and Benjamin get off and race up towards the house.

"If it is easier for you Drew, you can stay with me, as I said before; I already spoke to the Browns about it.

"No, thanks mom, I will stay at the motel then make arrangements to find a place to stay. Drury is too far away from my work."

From his motel room, that evening, Drew phoned Jessica.

"I won't be in to work tomorrow, but I expect to be there on Wednesday. Oh, and if your offer is still on the table, I would appreciate it if I can stay at your place. You can pick my brain and I will save myself bus fare," he said with a tired laugh.

Drew gave Jessica the address of the motel he was staying at and she agreed to pick him up the following day on her way home from work. He then left a message for Francine regarding the change of living arrangements and advised her he would let her know his new address as soon as he could.

CHAPTER EIGHTEEN

When he woke up the first day, Drew felt lost. He didn't recognize the room he was in by shape or design and for several moments he thought back to how he arrived at this place. Then he remembered he was now living at Jessica's.

As time went on, the move into the house progressed smoothly and the convenience of Drew living with Jessica worked well for both of them. Their passion for art and several other common interests became apparent the more they spoke. Jessica's positive supportive, attitude helped Drew as he took on more responsibilities at the gallery and before long he was calling on dealers and importers alone. Soon after the move, both realized that this arrangement would be more than temporary.

Jessica's house was large but utilitarian. The front had an interlocking stone walkway leading up to a concrete porch which spanned the width of the residence. The double-doors opened to a simple interior concept: a large living room subtly finished in black and white with a wood burning fireplace in one corner, a dining room which had been converted to an office and a large eat-in kitchen extending across the back. On the second floor, the L-shaped hallway accessed three bedrooms. The last bedroom, at the end of the hall, became Drew's. Opposite the bedroom door stood a grandfather clock which chimed every fifteen minutes.

On the morning of the fourth day, Drew approached Jessica with a problem.

"Do you think we can move the clock from the hallway? The chiming keeps me awake and I'm starting to feel like a bag of hammers. We can just move it down the hall if that is okay with you, but it needs to be away from my door."

Jessica smiled. "I'm surprised you lasted this long. I moved it down there after two days because the chiming kept me awake. But a grandfather clock that doesn't chime is like a cone without ice cream. It's an abomination. We can move it on Sunday or Monday."

"We will likely have to make it Monday because I am helping my mother move out of the house this weekend."

"That's right. I offered to give you a ride, didn't I?"

Drew nodded. "Yes, eight o'clock is when I want to be there. My mother will drop me off when we are finished, which shouldn't be too late."

"I'm doing some running around that day so message me when you are finished and, if I'm still out, I will drop by and pick you up. No reason for her to drive you if I'm in the area; I'm sure she'll have a lot of things to do after she is moved in."

The following Sunday was overcast. The heavy clouds churned out both snow and rain as the temperature hovered just above freezing. Jessica dropped Drew off at his parents' house. William was not there and Jean had most of her belongings packed. It was just the furnishings that hadn't been taken the previous move that she needed assistance with. The Browns showed up at noon and the van was packed by one o'clock.

"Andrew, I spoke to your father," Jean said as she started the car. "He will not give me the adoption paperwork. He would not say why but I think it is because he is afraid that you will abandon him once you have discovered who your birth parents are."

Drew shook his head, pursing his lips. He hadn't thought about it before but now that his mother brought it up, Drew could see abandonment being the outcome. And he was content with that.

"I don't get it, though, he's afraid of abandonment from a son he has treated with so much contempt over the years. That doesn't make sense to me. It isn't like we are ever going to reconcile our differences."

Jean looked at Drew but said nothing. Drew looked out the window thinking about what his mother had said.

"There has to be more to it. Just a couple of days before my move he told me to get out of the house. Maybe I should talk to him, see if he will be reasonable."

"No, I do not think that would be a good idea. He was very upset when I asked him about it. He even swore at me, something he has never done before. There was so much contempt in his voice, so much hatred."

"But mom, I just don't see..."

"Andrew!" She interrupted him, her voice sharp with irritation. "I told you he was very upset with me so I do not see how you speaking with him would produce a different result."

Drew looked at his mother with his eyebrows raised in shock, but didn't respond to her outburst. Jean calmed her voice and continued.

"How about you leave this with me? I will let the situation cool off a bit then try to reason with him. Yes, you want to have this information sooner rather than later but if you push the issue with your father he is likely to respond irrationally; childishly."

Drew knew she was right about his father, but still couldn't understand why he would react so vehemently.

The unpacking at the Browns' residence was done within two hours. Prior to finishing, Drew texted Jessica and she advised him that she could be at the house by five o'clock. Drew and Jean visited with the Browns while waiting.

When Jessica arrived, she pulled into the driveway and honked. Drew said his good-byes to the Browns and gave Jean a long hug before leaving the residence. He had the sense that the corner had finally been turned for both him and his mother; that they were free from the biggest hurdle in their lives, William. Getting into Jessica's car he was feeling celebratory and displayed a wide smile.

"You're looking rather happy," Jessica observed. "What's up?"

"Just about everything," he responded with a laugh. "I couldn't be happier for my mother, now that she is away from that prick of a husband; nor for me. I have a job doing what I love, I have enrolled for the winter semester night classes at the University, my living arrangements are fantastic and my boss is great...and, yes, I'm sucking up."

He paused for a moment his expression and voice changing in tone.

"Jessica, seriously, I can't remember ever feeling as contented as right now, about where my life is and the prospects for it going forward. In the short time working for you, you have been so supportive and positive. I'm so glad that you have given me this opportunity to work for you and you opened your home to me when my situation was so dire. My only hope is that I don't let you down."

Jessica looked at Drew grinning.

"If things continue the way they started, there is no way you will let me down. I'm glad that things are working out for you. And feel fortunate that John and Alicia referred you to me. As mentioned when we first met, you will be a great fit and in the short time you have been working with me you have continued to amaze with your knowledge and understanding of art and with how easily you have gone beyond simple university theory to praxis."

"Well, to celebrate the occasion I would like to take you out for dinner." With a wide smile Drew added. "Can you give me an advance on my next pay?"

The light snow that had been falling gave way to heavy flurries as they drove. The flakes were large and wet, sticking to everything they touched. By the time Drew and Jessica had reached the city, snow ruts had formed on the roads making driving difficult.

Entering the city, they saw lit Menorahs adorning the streets along with brilliant lights and displays in celebration of the holiday season. The mantle of new snow sat like beehive hairdos upon the nativity scene figures in front of a church.

When they left the restaurant after their dinner, the snow had stopped and the first snowmen were already built, standing along the sidewalk. As they passed a parked car, Drew stopped and grabbed a handful of snow. Packing it into a perfect snowball, he threw it at Jessica, hitting her in the back. As she turned to him Drew grabbed another handful and threw it. Jessica skimmed some snow off of a parked car and heaved it, hitting Drew in the head as he tried to dodge out of the way. Each then ducked behind parked cars and began making and throwing more snowballs. Several minutes of battle had passed when a voice boomed from the darkness of the apartments above.

"Get away from my car, you idiots!"

They ran down the street, laughing, to Jessica's car, which was parked in a nearby lot. Before getting in, they brushed the snow off their clothes and out of their hair. Inside the car they continued laughing. Drew pointed to Jessica's face.

"You missed a spot."

Jessica brought her hand to her face and wiped it.

"Nope, you missed it again. Do you want me to get it?"

Jessica nodded.

"Okay, but you will have to close your eyes."

As she did, Drew quickly brought a handful of snow he had scooped from the roof of her car and smeared it in her face.

"Oh my God," she shrilled as the white cold fell from her face down the front of her coat. "You bugger. I can't believe you did that."

Drew sat there with a silly smile on his face.

By the time they arrived at Jessica's house it was nearly midnight. Jessica removed her jacket revealing her wet blouse where the snow had melted. Drew couldn't hold back a chuckle.

"You think this is funny, do you?" Jessica spuriously reprimanded, a wide smile on her face. "Go ahead, laugh, but know that vengeance will be mine."

After she changed out of her blouse they retired to the living room and started a fire. Drew made them drinks and they sat near the hearth welcoming its heat.

"You know, I think the clock would look good in that corner, opposite the fireplace. It would balance the room out," he observed.

Jessica looked at the spot he had suggested and thought about the prospect.

"Okay, tomorrow we bring it down here first thing, unless you want to do it now so as not to have to listen to it tonight."

"Wow, you're full of energy. But I think I can handle it for one more evening. Fact is I'm so tired, it will take more than a chiming clock to keep me awake."

As the flames died down, they finished their drinks and closed the screen of the fireplace. They agreed to get up early and take care of the clock and Drew would go with Jessica down to the store to help her with some clean up and other odd jobs.

When they had finished breakfast the following morning, Drew and Jessica carried the clock from the upstairs to the main floor. Once in the corner, Jessica immediately realized, not surprised, that Drew was right.

The afternoon was spent at the store rearranging some of the exhibits and freeing up an area which would be used for a new display of artists of resistance from communist-era, Eastern Bloc countries. The idea was Drew's and both Jessica and Kimberley agreed it was a great chance for Drew to show his innate abilities and for the store to take on some art and artists whom they had never before considered. By mid-afternoon the area had been prepared and pizza was ordered. The meal was a good break from the work and gave them an opportunity to relax.

"Have you always lived in the area you are now?" Drew asked.

"Most of my early life was spent just outside the city. When I was young I was married, but it only lasted a short time. Both my husband and I realized that I had a drive that wouldn't work well in our relationship. The marriage was a good idea at the time. My ex had no interest in what I wanted nor, as it ended up, did I in him. That's the thing about getting married when you are young; you haven't established who you are or who you want to be. After the marriage ended I moved away with my parents but after getting my degree, returned here to start this business."

"You said it 'was a good idea at the time', does that mean that things have changed since then?"

"Yes and no. It was more a marriage of necessity than anything. So, at the time it seemed like a good idea. But, I've only been in a couple of relationships since my marriage ended, nothing has been too serious. Those relationships were never looked at as long term; more like trysts that satisfied the needs of both people involved." Jessica paused for a few moments and a smile emerged. "More recently, with the expansion of the store, I've found there isn't much time for a social life. So my chance of meeting anyone outside of the art world environment seems somewhat remote."

"And is that important to you? Meeting someone outside this milieu?"

Jessica laughed. "No I'm not that choosy. It's just as likely not to happen because my interactions are strictly for business purposes and never go beyond that."

Drew stared at her contemplatively. Jessica stared back and though she continued to smile, the area between her eyebrows creased and her expression took on a questioning look.

"What? Why are you staring at me like that?"

Drew gave his head a slight shake and his gaze fell away from Jessica and upon his can of cola sitting on the floor.

"Sorry. I was lost in thought." His cheeks took on a shade of red as the sensation of heat washed over him.

"Is that so? And what were you thinking about?" Jessica moved a bit closer and bent her head to try to look at Drew's face.

Drew continued to concentrate on the can in front of him.

"Nothing, really; you know how sometimes you just go off on a tangent by a single word or short phrase? That is what happened to me, that's all."

Jessica laughed, knowing that the line of questions she was asking was making him uncomfortable. Drew readjusted his seat, squirming with discomfort.

"Drew, I'm just playing with you," she laughed.

Drew gave an unconvincing smile and wanted to return to the conversation.

"If I might ask, why did you marry him in the first place?"

"We were young and impetuous. And we made a mistake, as young people often do. Luckily we realized it quickly and didn't fool ourselves into believing that what we had was anything more than teenage love. Unfortunately we didn't realize it until after."

There was a pause as both of them bit into their pizza and had a sip of pop.

"What about you? Have you been in any significant relationship?"

"No, the only females I have ever cared about have either been with another person." He paused. "Or is my mother." Drew let out a snorting laugh. Jessica joined him.

"Well, Drew, I think we are done for the day. Would you like to go home or are you up for going for a walk around the city?"

Though he was tired, Drew opted for the walk.

Christmas music was playing throughout the city and seasonal kindness had infiltrated people's consciousness as greetings were bartered with all whom they met along the streets. Adding to the ambience, snow from the previous night was still pristine; free from the effects of the dirt of the city. The temperature hovered around freezing and the sun was bright, its light glistened off the snow with the brilliance of stars on a moonless night. The effect produced warmth which accompanied them while they strolled. As they continued on, the sun descended behind the buildings, scoring the horizon and the sky took on a lapis lazuli hue; a breathtaking transition toward the blackness of night.

The drive home was quiet and Drew thought about the work necessary to put together the exhibit he envisioned. He had started organizing the layout and needed to begin researching artists from such countries such as Bulgaria and Romania.

When they arrived home it was late and they were exhausted. After a cup of hot chocolate they wished each other a good night and both went to bed.

CHAPTER NINETEEN

Christmas and New Year's came and went with little fanfare; Drew spent Christmas Day quietly visiting with his mother and exchanging gifts. William had called mid-day but the phone was left unanswered. In the evening they went out for dinner at a nice restaurant in the city.

That night, Drew arrived back at home just after ten o'clock to find the fire crackling and a bottle of wine with cheese and crackers on the table in front of the hearth. Jessica, who had spent the day with her family, had texted Drew to find out his return time and had prepared the cheese platter.

"What a nice surprise; a perfect finish to a quiet, relaxing day," he said to Jessica as she entered the room.

"I'm glad you like it. Do you drink Riesling? I have my favourites but wasn't sure what you liked and Riesling is a nice fall back."

Drew looked at her with a puzzled look on his face and shrugged.

"I don't have a favourite; one thing I am not is a wine aficionado. If it tastes good I'll drink it."

"We'll have to work on that."

Jessica poured each of them a glass then held hers up.

"Merry Christmas and to a successful collaboration; may we both continue to learn and grow within the relationship."

They sat quietly, sipping their wine and tasting the cheeses as the fire continued to crackle and burn. Finally, just after midnight, the fire had burned out and they went to bed.

Drew and Jessica spent New Year's Eve just as quietly, at city hall watching the fireworks before heading home to relax by the fire with some wine.

For the next two months, Drew continued to take on more responsibilities at work. Jessica had given him a company car, a VW Jetta, the style of which Drew loved and the drive he found comfortable. He was proud that in such a short period, Jessica had enough confidence to give him the opportunity to take on more responsibilities. Further, she ended his probationary period early and increased his pay. Drew spent much of his time on the road visiting with clientele and working on his exhibit. His main job, however, was to be Jessica's assistant and they continued to spend a majority of their time travelling to auctions and shows and working with their importers.

His night school courses were memorization intensive, yet enjoyable and, as with his previous years of university, he was able to maintain a high grade point average; a fact that was another source of satisfaction and pride.

Periodically Drew touched base with Fran but, having no further information to work with, the trail to discovering his birth parents had become protracted.

He and his mother got together often for dinners or weekend visits. When they spoke of William the conversation ended the same way; Jean would explain that, despite several requests, William still refused to assist in any way.

Over dinner one evening, Jean seemed particularly excited to see Drew. Their conversation was relaxed but Jean seemed distracted.

"Mom, is something going on?"

"Nothing too dramatic, Andrew, but I have been thinking quite a bit about buying a new house. The way property values have been dropping over the past several years, I believe it would be a good idea to buy before they start going up again."

"Sound planning, mom, when were you thinking of doing that? And what about our home? Have you spoken to William about him buying you out? That would make for a nice down payment."

"No, I have not talked to him about it just yet. I wanted to talk to you first. I was thinking that maybe we could buy it together. That way you are not throwing your money away on rent. You will be finished your university course and that would free up a lot of money for you. My hope is that you will have a good paying job so the mortgage will not be too much of a burden for you. I know I could not carry one on my own."

"I'll have to think about it mom. I don't think I would look at it as a place to live, though. As I mentioned the previous times you spoke to me about living with you, Drury is too far from the city. But it could be a good investment for me. Why don't we revisit the idea in a couple of years? For now I would rather concentrate on getting my degree."

Jean stared down at her plate, a look of disappointment on her face.

"Listen, mom, I know you are always looking out for me and trying to help but it just doesn't make sense logistically; I would have to drive three hours every day to and from work; and that is in good weather. My days can be long enough as it is, adding that much time to them would kill me."

"That's fine, Andrew," she sighed. "Now you know why I wanted to talk to you first. There is no point talking to your father if you are not interested." Jean's voice gave a hint of dejection.

Drew was beginning to tire of the discussion and his mother's tactics.

"Mom, I said I would revisit it and I will. But there is no way I'd consider moving back to Drury. It just doesn't make sense. I'm not rejecting you, I'm rejecting

Drury and the distance it is from the city. Now, can we talk about something else?"

For the remainder of the evening, the conversation was curt and cold. Drew was relieved when it ended and he was heading home.

Drew and Jessica began spending much of their time together outside of work as they found many similar personal interests. Dinners were eaten together and most of the free time they had was spent going out to movies. Jessica also introduced Drew to live theatre, which he enjoyed, and opera, which he didn't enjoy as much. When they didn't go out they would spend hours in front of the fireplace reading or enjoying wine and cheese while light and crackling warmth emanated from the flames. Drew's pallet had become more refined and he was showing signs of becoming a wine enthusiast, though much work was still needed. When necessary, Jessica would help Drew with his studies.

Drew felt a closeness and fondness for Jessica he had never experienced with anyone before. The open, honest relationship they had developed and the ease with which they were around each other were things he looked forward to when they were apart.

After returning from an evening at the theatre, Drew started the fire while Jessica poured each of them a glass of Icewine and cut up some Manchego cheese to go with crackers. When she returned to the living room they sat on an area rug near the hearth. The dancing glow of the flames produced the only light in the room. They settled in quietly, taking pleasure in the warmth and beauty of the moment. Drew closed his eyes, bathing in the fire's gleaming radiance.

Jessica moved closer to him. She leaned forward and gently kissed him. Drew pulled away, alarmed.

"I'm sorry; I didn't mean to upset you," Jessica said self-effacingly.

"Don't be sorry, you just caught me a little off guard. And it certainly didn't bother me."

A long moment passed. They sat before the fire motionless, gazing at each other. For the first time in his life, Drew experienced a physical attraction which was enhanced by a strong emotional connection.

Surging excitement flushed over Jessica. She slowly leaned forward, lips slightly parted, and met Drew, bringing her hands up and cupping his jaw. Their lips parted further as tongue met tongue, dancing. A rush of anticipation coursed through Drew's body.

Drew moved from kissing Jessica's lips and gently bit her chin and neck before moving to her ear. Jessica quivered a low moan and trembled as he nibbled her lobe and began running the tip of his tongue along the contours of her ear.

Jessica withdrew slightly, gazing at Drew.

"I haven't been with a man in a long time," she whispered.

Drew looked at her with a devilish smile.

"That's okay, we'll explore together. But let me know if you aren't comfortable."

Jessica lay back on the rug and Drew lay on his side, beside her, his head supported by his hand. He began running his fingers delicately over her face, from her forehead over her closed eyes and down the bridge of her nose, along her jaw line to her chin before stopping at her mouth. With his index finger he lightly outlined her soft, full lips before replacing the finger with his own lips. Seconds passed as they delighted in the yielding warmth.

Drew unbuttoned Jessica's blouse and fondled her breasts above the bra, slowly working inside the cup, lightly brushing her erect nipple. A soft sigh. Jessica removed her blouse and bra and helped Drew remove his shirt.

She explored Drew's torso with her hand as he lay back down on his side. With her middle finger she tenderly outlined the scar on his chest. She looked up at him to search for reassurance and he nodded to indicate it was alright to touch it. Drew lay on his back. She lowered her head and began kissing and licking his chest, and lightly bit his nipples. As she moved towards Drew's abdomen, Jessica positioned herself so that he could play with her breasts, tenderly squeezing and rolling her nipples between his index fingers and thumbs.

Jessica moved down to Drew's waist and undid his pants. Reaching inside his underwear she slowly began stroking his hardness. Drew closed his eyes, feeling the gentle pleasure. He pushed his pants down to his thighs then removed her pants and panties. Escaping moans rose to hush the hissing and crackling blaze.

As Jessica took Drew in her mouth, he began to rub between her legs and penetrated her with his fingers. He luxuriated in Jessica's aroma and began licking her, tasting her desire. Spreading her lips he ran his tongue over them, periodically flicking inside her, each time producing a shuddering gasp.

Jessica brushed her lips along Drew's shaft while she stroked and caressed it with her hand. Opening her mouth she swept her teeth against his erection, lightly biting as she moved along its rigidity. Her tongue skimmed his testicles as she slowly took them into her mouth. Drew experienced frissons as his body indulged in Jessica's attention.

Drew tenderly held Jessica's clit between his teeth and grazing it with his tongue while delighting her inner walls with his index and middle fingers. Jessica's juices trickled down the back of her leg.

"Oh yeah, eat my hot pussy," she moaned, her voice elevated and throaty.

Removing his fingers from inside her, Drew reached around to Jessica's buttocks and pulled her tight against him, passionately smothering himself in her vulva, delighting her labia and clit, feeling her tighten and release, drinking in her sapid nectar.

Jessica's body was overcome in an outburst of minute orgasms. She stroked Drew's firmness passionately while licking and sucking the smooth throbbing head.

"I want to fuck you like a dog," Drew growled lustily.

Jessica repositioned herself and reached down between her legs taking Drew's hardness and guided it into her engorged passage. With each thrust, Drew's scrotum struck Jessica's clit, radiating jolts of ecstasy through her groin and into her stomach. Drew grabbed Jessica's hair and pulled it, jerking her head back each time he penetrated. His thrusts came hard and fast, punctuated by grunts and heavy breathing. Jessica extended her hand down between her legs, rubbing her clit and caressing his sack.

Reaching her zenith she let out several loud moans. Her rapturous climax hit so intensely she had to lower her head down to the rug for fear her arms would give out in the euphoria. The initial rush was followed by multiple tremors as her legs began to shake, weakened by the experience.

His body shimmering with sweat, Drew lay back down and Jessica resumed passionately osculating and caressing his phallus. Approaching orgasm, Drew's breathing became shallow, his face flushed, his body tensed.

Drew surged. With her index finger, Jessica pushed against Drew's perineum, intensifying the sensation as he pulsed. Jessica removed him from her mouth and continued stroking him vigorously as his warm release covered her bosom, glistening in the glow of the fire. Squeezing her breasts around his still hard form she licked the last drops from the head.

Blissfully spent, Drew and Jessica fell asleep in each other's arms.

Except for putting more logs on the fire, they remained on the rug for the night, neither wanting to be out of the other's company.

At breakfast, Jessica stared at Drew with an odd expression on her face.

"What?"

"Oh, nothing really; I'm just wondering about the sleeping arrangements, that's all. Do you think it would be inappropriate if you were to share my bed?"

Drew had just spent an emotional, passionate night with Jessica but the implications of what she was suggesting was well beyond any thought he had given to the relationship. At the same time, the prospect excited him. He didn't know what to say, but didn't want to offend her.

"I like the idea, but do you mind if I give it some thought and we discuss it further? You know how I like to consider things thoroughly before I make a decision."

Over the years of living at his parents' home, Drew had been subjected to knee-jerk reactions and spontaneous decisions by his father. As a child and youth he had allowed himself to commit the same mistake and had paid for it. During his years in prison, through the direction of John, he learned to be more thoughtful, more reflective, before making any determinations or deciding on courses of action. Being out of prison did nothing to change that approach.

"Of course, when you are ready, let me know. Until then the current arrangements will remain."

A self-conscious silence hung between them.

"Drew, I want you to know this isn't about last night. I found myself quite attracted to you very early on. You are funny, articulate, sensitive, thoughtful and, quite simply, a decent man. You have passion and appreciation about you that transcends your knowledge and education. And, yes I'll admit, you are easy on the eyes."

Despite his discomfort in receiving the complements, Drew kept his eyes on Jessica, fighting the urge to look away. His head swirled with thoughts and emotions.

"I have felt an incredible connection to you as well. You have given me the confidence to be myself and that has allowed me to grow as a person. I look forward to being with you every day and feel a near emptiness when we are apart. It's funny; John once told me that when you are part of someone's life, not being there takes away an element of who they are. I now understand what he means. I don't know how to say it except that I love being around you, spending as much time as I can with you, whether it's at work or outside of it."

Drew paused then took Jessica's hand.

"Jessica, I think I am in love with you, but I don't know; never having felt this way, this intense before about someone in my life."

Jessica's eyes were affectionate. While still looking at him, she brought Drew's hand up to her lips and lightly kissed each of his knuckles.

"As the Italians say, *Ti amo.*"

Drew leaned across the table and kissed Jessica. As they parted, a tear of joy trickled from his eye.

"I think you have my answer regarding the sleeping arrangements," he laughed, wiping his cheek.

The remainder of the morning was spent moving Drew's belongings into Jessica's room.

That afternoon, Jessica went out to run some errands while Drew remained behind, putting the last of his belongings into drawers.

When he had finished Drew wandered to the living room and kindled the fire. He watched for several minutes while it grew from a spark to a blaze. As he stood before the flames he reached back and removed his wallet from his pocket. Filing through it Drew found his Prison Discharge Slip and took it out. He kneeled down looking at it for several moments before holding it to the fire. As the flames enveloped the slip, Drew couldn't help but think that it represented a cremation of the old Drew and his resurrection, his baptism; a new beginning.

When Jessica returned, several hours later, she found Drew asleep on the rug in front of the fireplace, a slender upward curl to the corners of his mouth. As he lay there, her eyes smiled in delight, wondering what he was dreaming about.

Jessica went to the kitchen and began preparing roast and potatoes for dinner. Having placed the meal in the oven and the table set, she returned to the living room with two glasses of wine.

"Drew," she whispered as she nudged his foot with hers, "wake up."

When Drew woke, Jessica invited him to snuggle up with her on the couch in front of the fireplace and enjoy a glass of wine before dinner was ready. The meal was delicious and the conversation animated. As usual there were a variety of topics which allowed for serious discussion and frivolous banter; all of which each found enjoyable.

At the conclusion of the meal they returned to the living room with wine and their dessert, chocolate lava cake. Nearing the couch, Drew stopped and turned towards Jessica.

"What about the grandfather clock, Jessica? Do we put it back by the bedroom where I use to sleep?"

Jessica looked over at the clock towering in the corner with great dignity and authority.

"I don't know; I think I like it where it is, there in the corner."

Drew nodded in agreement. "It does look good there."

CHAPTER TWENTY

Just after eight o'clock in the evening, the telephone rang.

"Good evening, Jean."

"Hello, William," Jean answered coldly, "what's the reason for the phone call?"

"Jean, I know you spoke to me about helping Drew and maybe it is time for me to get on board. It's about time we ended this power struggle, I'm willing to give Drew the adoption paperwork and co-operate in any way that helps him discover who his parents are. "

The phone remained silent for several seconds as Jean weighed William's words.

"Why the sudden change of heart? What are you trying to get out of this, William? We have been asking you for the information since October when Drew first broached the subject. And you have been nothing but an impertinent, little child. Or is your offer of assistance because you are making one last pathetic attempt to regain everything that you have lost?"

"Hold on there, you asked me once. And we both agreed in October that it wasn't a good idea to give Drew the paperwork. Yes, when we spoke in December I was uncooperative, but can't we just put all of that behind us. We should look forward. Actually, I don't know if you noticed; this is our anniversary. Maybe, the occasion has given me a reason to pause and reflect on what I want and what needs to be done. I miss you and if we work together to help Drew, hopefully you can see fit to talk to me, to let me be part of your life again. Jean, we had so much..."

"No, William," she interrupted, her voice flat, emotionless, "there will be no discussion on that subject for us. Reconciliation is not even on the table. How about if you give the information to me because Drew needs it to help find his birth parents; because it is the right thing to do."

William felt the anger in his throat.

God damn it, I'm here trying to make some sort of peace, to compromise and you stonewall me. Is our marriage that easy to toss aside?

William closed his eyes and counted five heartbeats to calm down.

"If that is the way you feel about us, Jean, I won't force the issue. I will just contact Drew and arrange to meet him with the information."

"No, it would be better if you handed the paperwork over to me to pass on to Drew. I would hate for something to happen between the two of you and Drew not get the documents."

"Really? What could happen? Like I just said, we'll simply arrange to meet someplace and I'll give the envelope to him. There will be no need for you to be a part of it. If you could just give me his phone number..."

"William, I will not give you his number; Drew would never forgive me. I will tell him that you wanted to help but you cannot contact him."

Jean's response roiled William once again.

"Don't you think that decision should be his? What the hell is it with you? Who are you to decide whether I can see him or not? I'm his father. You've controlled us his entire life, when will it..."

Jean hung up.

Moments later the telephone rang again.

"Sorry Jean. It's just that I'm feeling a lot of stress and overreacted. Please, don't hang up on me again."

Jean was quiet; William waited nervously.

"Okay, William, the choice is yours; either you give me the paperwork to pass on to Drew, or I tell him you continue to refuse to give any assistance. Forgive me if I do not trust your motives, I have been around you long enough to know the man you are. Besides, Drew told you he never wants to talk to you again."

"Please, hold on a sec, Jean."

William, frustrated, knew she was his only avenue to contacting Drew. He placed his hand over the telephone's mouthpiece as he moved it from his ear.

"You bitch! You fucking controlling bitch! You know you have the control. You and your fucking smug attitude. You're stifling me. You are going to ruin my life! Take everything from me. All I want is to talk to Drew," he snarled through clenched teeth.

Again, William had to fight to calm himself.

"Fine, I will give you the paperwork. When would you like to drop by the house? We can go over everything and make sure what we have is complete."

"I will not go to the house. You will have to drop it off here. And I can go over the documents, myself, to ensure they are complete."

"But Jean," William said mockingly, "you had so little to do with the process those, oh so many years ago. How will you even know what's correct; unless, of course, you have suddenly remembered all of your involvement in the adoption?"

Jean ignored the taunt; returning her own jibe.

"If you are available tomorrow, I will be here all day. You can drop off the envelope on your way to the bar. I'll say good bye to Andrew for you."

"So there will be no compromising with you, eh? Fine," William's voice carried the loss he felt, "I need the address. Is there a separate entrance to the apartment where you are living; or do I just go to the front door?"

"I am house-sitting while the owners are gone for the long weekend. You can knock at the front door."

Jean gave William the address and they agreed that he would be there by noon the next day.

After he hung up, William poured himself a drink before he retrieved the documents. For the next several hours he read them over and made notes, filling in some of the information that was not written down. When he had finished, just before midnight, William went to bed. He tossed for a long period while thinking about the conversation he had had with Jean.

Why does she need to be in the middle of this exchange? How does it benefit her? I have to figure this out. She's been so insistent. But why?

"Hello William, hope you have a good life." A young, pregnant Jean stared at him with venomous contempt as she stood in the doorway to the house.

"What do you mean by that? I'm only here to give you the envelope." William replied.

"How can you be here to give me the envelope? I have it already."

Glancing down William saw he was no longer holding the package. Jean's sneering growl coerced his attention back to her. She stared at him with black pools for eyes, a maniacal smile splitting her face, escorted by a demonic, rough laugh. Jean ripped at the envelope with clawed hands, shredding it and the paperwork inside.

"There is no need for this. The paper cuts and will only hurt him," she snarled.

William tried to move toward Jean only to have his advancement halted by an invisible barrier. Frantically he searched for a seam, an opening, but the imperceptible barricade offered no weakness. In desperation William hysterically began punching and kicking it until he was left with nothing but mangled fingers and broken and bloodied stumps where his feet once were. Still the fortification remained unblemished and impenetrable.

When William again focused on Jean, she was nude and recumbent, her face having distorted from abhorrence to distress as she strained to push. Sweat covered her, matting her hair and dripping to the floor.

Slowly a head began to emerge from between her legs. It had dark brown hair and was unusually large for a newborn's. Repulsed, William watched, powerless to look away as Drew materialized from Jean's womb and began suckling at her teat. William let out a voiceless scream, his hands cupping his face, fingers cleaved, allowing him to continue watching. Immediately Jean and Drew began to copulate and, as though by osmosis, Drew's body merged with Jean's until only his head remained separate.

"You see William; we are one and will always be." Loathing clung to Drew and Jean's words.

As William continued to stare, they began to drift away, both laughing.

"No! You can't leave me; you can't. I have nothing," William screamed toward them as they disappeared into darkness.

William awoke from the dream drenched in anxiety. He got out of bed and went back to the dining room where the adoption paperwork remained. He sat down, elbows on the table, hands grasping each side of his head.

I'll have nothing. She will take this and it will all be over. I will never see or hear from her again. She will win. Drew will live the rest of his life ignorant. Unaware of a truth he should know. How can I get through to him? How do I make him understand?

After a long pause an idea came to William.

I will get his attention through his mother. He will want to find me. Drew, you may hate me for what I must do, but you need to know.

William considered how to best achieve his course of action. Thinking about the dynamics of Drew and Jean's relationship he knew what was necessary was dangerous to everyone involved. It was critical that his next move be adequate in order to set the required sequence of events in motion to allow him the opportunity to speak with Drew.

Finally, William returned to bed.

The following morning William gathered the documents from the dining room table and placed them back in the manila envelope. His anxiety was nearly crippling. He had had a difficult night of sleep after the dream, and was nervous about his plan. He left the house at ten o'clock and did some shopping before driving to see Jean.

At noon, he parked his car a half a block down the road from the house where Jean was living and walked the remainder of the way, the snow crunching beneath his feet.

The sky was cloudless but the cold temperature and blowing wind negated any warmth the looming sun cast down upon the town.

Jean opened the door and looked at William, a bit surprised.

"That is a new jacket."

"Yeah. May I come in for a bit? It is bitterly cold out here."

Jean stepped back and William entered the house, removing his winter hat once he was inside. He began to unzip his coat.

"Please, William, leave the jacket done up, I just want you to give me the papers then you should leave."

"Really? I can't even visit for a few minutes? Is this what has become of our relationship? You are going to cut me completely out of your life? Leave me with nothing? Jean, once I give you this paperwork I will have nothing."

Jean looked at him impassively. William could feel his anger beginning to smoulder.

"I wish I could say I am sorry, but I am not. You were, and still are, evil. Even your offer to help is founded on trying to get back with me, not on assisting your son."

"Help my son? I won't be helping him because he won't know I did this. I have you figured out, Jean; just like I told you I would. I wouldn't be surprised if you already have the black marker ready for your editing. And once you have censored it, you will hand the half document over to our son; if you give him anything at all. And, again, you'll look like the heroine. Even if you give him the paperwork, do you expect me to believe you will give me any credit? The situation will remain the way it always has been; you pitting Drew against me."

"This conversation is over. You believe what you want, you paranoid, little man. I will give Drew the information he needs to know. Period. And what he needs to know is the identity of his birth parents, if he can divine the information out of what paperwork he receives. He is not Drew's father, she is not his mother. They simply brought him into this world. Drew has no father and I am his mother."

"You're so delusional you've even convinced yourself. He, she...you speak of Drew's biological parents like they are meaningless extras in a movie. All these years of suppressing the truth out of fear for the child you couldn't have. You coddled and smothered Drew; not out of love but dread, dread he would love you less if he shared you with his real parents, or even shared you with me. And that ate at you. I could not love him like you loved him because I didn't fear losing him. The guilt you felt from losing your brother and being infertile drove you away from me and towards Drew."

"When did you become a psychiatrist?" Jean snorted. "Physician, heal thyself, and then come talk to me."

"I *know* I'm not perfect; and there are a lot of things in my life I am not proud of. Two of my biggest regrets, however, are how I misdirected so much of my anger towards Drew and that I consented to your pact, only to see you use it against me all these years later. But my biggest regret of all is that my love for you didn't allow me to see you for who you are until it was too late; too late for me and too late for Drew."

Jean scoffed.

"My only regret is that I consented to marry and stay so long with such a stupid, weak, little man. Now, give me the paperwork and get out of this house; get out of our lives."

Jean held out her hand to William.

William lunged at Jean.

CHAPTER TWENTY-ONE

Lying in bed, Drew gazed at Jessica as she slept so peacefully, so beautifully, beside him; her arm draped across his chest, her soft breathing the perfect sound in an otherwise silent world. He contemplated the events of the previous thirty-six hours. The intensity of emotions he felt for Jessica, the passion of their love-making. The happiness he felt; contentment he had never before achieved. Knowing that this was where he was supposed to be; with Jessica, his kindred soul.

As Jessica awoke a yawn embraced her body, compelling her to stretch rigid from fingertips to toes, her back arching. As her body released she looked at Drew, an angelic quality to her smile.

"Good morning," her voice still lithe with the delicate sound of sleepiness, "did you have a nice sleep?"

Drew brushed away the hair from her face and kissed her.

"Yes, it was wonderful. How was yours?"

Jessica did not answer, choosing instead to climb on top of Drew and passionately kiss him. She placed her head on his chest and listened to the sound of his heartbeat content to be in the moment with her man. They remained silent and still for several minutes.

"I am a little peckish. How does French toast and bacon for breakfast sound?"

Drew ran his hand down Jessica's bare back before rolling her onto her back and spreading her legs.

"Soon."

As Drew stepped out of the shower, he smelled the tantalizing aroma of the breakfast Jessica was preparing. Entering the kitchen he found the table was set; orange slices, coffee, French toast and bacon ready to be shared.

After breakfast Drew cleaned the kitchen while Jessica showered. As he was filling the dishwasher his cell phone rang.

"Hello, Drew speaking."

"Is this Andrew Parsons?" The voice at the other end was official.

"Yes, who may I ask is calling?"

"Mr. Parsons, this is Detective Jones with the Metro Police Force."

There was a long pause. Apprehension clawed at Drew as he thought about Alicia and the children.

"Mr. Parsons?"

"Yes, yes, I'm here. How can I help you, Detective Jones?"

"Mr. Parsons, I need you to come down to Princess Hospital; there has been a serious incident involving your mother and she is currently here being treated by the doctors."

Drew groped for the chair at the kitchen table needing to sit down.

"What happened? How bad is it? Is she okay?"

"We are still investigating the matter; however, it appears as though someone broke into her house and assaulted her. Her condition, from what I understand, is serious, but stable. Can you come in to the hospital on your own or should I send a cruiser to pick you up?"

"No, I can make my own way down. How soon do you need me there?"

"The sooner the better; we would like to speak to you, as would the doctor."

"That's fine. I should be there within thirty minutes. Where should I go to at the hospital?"

"Your mother is in the intensive care unit. I can meet you at the nursing station in that ward. After we have spoken, and if the doctor allows it, you can see your mother."

Drew thanked Officer Jones, hung up the phone and ran up to the bedroom to get changed. As Jessica exited the washroom he met her, his eyes consumed with worry.

"Jessica, my mother is in hospital, she has been badly beaten. Can you give me a ride down to Princess Hospital?"

"Oh my God, Drew, of course I can. Did they give you any details of what happened?"

"They said it looks like someone broke in and assaulted her, but I know that someone was William. I just know it."

Arriving at the hospital, Jessica accompanied Drew as he rushed to the ICU where Detective Jones was waiting at the nursing station. Drew introduced Jessica and Detective Jones escorted them to the Quiet Room where they could speak in private.

"Drew, it appears that early yesterday afternoon someone entered the house where your mother lives and assaulted her. The motive for it is not clear but there may have been some property taken as well, so it may be a situation of your mother being in the wrong place at the wrong time. Unfortunately, the beating was severe and your mother wasn't discovered until the owners of the house returned home early this morning."

"Were there any witnesses? Have you talked to my father? If you haven't, you should."

"We have spoken to some witnesses who recall seeing someone at the front door at roughly noon, yesterday. They didn't get a good look at the person as the winter clothing obscured their views. One thing several of them recalled, though, was the person was wearing a sky-blue winter coat that came down to the waist. Also, no vehicle matching your father's was seen in the vicinity of the house.

"You mentioned your father, why is that?"

"Because he abused both me and my mother and it wouldn't surprise me if he were to do something like this."

"Do you know if your father has a winter coat that matches the description given by the neighbours?"

"No, from what I remember he has a green parka that went down to just below his butt."

"Yes, that is the coat he showed us when we spoke to him. We have already interviewed him but he states he was home at that time, having returned from doing some errands. He showed us a receipt from the grocery store he shopped at, which showed a time of eleven forty-five, and said he was home putting the groceries away at the time which the other witnesses say they saw the person at your mother's residence. Further, we checked his hands for signs of trauma and found no cuts or contusions which would normally be found in a case where significant injury is done to the other party. That being said, the investigation doesn't end there. We will be following up with him to substantiate his story."

"And you say the person stole things from the house?"

"We aren't sure at this time. Whoever it was, he or she did significant damage to the inside of the house. The owners are going through it right now assessing the situation and to determine whether or not anything has been taken."

There was a short pause.

"Drew, can you tell me where you were yesterday afternoon between twelve and one o'clock?"

"I was at home with Jessica; we were re-arranging some furniture in the morning."

Jessica nodded in agreement.

Detective Jones looked at Jessica for the confirmation then turned back to Drew. “Now, please show me your hands.”

Drew extended his arms and Detective Jones examined them for any signs of trauma. Seeing no evidence of damage, he released them.

“Okay, thank you. I have spoken to the doctor and she has consented to you going in to see your mother. But I must warn you, she was severely beaten about the head and her face is badly bruised and swollen. The doctor can answer more questions you may have but, understand, your mother is in a medically induced coma. She will not speak or respond to you.”

Detective Jones walked them towards Jean’s room where Dr. Banerjee, a slight, Indian woman, stood down the hall from the door. After introducing Drew and Jessica to her, Detective Jones left, allowing them to speak privately. Drew told Dr. Banerjee what Detective Jones had explained to him.

“But, I don’t understand, why did you put her in a coma?”

“Unfortunately, your mother was so severely beaten that she sustained a serious brain injury. In the case of traumatic brain injury doctors sometimes need to induce a coma. This shutdown of brain function naturally occurs in cases of extreme trauma so, as doctors, we seek to temporarily mimic it in patients who have experienced the type of injury your mother has encountered. The reduction of the blood flow allows the vessels in the brain to narrow, taking pressure off of it. Put simply it’s like letting a little air out of an overfilled tire.”

“Thank you Dr. Banerjee, I understand. Let’s pray the coma works the way it should.”

Dr. Banerjee smiled and led them towards the sterile hospital room where his mother lay. As she stood at the hospital room door, she turned to Drew and Jessica.

“Drew, I have one more item I would like to discuss with you. While I am confident that the outcome for your mother will be positive, with head traumas one can never be certain. I would like you to consider organ transplant as an option should your mother not recover from her injuries."

The thought of his mother dying and of donating her organs had Drew's mind in upheaval. As they entered the room and Dr. Banerjee rolled back the drape surrounding Jean's bed, Drew's legs buckled at the sight. Jessica helped him to a chair in the corner.

Jean's face was beaten almost beyond recognition: her eyes were black and swollen; her nose obviously broken and her lips distorted by the swelling. Her entire face was black and blue and bandages crowned her scalp. Tubes and wires jutted out from her mouth, arms and nose. The respirator in the corner wheezed with the rise and fall of Jean's chest while the steady beep from the heart monitor taunted Drew's soul.

The severity of the situation became too much for Drew. The room began to spin and the din of blood coursing through his ears turned into a roar. Getting up from the chair, Drew raced from the room.

"Drew...Drew...stop!" Jessica called as she followed him out of the room.

In the hallway Drew leaned his back against the wall, slowly lowering himself to the floor. All at once tears burst forth in a torrent accompanied by an uncontrollable moan. Jessica held him in her arms.

Drew only had one thought in his mind: *You bastard, you fucking bastard. I'm going to kill you.*

Drew and Jessica returned to the room and sat by Jean for several hours, as sadness and anger fought for supremacy before bracketing in Drew's psyche.

The drive home was silent. Drew couldn't get the image of his mother out of his head. What William had done was barbarous and unconscionable. Drew thought about the words he had spoken to William the night Jean had left the house: *'If I find out that you have acted contrary to what I have said here to you tonight, understand that my retribution will be swift and absolute.'*

As they walked up the front steps to the house, Drew stopped and turned to Jessica.

"I have to go talk to a friend. I won't be too late but don't wait up, if I am."

Jessica's forehead creased with concern.

"Drew, please, don't do anything rash. Let the police do their job. I'm sure the person responsible will be found."

Drew ran his hand through Jessica's hair and caressed her cheek. The glint of a smile appeared on his lips. Then he kissed her.

"Don't worry; I'm not going to do anything rash. You know me; I like to think about things first. I just need to speak with my friend. He is a guy I have known for a long time and is someone I can talk to. I just need to see him, that's all."

As Drew pulled his car to a stop on the main street, he knew exactly where to find Mickey. He got out of the car and crossed the road to Mack's Pub. Like every other night, the pub was loud and smoky with the jukebox blaring classic rock. Tonight's assault as Drew entered was 'Radar Love.'

Looking about the pub, Drew saw Mickey sitting in the corner with his friends. Mickey stood to meet Drew as he approached.

"What the fuck? Where you been lately?"

"Long story; got a job working in the city."

"Fuck me, that's great. Come on, you can buy me a drink this time."

"Not now, Mickey. Can we go outside for a few minutes? I have something I need to talk to you about."

"Fuck, sounds serious. Sure, man, let me get my coat on."

Standing in the frigid evening air, Drew explained to Mickey what had happened to his mother and his suspicion of William's involvement.

"Do you still stay in touch with Doug? I need to get my hands on a gun."

"That's fucked up, man. For sure, I can get you one. But it will take me one or two days. I ain't seen Doug since the trial but I can get hold of the guy who sells them. Fuck, you sure it was your dad?"

Drew nodded his head.

"Never been so sure. That motherfucker has sealed his fate. I warned him not to touch my mother but he didn't listen. Now I'm going to kill the fucking bastard."

"How much you willing to spend? There's lots of fuckin' bazookas you can choose from."

"That's just it; I don't have a lot of money. Will four hundred be enough?

Mickey rubbed his chin between his index finger and thumb.

"Fuck, yeah I can make it work. Just give me your phone number and I will give you a call as soon as I have the piece. Fuck me, this is nuts, man, why is he such an asshole?"

Drew simply shrugged.

Arriving back at home that evening, Drew entered the front door to find Jessica sitting by the fireplace; the fragrance of burning wood filled the living room, its walls awash in a flickering auburn glow. She got up from the love seat and walked over to Drew, giving him a hug as she met him.

"Did you talk to your friend?"

"Yeah, it was good to see him; it really helped me deal with what happened to my mother. Unfortunately, he couldn't talk for long so I may go see him again in a couple of days."

"That's good. I contacted Kimberley and told her about what happened and that we wouldn't be coming in tomorrow. She can cover the store by herself. Come sit on the love seat, I'll give you a massage and help relieve your tension."

"Jessica, if it's okay with you, I would just like to hold you. Can we sit by the fire and just be?"

Jessica took his hand and led him to the love seat where he held her for several hours. Finally, just after one o'clock in the morning, they went to bed.

Early the following morning, Drew's phone rang. It was Mickey.

"I got the fuckin' piece, when can we meet?"

"I can be there by noon, if that works for you."

"No problem, I took the day off so I'm free whenever you can make it. Just call me when you are getting close."

Drew ate breakfast quickly.

"I got a call from my friend. He is off today so I am going to visit him again, if that is okay with you."

Jessica put her coffee down and gave Drew an understanding look.

"That's fine; I will be running around today, anyway, so go visit with him. I'll see you when you return. If you are going to be late, just let me know."

Drew got up from his seat and walked around to where Jessica was sitting, giving her a long, passionate kiss.

"I love you."

As Drew entered Drury, the muted low-lying, hoary sky remained suspended over the town like the hovering, smoky haze of a bar. Heavy snow continued from the night before, its mantle of white giving an unsullied illusion to the surrounding landscape.

They met at the back of Mack's, which hadn't opened for the day. Drew parked so that his door window was adjacent to Mickey's. Mickey handed Drew a small canvas bag containing the gun and ammunition. Drew checked the contents before giving Mickey the money. He let out an ironic laugh.

'Glock 9', the same gun Lorne had used the day of the shooting.

Once the exchange was complete, Mickey left while Drew idled in the parking lot, putting bullets in the gun's magazine clip.

After finishing, Drew removed his cell phone from his pocket and called Jessica. The answering machine picked up.

"Hi, just want to tell you that I'm so happy to have met you; in fact, never been as happy as when you're with me. You have filled a missing part in my life. I'm in Drury and just visited with my friend again. And Jessica, I really do love you."

Drew ended the call then dialed again.

"Hello William."

CHAPTER TWENTY-TWO

Fifteen minutes after the phone call between Drew and William ended, Drew stood on the front porch of the house. He knocked on the door and waited several seconds. When William hadn't answered Drew knocked again and waited. Then he opened the door and entered.

"Hello Drew."

William sat on the couch in the living room, a large manila envelope to his left on the seat cushion beside him. On the coffee table to his right sat a half-empty bottle of Canadian Club Whiskey and a shot glass filled to the brim. In his left hand William held the pistol from his bedside night table. He was wearing a sky-blue winter jacket. William brought the glass to his lips and downed all of its contents before pouring himself another shot.

Drew removed his boots and coat and, carrying his coat, calmly walked to the chair opposite where William sat.

"How drunk are you?"

"Drunk enough to numb the pain."

"So I was right, it was you. God, you are predictable William."

"I was counting on *your* predictability, Drew. I knew the only way to get you to come here was through your mother, one way or another. And here you stand."

"So you almost beat her to death to get me to come here? You are seriously fucked up William," Drew spat.

William sighed and gave a resigned nod.

Drew continued.

"Why couldn't you just leave mom alone? Why couldn't you let us live our lives? Everything had been going so well over the past several months. But you are a miserable, spiteful man so you had to screw up our lives, just like you always have."

"I could almost say the same thing about your return from prison, Drew. But it isn't that simple. There are things here that you aren't aware of. Your mother has filled your head with half truths and complete lies. She is not the woman you think she is."

"Really? Did she fill my head with the beatings, or the humiliation and degradation you put me through?"

"I have no defence for that. I know it was wrong and, realizing this won't mean anything to you, I do apologize for what I did to you and the pain caused."

Drew scoffed, rolling his eyes.

"But the truth is your mother has harmed you as well. Not like I have; more subtly, more insidiously. She smiled and hugged you while doing her damage."

"Harmed me? How, by protecting me from you?"

"That is exactly how she harmed you. Your mother pitted us against each other. She has played the victim. Making you look at me as the villain. Admittedly, I did little to contradict that view you had and still have of me, but I was nowhere near as bad a she has made me out to be."

"You are though. How often did you beat or threaten? My God, I could never be like that."

"Then if I have taught you nothing else, I've taught you to be a better man than me."

Drew let out an acerbic laugh, yet, somehow, those words rang true in his ears.

"And she was there to make things better. She protected me; treated me right."

"The way she treated you was not natural. Are you aware of how often she rejected our bed to be in yours?

She was so afraid of losing you she built a protective bubble around both of you, not letting anyone else, not even me, in. My God, the day you were released from jail, she drove to pick you up without calling me before she left. The bubble was being rebuilt."

William paused to pour himself another drink and to allow Drew to think about what he had heard.

"Why do you think the picture of your birth mother was lost? Don't you find it odd that your birth father's picture was given to you on your birthday but not your birth mother's? More than anything she feared the idea that your biological mother may somehow compete for your affection, even if you only had a picture of her. Over the years she became delusional. Think about it Drew. Think hard about it."

Drew slammed his hand down on the arm rest of the chair, his face red with anger.

"Enough of your goddamned lies. You are a pathetic excuse for a human being. I will not sit here and have you berate her or have my intelligence insulted."

"Drew..."

"No, shut the fuck up, you bastard. I could kill you for what you did to her."

Drew scratched his forehead with his fingers and pursed his lips while staring down at the floor. William finished his drink and poured himself another, spilling onto his shirt as it washed over the brim. He waited, watching until it appeared the anger Drew displayed had subsided.

"Drew, can I ask you something?"

"Yeah, whatever, go ahead."

"Do you remember the year, I think you were eight, when we went down to Florida for March break? We were there ten days."

"Yes."

And do you remember spending time with that older couple?"

"How could I forget? It seemed like we spent the entire time with them."

"We spent two days with them. But the way your mother kept going on about it, even years later, it's no wonder you think it was longer. Anyway, that's beside the point. Is there anything else you remember? Do you remember them, the couple at all?"

Drew thought about it for several moments but couldn't recall anything about them.

"Obviously I remember going to the amusement parks and down to the ocean. But I can't really remember them as individuals. The only other thing was that you and mom had a big argument, maybe the biggest I ever heard. Mom told me it was because you were drunk again and she was afraid for our safety. Of course, that was what most of the arguments were about, weren't they."

"She lied. Your mother and I argued over the visit with that couple. I had made arrangements to see them without her knowledge. It was done that way because if she knew, there was no way on God's green earth we would have visited with them."

"And that would have been a *bad* thing?"

"Yes, it would have. Drew, they were your grandparents; your father's parents. They were so excited to see you. But I made them promise not to divulge who they were to you."

"But I can see why you don't recall anything. Do you remember how your mom reacted?"

Drew gave a vague shake of his head and a vacant stare.

"Of course you don't." William muttered to himself.

"She kept you by her side, literally, the entire time we were visiting. She slept in your bedroom; in your bed. Again. She was fearful that somehow they would try to take you away from us. She wouldn't even let them touch you; hug you. The night we left their house was the night of the argument, and she wouldn't talk to me for the remainder of the trip. The fact is many of the arguments your mom and I had were about your adoption and whether to tell you. I had agreed to a pact but was never comfortable with it."

Drew was stunned. He recalled snippets of that time: his mother sleeping in his room and telling him the couple were friends of his dad and that she didn't trust them; of her sitting beside him the entire time they visited.

"Son, when you were a child your mother asked me to keep your adoption from you with the understanding that we would tell you when you were at an age to understand. As you got older I intended to let you know your background because, unlike her, there was no fear of losing you to them. But I agreed to continue to maintain the secret because my love for her was greater than my fear of losing you. It didn't matter to me what I did as long as she and I remained together. It wasn't until too late that it struck me I could *never* do enough to win her back. I lost her to her world; and you in the process.

"When you talked about finding your birth parents after you got out of jail, my response was a result of wanting to protect her secret; to protect our pact. But your mother's response to your request made me realize what was happening. As soon as she walked over to you, I knew she was somehow going to use your desire to find them as another way to shore up her relationship with you; to make her appear to be the only person on your side. She told you she had a faint memory of things. But do you really believe that she had nothing to do with the adoption? Or that she would ever forget the names of the people who gave birth to you?"

Drew looked up at William confused. He didn't want to believe what William was saying but couldn't deny the possibility of its truth.

"What about all the beatings? The drinking? What about me not being of your blood?"

"Again, there is no excuse for the actions I have committed against you in my frustration over the years. You are right, I was a little, spiteful man falling into your mother's trap. And I was too weak. Rather than seeing what I truly knew and standing up to her, I turned to the bar and my friends or used you as my scapegoat. She was aware that my love for her would allow her to manipulate me and she did so by manipulating you. And because she knew I would lash out. In turn, she manipulated you by her manipulation of me. And her plan worked to perfection. She was your protection then someone you wanted to protect. I was the monster. Every time she doted over you it was a stab to my heart and every time she told you a lie about me, every time I lashed out in response to her relationship with you, you hated me a little more."

William adjusted himself on the couch before having more to drink. Drew stared at William while trying to understand what he was getting at.

"Hold on, hold on," he insisted, eyes closed, shaking his head and extending his hand towards William. "So you're saying that she controlled both of us through the other? She played us."

"Exactly. But those are fragments in a long life. Yes, there were abuses, for which I can't tell you enough how sorry I am, but there was so much more. Unfortunately, you were nurtured on your mother's terrible stories of me – some true, though many of them were lies; but there was so much good we shared. Her deceptions starved you of the pleasant memories: our Florida trip; going skating together; the comic book conventions are just a few examples. It was all part of her need; her desire. Over time though, her scheming became so engrained in her that she started to believe the lies; that she needed to protect the both of you from me; the pure evil.

"And when you returned from jail, she put that deceptive mask back on. The only difference was that this time she made you want to protect her from my evil. And you can't deny it; you did wanna protect her. Protect her from the monster that you believe I am."

Drew looked at William with the intensity of a boxer studying his opponent in the center of the ring. Several moments passed.

"Then why did you refuse to help me with the adoption paperwork? If you were so intent on getting the information to me, why didn't you contact me?"

William threw back another shot.

"Again, that situation didn't happen as you believe it did. As soon as I saw your mother's reaction, I knew that her nex' move would be to turn the situation in her favour. My first reaction was to keep the information from you but then I decided to give it to you. I knew it was the right thing t'do. As you sat outside, on the back porch, I suggested giving you the information, despite the pact we had agreed upon." William stopped speaking and looked towards the ceiling trying to formulate his next thought. His eyes blinked slowly. After several moments he continued. "I knew she would realize what that would mean. She was the one who didn't want to hand the information over to you. And do ya know why? Because it would have discredited her; made you realize that what she had told you, just a few minutes before, was a lie; that she was a fraud. When I left I took the file with me because I couldn't let her use it to further manipulate you for her purposes. Though, I mus admid, I also used it to gain some power over the situation. But after thinkin' things over, I decided that givin' you the information was the best thing to do."

William paused to allow Drew to get his head around the explanation being proffered and took another drink before continuing. The effects of the alcohol were beginning to show. Looking at William, Drew's ossified glare had begun to soften.

"Then, later," William continued, the effects of the alcohol more apparent, "I contac'ed her about givin' you the paperwork but she refused, saying she would give ya what ya needed to know. I guar'ntee you her intention was to black out or destroy anythin' that would make you aware of her involvement aff'er she had denied it." William paused to belch. "Though it wouldn't've surprised me if she just inten'ed to destroy it all and tell you I wou'n't agree to hand it over. If the question came up at a later time, she would've accused me of destroyin' it; and who'd you believed, your angelic mother or you bestial father?

When the issue was pushed, she threa'ened to tell you that I wasn't willin' to hand over the info. She really pain'ed me into a corner, knowin' that I had no way of contac'in' you without her bein' involved."

"How many times did she call you about giving me the adoption papers?"

"Other than the day she began movin' her things out of th' house, I nev-ver heard anything from her. The fact is, *I* called *her* the other day about geh'in together, even off'rin' to go over ever'thin' and fill in some of the gaps. But she refused, saying she'd do it herself."

Drew shook his head unable to assimilate what he was hearing from William.

"No, no, I don't believe it. She has been there for me through everything: protecting me from you; visiting me in jail and helping me get back on my feet. You have done nothing other than abuse me and her. I can't believe that you are suddenly the angel and she is the devil."

"Drew, please, it isn't that black an' white." William paused to belch again. "I'm nowhere near as evil as you think and your mother is nowhere near as perfec' as you think, either. My sishuation is desp'rat. I din'n't want to lose you or your mother, yet both of you are gone; you and she will never patch thin's up with me. I am culpable for the things I did to you but she, too, is complicit in what has happ'ned to you, to our fam'ly."

William wiped his chin after knocking back another mouthful of whiskey. He shook his head trying to clear his mind then squeezed his eyes shut and opened them again in an attempt to refocus.

"And now I have nothin'. But my goal is for you to see the truth; to look at it with clar'ty; to see her for what she is. Not out of spite for her but out of my love for you."

"But I still don't see why you had to beat her so viciously? How was that going to make matters any better?"

"You won't likely believe me about this either, but I din'n't inten'ta hurt your mother that badly. It was an accident. As we were strugglin', she fell back and hit her head agains' the corner of the wall. Then, when she fell, her face hit the floor direc'ly. My plan was only to hit her, to bloody her nose, knowin' that she'd call you and you'd come for me. When she got hurt I panicked."

"You're right, I don't believe you. I can't believe anything you have said. How convenient it is that you can so quickly explain everything away: mom's delusional; I don't understand; it is all a plot on her part and you present yourself like the knight in shining armour here to protect me after all these years. And to tell me you love me? That's just too fitting. So, yes, if I had the adoption paperwork, you would never again be a part of my life."

William moved, placing the pistol on his lap. Reaching to his left he picked up the manila envelope.

"I'm truly sorry you don't believe me. But if that's how you feel, you don't need these adoption papers an'more; for they hold the truth. In them are the sig'tures of your mother and me. In them are the sig'tures of your biological paren's. Their names have been blacked out, but there is some good info in here. Notta mention the notes your mother and I took durin' the pr'ceedin's along with some more I added the other night."

As he spoke, William reached behind the bottle on the side table, knocking it over, and produced a lighter. After flicking the wheel several times, he brought the flame to the envelope. Drew looked on in alarm as the bottom of the envelope caught fire. He leapt from his chair and charged William, knocking the file from his hand to the floor. Pouncing on the envelope, he smothered it with his coat until the flames went out.

He looked back at William who was again holding the pistol, tears falling from his eyes.

"I have nothin' to lose. I have nothin'," his voice was heavy and despondent as he stared at the pistol.

Drew held his hand out to his father.

"William, put the gun down."

"No, I have nothin'. I hurt your mother. I never wann'ed to hurt your mother, don't ya see?" William said, shaking his head. "But she wou'n't listen to me; she wou'n't let me see you. All I wann'ed to do was see *you*, to let you know the truth and let you decide for yourself. But I'm too weak. Too damn weak. Always so, so weak."

Drew now turned to face William who sat on the couch completely distraught.

"Please, William, give me the gun. We can talk some more, maybe we can work things out."

"I know I rambled on in my drunkness but you should know the truth," he said through his tears, ignoring Drew's pleas. "She knew, son, she knew all along. Ask her. She won' be able to deny't. I have nothin' more to lose, I am naked before you; there is no poin' in me lyin'. I have nothin' else."

William reached into his coat pocket and pulled out his cell phone.

"Listen to the voice recorder aff'er."

Drew looked at him confused.

"William...!"

He cocked the gun's hammer.

William squeezed his eyes tight; his face strained and contorted, his neck tensed.

"Good-bye."

"No, dad!" Drew yelled.

Hearing Drew's words, William's face became placid and he looked directly, focused, into Drew's eyes. Then he smiled; a sincere, contented smile.

"Thank you, Andrew."

The gun fired and William jerked violently to the side collapsing into the couch, blood hemorrhaging from his temple.

As William's limp body slid to the floor Drew moved to cradle it. The wound on the left side of William's head was mirrored by one on the right side.

"9-1-1, what's your emergency?"

"My father, he shot himself in the head right in front of me. I think he's dead."

CHAPTER TWENTY-THREE

When emergency services arrived they entered into a violent, bloody scene. Drew sat on the floor leaning against the couch holding William's corpse between his raised knees, its bloody head leaning back, positioned on Drew's right shoulder. The blood from the wounds continued a sluggish flow, running down the side of his head and into his ears before continuing down his neck to his shoulders. Drew's clothing was stained with cruor and his hands were sticky from the congealed fluid he had tried to stop as it spouted from William's temples. The lamp to the left of the sofa lay shattered on the table, destroyed by the same bullet which had ripped through William's head. The bottle of Canadian Club was lying on its side, its contents soaked into the rug.

Paramedics and fire fighters attending to William immediately recognized he was deceased and that they were helpless to do anything to change that fact. They removed the body from Drew's grasp, placed it on the floor and attempted to resuscitate it; more an act to comfort Drew than to bring life back to William.

Police officers spoke to Drew. The gun was seized along with other evidence. Paper bags were placed over William's hands to preserve any gun powder residue that may have been on them. The presence of the residue would support Drew's claim that William had shot himself.

What weren't seized were the cell phone, which remained in Drew's pocket, and the partially burned manila envelope Drew had removed from the house and put in the trunk of his car while he waited for the emergency services.

The coroner's office was notified and the coroner arrived twenty minutes later to determine death and order the removal of the body.

Drew was transported to the police station.

On the way Drew called Jessica and told her what had happened. She showed up at the station within the hour with a change of clothing for Drew and waited for his release.

When Drew left the interview room, Jessica met him by the front desk of the station.

"Thanks for coming Jessica. Sorry you had to wait out here. I didn't expect the interview to go on for so long. It must have lasted for at least three hours. They just kept asking me the same questions: why'd I go there; what happened just before he shot himself; where would he have gotten the gun; why was I on the floor near him and so on. Man, it was gruelling."

"Don't worry yourself about it or me, Drew. The police are just being thorough. They need to ensure what you tell them is consistent with the physical evidence they discovered at the scene and what the forensic examinations will determine."

Drew looked at her with puzzled amazement.

"I used to watch a lot of police crime scene shows," she answered off-handedly.

"I'll tell you, they were thorough all right. I'm exhausted and can't wait to go home. Did you bring a change of clothes?

Jessica handed him a paper bag containing a shirt and a pair of pants. Looking at him she could see the strain written all over his face.

"Drew, I am so sorry. I know these past couple of days have been terrible for you."

She gave him a hug, caressing the nape of his neck as he rested his forehead on her shoulder.

"Jessica," he whispered, "this is all fucked up. My head is reeling and I don't know what to believe anymore."

"Shhh...We can talk about it later, when things have settled down a bit. Once you have a chance to rest you can look at it with fresh eyes. For now, let's just get you home."

"My car, it's at my parents' place. I have to get it."

"We can get it tomorrow, Drew. Let's not worry about that just now. We need to get you home and rested. You look exhausted."

"But..." Drew's voice trailed off, he knew that Jessica was right. It would be better to leave it and pick it up the following morning. The envelope could wait another day. Right at that moment he needed to get away from Drury, from his parents' home, from everything.

During the drive home, Drew sat contemplatively, mulling over the recent events involving his parents. Jessica didn't interrupt. He reflected about the beating he thought William had laid upon his mother and the vision of her in the hospital with all the machines around her, possibly keeping her alive, and the blood that streamed from William when he shot himself in the head. But above all, he thought about what William had said to him.

Drew also thought about confronting his mother.

I need to know that what he told me were lies; that there is no scheme on her part to keep me to herself. That she didn't know more than she told me about the adoption. She is my mother and she only wanted to protect me, to keep me safe from him. If she says there is no truth to his claims, I will believe her. I must believe her. But if what he told me were truths...no, no they can't be.

When they arrived home, Jessica walked Drew into the house. She directed him to the chaise lounge in the living room and had him lie down putting a heavy blanket over him.

"You just lie here; I will get the fire going and make you something to eat."

When the fire was blazing, its warm, comforting glow enticed Drew to fall asleep while Jessica prepared the meal.

After they had finished eating dinner, Jessica and Drew curled up on the love seat in front of the fire.

"If you want to talk about anything, Drew, I am here to listen. I don't want you to think that you have to deal with this on your own."

Drew ran his fingers through Jessica's hair.

"Thank you, but I just need to get away from all of it for the night, to take my mind off of things. I need a nice distraction."

Jessica moved closer to Drew sliding her hand up the inside of his thigh.

"I think I can be that nice distraction you need. Your will is my command, whatever your pleasure?" Her voice was playful.

Drew looked at Jessica for several moments before he gave a lubricious smile. Taking her by the hand, he yanked her up from the couch and pulled her up to the bedroom where he pushed her onto the bed. Jessica was shocked by his sudden actions, but aroused.

"Now get undressed and lay there. I'll be back in a moment."

As Jessica stripped, Drew walked into the closet and emerged moments later carrying a bandana, the belt from her nightgown and two other leather belts. Jessica was sitting on the side of the bed.

"I said lie on the bed," he commanded, his voice trenchant. "Put your hands over your head and spread your legs. Now!"

Jessica obeyed. Her heart was pounding and she began getting wet as he fastened her hands to the headboard. Once he had secured her hands, Drew tied the bandana around her head, covering her eyes. Her nipples hardened as Drew brushed against them with the leather belts. Jessica let out a soft moan. An unexpected belt lash across her stomach produced a slight yelp from Jessica, but not one of displeasure.

Once he had restrained her legs, he began at her feet, sucking on each toe and biting the arch. She hadn't known that what Drew was doing could be so erotic. Jessica's breath caught in her throat with the suddenness in which Drew's hand was between her legs, rubbing her sultry warmth.

Abruptly, Drew got up from the bed and left the room. Jessica could hear him walk down stairs. Then there was silence. Simultaneously, anticipation and apprehension began to grow in her.

By the time Drew returned, several minutes later, Jessica's apprehension had turned to worry.

"Where did you go? Why didn't you tell me you were leaving?"

"Shhh, shhh, shhh," he replied, placing a finger on her lips. Then his voice darkened, "I just had to grab the whip."

Jessica was dumbstruck.

Before having a chance to object, she felt the cold of the cream as it sprayed from the can onto her nipples. The trail followed down her stomach to her mound. The sensation as he continued emptying the contents of the can on her was exhilarating.

Drew placed the can on the floor and began to spread the cream over Jessica's body; first with his hands, then with his tongue and mouth.

Each touch of Drew's fingers, each lick of his tongue, each bite heightened Jessica's passion. Being controlled, along with the anticipation and excitement of not knowing where he would pleasure her next, only added to the sensuousness.

As Drew licked between her legs, Jessica felt an object enter her. It, too, was cold and the pleasure was immediate. A small shock embraced her entire body as Drew moved it in and out of her.

"Oh my God," she said, breathlessly, "What is that?"

"Don't talk," Drew whispered but with an air of enmity.

Jessica let herself go, allowing the ecstasy to control her, moving her to and from each pleasurable moment: the contours of the object as it probed deep inside her; Drew's tongue delicately circling her clit; the squeeze and release of her nipples.

With a shudder, her body and mind yielded to the euphoria of an orgasm that left her wondrously exhausted.

"That was amazing," Jessica said, her serene voice fluttering from her lips, "how did...where did you learn to do all..."

Drew placed his hand over her mouth to muffle her speech. "Didn't you get the hint the first time? Now shut up, or else."

Jessica was shaken by the tenor of Drew's voice.

"I gave you your pleasure, now I'm going to *take* mine. And I don't want to hear another word from you, do you understand?"

Jessica nodded.

Straddling Jessica's torso, Drew grabbed her hair, pulling her head down until her chin skimmed against her chest.

"Open your mouth," he demanded.

Jessica hesitated momentarily as she thought about the situation; though, she was surprised by his tone, she wasn't concerned for her safety.

He needs to feel in control; needs this release. He's just playing the part. He is controlling without being degrading. Thank God he hasn't called me a bitch or a cunt.

"I said open your mouth, now."

Jessica submitted.

Drew plunged his erection deep into her mouth, pushing against the back of her throat and causing

Jessica to gag slightly. He pulled back before thrusting again. She noticed that Drew's phallus felt much harder than it had the previous times they had had sex. As Jessica thought about it she felt a ripple of exhilaration pass through her. She was always in control and had never played the submissive before. Now she found the role thrilling. Drew withdrew from her.

Please, please fuck my mouth. Let me suck your hard cock, her mind begged.

"I'm going to cum on your face." Drew's voice was strained and aggressive.

Jessica demurred but continued to accept that he was just playing a role. Still she didn't speak, yielding to his earlier warning.

He removed the bandana from Jessica's eyes. She gazed up at his voluptuous, Adonis-like form, towering above her, rigid and straining. Jessica opened her mouth again and Drew entered her. Pulling her hair, he quickly rocked her head back and forth in concert with his driving pelvis.

Holy shit, I'm so wet; this is amazing.

Several seconds later, Jessica felt the pulsing of his erection before Drew orgasmed. As he climaxed, Drew withdrew himself from Jessica, groaned and ejaculated; shooting his semen onto her face. Jessica bathed in the warmth of the juice as it masked her; a trembling moan escaped her lips.

Drew collapsed on the bed beside Jessica, emotionally and physically exhausted.

He kissed her lips softly, passionately.

"Thank you," Drew whispered still with a mournful emptiness in his voice. He kissed her again.

"Drew, is it okay for me to speak again?" Jessica said in a soft, hesitant voice.

"Yes."

After Drew untied Jessica, they showered together before going to bed for the night where Drew held Jessica tight.

The following morning, Drew woke early and prepared breakfast for both of them. Entering the kitchen wearing nothing but one of Drew's t-shirts, Jessica walked up behind him and wrapping her arms around his waist, drawing him close.

"Sleep well?" Drew asked, at ease in her embrace.

"Very," a soft smile decorated her face.

While they ate, Drew and Jessica planned the day. Jessica would drop Drew off at his car and he would go to see Fran with the adoption paperwork.

"Hi Fran, its Drew calling. I know this is short notice, but do you have time to meet this afternoon? I got the adoption paperwork and was wondering if I could drop it off."

"That's great news, Drew. I can see you this morning if that works, or sometime later this afternoon."

"Thanks, but it will have to be later in the afternoon. I am heading to my parents' house this morning. Would two o'clock be late enough?"

Fran checked her calendar for a moment before responding.

"Yes, two should be fine."

Drew gave Jessica a kiss before he got out of the car at his parents' house.

"I hope to be home by dinner, but I will call you later and let you know what's happening."

Jessica wished him luck and drove away as Drew opened the trunk to his car and removed the envelope. Sitting in the car he opened it and took out the paperwork. The flames had done some damage to the documents but, for the most part, they remained unscathed. Within the paperwork Drew found some notes in William's handwriting. Fighting his curiosity, he placed the documents back in the envelope and set it on the front passenger seat. Looking in the center console Drew found his gun where he had left it the day before. Closing the console, he drove to his appointment with Fran.

While on route, Drew remembered his father's cell phone which was still in the jacket pocket. Pulling over to the side of the road he took it out and turned it on, scrolling to the voice recorder. Drew hit the play back button.

"That is a new jacket."

"Yeah. May I come in for a bit? It is bitterly cold out here."

Drew listened to the entire recording. Then he listened to it again; the second time, fast forwarding the conversation to the part that intrigued him the most.

"This conversation is over. You believe what you want, you paranoid little man. I will give Drew the information he needs to know. Period. And what he needs to know is his birth parents, if he can divine the information out of the adoption paperwork he receives. He is not Drew's father, she is not his mother. They simply brought him into this world. Drew has no father and I am his mother."

"You're so delusional you've even convinced yourself. He, she...you speak of Drew's biological parents like they are meaningless extras in a movie. All these years of suppressing the truth out of fear for the child you couldn't have. You coddled and smothered Drew; not out of love but dread, dread he would love you less if he knew his real parents, or even shared you with me. And that ate at you. I could not love him like you loved him because I did not fear losing him. The guilt you felt from being infertile drove you away from me and towards Drew."

And again.

"I will give Drew the information he needs to know. Period. And what he needs to know is his birth parents, if he can divine the information out of the adoption paperwork he receives. He is not Drew's father, she is not his mother. They simply brought him into this world. Drew has no father and I am his mother."

Drew tried to convince himself that the recording proved nothing.

She didn't admit anything. It was just him throwing out speculation and accusations. This means fuck-all.

Still, as he sat in the car, Drew couldn't get out of his mind what he perceived to be a nuance, the minutiae in his mother's voice that contradicted what she was saying; to what he wanted to believe.

Fran met Drew in the waiting area of the Department of Family and Social Services.

"Hello Drew, it is great to see you again."

"Hi Fran. Thanks for seeing me on such short notice. Like I said to you when I phoned, I got the adoption paperwork."

"That's fantastic; did your dad finally decide to become a nice guy?"

Drew explained the events from the previous two days to Fran, who sat in astonished silence.

"I am so sorry Drew, I didn't realize. I shouldn't have made a joke."

"How could you have known, Fran? Don't worry about it. How about we get to the documents."

After a cursory look at the paperwork, Fran asked that Drew give her a couple of days to do an in depth examination. She would contact him when she had completed the task.

On the drive back home, Drew's phone rang.

"Hello, Drew speaking."

"Hello Drew, this is Dr. Banerjee. Drew, I have some good news; your mother is awake and communicative. While she can't speak, she is responding to stimuli. It would be of benefit if you could come to the hospital and visit with her."

"I'm almost home but will come to the hospital after my dinner."

It was just after seven o'clock when Drew and Jessica arrived at the hospital. Dr. Banerjee met them at the ICU desk.

"Your mother is still on medication but should be able to recognize you and respond to your voice. You will have about thirty minutes to visit with her. If you have any questions, I will be on the ward or you can have me paged."

"Thank you Dr. Banerjee."

When they entered the room, Jean's eyes were closed and she appeared to be asleep. Drew immediately noticed there weren't as many tubes as there had been the previous visit, and for that he was relieved. But the bruising and swelling persisted, making her difficult to recognize.

As they moved chairs close to the bed, Jean's eyes flittered open and a slight smile appeared in them.

"Hi mom, I'm glad you are feeling better. I know you can't talk, but can you respond in other ways?

Jean moved her hand, which lay on the bed beside her, slowly up and down in response.

"Good. Mom, I would like to introduce you to Jessica. She is the woman I have been living with and we have become close."

Jessica stepped closer to the bed and placed her hand on Jean's arm.

"Hello Jean, nice to meet you, though I wish the circumstance was different. Drew has told me so much about you."

Noticing the birthmark on her neck and that Jessica was quite a bit older than Drew, Jean's eyes widened in alarm as she looked Jessica up and down. Though she wanted to, Jean couldn't speak.

Jessica turned to Drew and kissed his cheek.

"I will be down the hall in the waiting area until you are finished talking to your mother."

As the door closed, Drew turned to his mother and held her hand.

"I'm so sorry William did this to you. I spoke to him and he admitted to the assault."

Jean weakly squeezed his hand.

"He and I talked for a while and he explained what happened, how you hit the wall with your head as you were struggling. Not that it makes a difference because he attacked you."

Again, Jean squeezed.

"So he told me the truth. Well, I will give him that much."

Several seconds passed as Drew stared at Jean, preparing himself for what was to come next.

"Mom, he gave me the adoption paperwork with all the notes that had been made by you and him. And we talked mom, dad and I talked a lot about it and about other things."

Jean's eyes widened, again, as fear gripped her. Drew noticed the look and it confirmed to him that William had told the truth.

He let go of his mother's hand and walked a few paces to the corner of the room.

"Mom, you knew didn't you? You knew, yet you kept all that information from me. The pact you and he shared. What else have you hidden from me? The picture of my mother? Their names? You have always known their names, haven't you? How about where they lived? The things you told me that first day I spoke to you about finding them, were they all lies?"

Jean slowly held her hand out but Drew ignored the gesture as he stared at her in dismay.

"And how many times did you approach dad about getting the adoption papers? Outside of the day I asked, did you ever talk to dad about them?"

Jean's brow furrowed and tears glistened in her eyes. She saw her world beginning to crumble. Everything she had done to protect them was vanishing, as was Drew's adoration of her.

"My God, mom, everything he told me was the truth. You didn't protect me, you imprisoned me, enslaved me in your frail, delusional world."

Drew stepped closer to Jean.

"When I look back, even over the past few months, it becomes clear. You had to speak to dad about the adoption paperwork and when I suggested talking to him you got upset; you arranged for me to continue living with you when you moved out, getting the Browns to okay it, without asking me first; the attempt to get me to buy the house with you. Even the day you picked me up from the penitentiary you lied about why dad wasn't there. It was just a continuation of a life you wanted for us. It has been this way since I was a child. You wouldn't even let me hug my own grandparents. You haven't been there for me; you have kept me for yourself. My God, what is wrong with you?"

The tears trickled down Jean's face, her look had gone from fear to despair. There she lay, unable to defend herself, unable to explain why she had done what she did. He needed her protection. She had to shelter him from William, from his birth parents, from a world full of dangers; one which tried to tear them apart. And again from Jessica.

"Dad was right, mom, you have conspired and deceived me my entire life. You didn't protect me. What you did, you did out of fear, out of some distorted view of our lives. Your hugs weren't hugs of love but manacles to confine me, to keep me at your side, to manipulate me so I wouldn't leave you."

Drew's face reddened and he began to pace about the room. Then he stopped and turned to Jean.

"Why couldn't you trust me? You were my mother. I was your son. I would have loved you. I would have revered you. It wasn't a competition; it wasn't a matter of spreading my love. My love for you was unyielding and having my biological parents, or dad for that matter, in my life wouldn't have changed a thing. Yet your fear delayed or ruined those opportunities in my life. Now…now your love means nothing to me. It was all a lie. Our relationship is an absolute lie. And now I have no parents."

Just as had happened so often, Drew was reliving the scenario of the abandoned and abused child, imprisoned by circumstances he couldn't control; inexorably tied to a world of lies and omissions. The totality of it tore a hole in Drew's mind. The woman who had been his protector, his confidante, his rock…his entire life, was gone. And he was lost.

Like so many times so many years ago, tears formed rivulets down Drew's face, the consequence of abuse. He couldn't bear to look at her. Wiping the tears from his cheeks, Drew spoke to Jean, his voice soft and wounded.

"Good-bye mom."

He opened the door and left the room. Meeting Jessica in the waiting room, he directed her towards the elevators passed the nursing station where Dr. Banerjee stood.

"Drew?" Dr. Banerjee called to him as he passed. He did not respond.

"Drew, what's wrong? What's happened? Jessica asked, seeing the sadness displayed on his face.

"Not now Jessica. I'll tell you soon, but I just need some time to digest everything that is happening."

Jean lay there devastated her entire world a scorched, desolate ruin. She needed to talk to Drew; to make him understand. But how?

I will get hold of William; he will want to help me. That weak, little man will do anything to assist me. I will get him to speak to Andrew; to help me win my son back. And Jessica must go. All of this can be straightened out and things will be better. Drew will understand, I am his mother, his real mother. I just need to speak to William.

Unlike the release from his previous imprisonment, Drew found no pleasure, no relief as the doors opened and he walked out of the hospital into the bitter cold of a moonless March night.

CHAPTER TWENTY-FOUR

Kimberley met Drew with a solemn smile when he returned to work a few days later. A genuine concern showed as she listened to Drew talk about what had happened. Before they realized it, the morning had bled into the afternoon.

The incidences of the previous week, including the preparation and funeral for William, had put Drew far behind on his plans for the display of Eastern Bloc artists and he would need to put in many more hours and work through the weekends to get caught up. Jessica and Kimberley assisted where they could but Drew needed to immerse himself in his work to try to take his mind off his personal troubles. He worked well into each night, usually arriving home long after midnight, only to get up at dawn and head back to work. He wasn't eating properly and his body was beginning to feel the effects of the stresses he was putting on it. He was having difficulty concentrating on his work as the suicide of his father and the truth about his mother continued to creep into his thoughts.

Midway through the week, when checking his messages, Drew saw he received one from his mother.

"Drew, please call me back. I need to discuss your relationship with Jessica. She is not good for you. I think..." Drew deleted the message.

To protect himself from her, he ignored future phone calls from his mother, deleting any messages she left without listening to them. Finally he blocked her number.

Early on Monday, Drew's phone rang. Looking at the call display he recognized the number.

"Hello Fran, how goes the battle?" Drew tried to sound upbeat but his voice came out flat.

"Hi Drew. Continuing the fight, how about you?

"Not lost yet. Any news from the home front?"

"As a matter of fact, lots. We need to meet and go over what has been found. The adoption documents on their own were of limited help but your father and mother's notes which you found in the paperwork, were invaluable. I think you'll be very pleased with the outcome of my findings."

"I'm working in the gallery today but we are closed. Do you want to meet somewhere or would you prefer I came to your office?"

"I think meeting here would be best. How soon can you get here?"

"Give me half an hour."

Just after ten o'clock Drew arrived at Fran's office. As she welcomed him she immediately noticed there was something different about him. He looked fragile, melancholy. She led him to a room which contained a large oval meeting table surrounded by a dozen chairs.

"Are you sure you are all right, Drew? You look under the weather."

"I'm fine, thanks, just a little worn out; have been putting in a lot of late nights these days. I am way behind on a work project and just need to catch up."

There was a long pause as Fran continued to study him. Finally she spoke.

"Drew, as I told you on the phone, your parents' notes on the file were very important to me putting together the information. Your father, in particular, was very thorough in his note-taking and it was because of those notes that everything fell into place. His notes contained a lot of short forms and initials but, using that information along with the documents from the adoption, it all came together fairly easily."

A nervous excitement grew in Drew's stomach. But with the information he longed for so close, there was a certain amount of apprehension.

Fran began spreading the paperwork over the table then opened her notes for reference.

"There was some damage done to the legal documents when your father set them on fire. Since he started the fire at the bottom of the envelope, lines where the signatures were located got damaged. Fortunately, I was able to distinguish enough lettering to figure them out. I have to admit, it's unusual for a document which has been censored to contain the signatures of the people. The authorities are far more diligent to ensure nothing has been missed. It's fortunate for you they seemed to have taken a vacation when editing this paperwork."

Drew looked up from the papers to Fran, eyes tired and tormented.

Reading the anguish on his face, Fran hastily continued.

"Rather than me going over the process let's get right to the meat and potatoes of my findings. I believe I was able to establish your birth parents' names. Well, to be more exact, their surname. Both the documents and your parents' notes only have initials. Puzzling out their last names didn't pose any real problem. They were married and were young. The documents indicate that they gave you up for adoption, well guardianship originally, because they were not fit to bring up a child. The notes suggest it was because of the financial burden. Nothing suggests they were unfit otherwise, though there are notes about your biological father being in trouble with the law. But even those crimes don't appear to be anything serious or the basis for the wardship. Social Services, as they were named at the time, removed you from them and the Parsons received you as your guardians soon after."

A perplexed look shadowed Fran's face.

"Now here's the odd thing: somehow during the time between William and Jean becoming your guardians and the adoption, your date of birth was changed to the day they became your guardians. For all the research I did, I was unable to determine how that happened. Somehow, somewhere along the line, someone was able to make the change or convince someone else to make it. The year of your birth stayed the same but the day and month changed. Anyway they also changed your name, which isn't uncommon with adoptions."

Drew interrupted, "They changed my date of birth *and* renamed me? It's no wonder the hospital couldn't find any info on me. What was my name before that?"

"David. Jean and William made that your middle name and, according to the notes your parents wrote, named you Andrew after Jean's youngest brother who had died when she was young."

Fran took a duotang from the accordion file and pushed it across the table to Drew.

"All the information you need is in there. I have summarized everything using the adoption documents and your parents' notes to support my findings and assumptions. I will give everything back to you but the summary brings it all together in a neat, chronological fashion."

Fran reached across the table placing her hands on Drew's.

"Drew, while you may have detested your father, it was he who made this possible. From what you told me at the last meeting, I believe that, in the end, he truly did have your best interests in mind."

When they stood from the table, Drew hugged and thanked Fran for all the assistance she had provided him. He wanted to take the information back to the shop where he could look at it in private.

"Drew, one more thing; the information your parents added to the adoption paperwork contravened the wishes of your birth parents. They had clearly stated that they didn't want their names to be released. I used that information in my investigation rather than seize it as should have been done. The official document will not include most of what has been included in the summary given you. Being such, if anything comes back on this, I never had your parents' notes and will deny any knowledge of them."

Drew looked at Fran with admiration and appreciation.

"You are safe with me. I only gave you the adoption papers."

Back at the shop, Drew sipped the coffee he had picked up across the street. He set the accordion file on the counter but didn't open it. Picking up a notebook and a pen, he stared at the file. He walked to the back office and turned on the stereo. Looking for something soothing he found a Moody Blues CD. As the music piped into the gallery he returned to the counter. With his stomach tumbling and his heart pounding hard, Drew became light-headed and had to sit down. Perspiration trickled down his back as he removed the duotang from the file. While holding it with his right hand, Drew ran his left hand across the front cover, stopping halfway down before setting it back down on the counter, his left hand still sitting on the cover.

Minutes passed and Drew still couldn't bring himself to open the duotang. Finally, accompanied by a deep breath, Drew turned to the first page.

For the next hour Drew read and re-read the summary and examined the supporting documents and notes Fran had included. He was impressed with the thoroughness of her work but devastated by the findings.

All that time, he was right there, right within reach.

It was mid-afternoon when the Jetta pulled to a stop along the laneway. Drew got out of the car, with the duotang in hand, and walked across the lawn. As he approached, his legs became cripplingly weak and he had to steady himself against a tree. The sky was brilliant blue and the warmth of the March sun had begun to chase away winter's white grip. The sound of water droplets falling from the trees to the snow below filled the otherwise sombre air. When Drew regained his strength, he continued advancing to the headstone.

Drew looked at the inscription:

John David Benjamin Musgrave

January 28, 1971 – April 19, 2012

In Loving Memory of a Father, Husband, Son

Then he opened the summary book.

Birth father:

J. Musgrave (other initials: J.D. and J.D.B.)

DOB: 01/28/71 Age: 18

Drew hugged the headstone; tears streamed from his eyes. Misery boomed from him like the voice of some ancient God.

"Father."

In the midst of his bereaved hysteria, at the height of his anguish, Drew was struck by rational, free flowing lucidity. The memories flooded him.

"What about the one on your stomach: David?"

John looked down at the name. "David was my first son, he was a cute kid. Unfortunately he was taken away from us when he was one."

Several more memories followed but his final recollection cut Drew the deepest.

As he held John, dying in his arms, with all the chaos going on around them, John's inaudible spoken words came back to Drew with resounding clarity:

"You are of <u>my</u> blood..."

Drew dropped to the ground, curling into the fetal position. Tears came unconstrained; his wailing hit a fever pitch as his body convulsed in its torture. He remained at John's grave for several hours. At last, cold and stiff, Drew rose and walked, shivering, back to his car. He sat in the driver's seat, his thoughts still disheveled. He called Jessica to tell her what he had found. There was no answer. He left her a message, his voice weary from exhaustion.

"Jessica, it's me Drew. I have something important to tell you; I am going over to see Alicia, having just been at the grave of John Musgrave; the grave of my father. I am going to confront Alicia as I believe she is my mother...I don't know." Drew paused as the scope of the situation struck him.

Jesus Christ, I had sex with my mother.

Drew ended the phone call. Opening the car door he fell to the laneway vomiting on the asphalt. Moving slowly, he crawled his way to the lawn and, taking a handful of snow from the ground, cleansed his mouth to rid it of the bile. A second handful cooled his face and calmed him for a moment.

Jesus Christ, I had sex with my mother.

When Drew pulled into the driveway at Alicia's house he took the photo from his wallet and studied it. Standing on the front lawn, he held it up towards the house and was able to position the picture so it matched perfectly with the front porch and wall. The only difference was the colour of the aluminum siding.

This is where the photo was taken.

Drew knocked on the front door and waited. He could hear movement from within the house. Then the door opened. Zoë stood gazing at him before a wide smile crossed her face. She jumped to Drew hugging him tightly. Benjamin ran down the hall and, he too, jumped up on Drew, hugging him. When Drew looked up, he met Alicia's eyes. Hers were warm and welcoming; his emotionless.

"It is so good to see you, Drew. The children have missed you; I have missed you."

Drew offered a weak smile.

Sensing that something wasn't right, Alicia sent the children to play in the basement, wanting to speak with Drew alone. Drew took a seat in the living room. Alicia wanted to tell him that she had taken what he had said to heart; had done a lot of soul searching, and had stopped dealing in drugs. But, first, she needed to know what was happening with him. Concern marked her face.

"Drew, what's wrong, what is going on? Is there a problem with your parents? With work?"

He snorted a sinister, angry laugh.

"Yeah, there is a problem with my parents. But one you won't believe."

Alicia leaned forward in her chair. Drew pulled away as she tried to take hold of his hand.

"Please tell me what's wrong, Drew. You must think I can help or you wouldn't be here."

Drew removed the duotang from inside his jacket, opened to the first page and began to read aloud.

"In the investigation of the adoption of Andrew David Parsons previously named David Colin Musgrave DOB 02/18/89."

He glanced at Alicia then back at the booklet.

"Birth father, J. Musgrave (other initials: J.D. and J.D.B.), DOB: 01/28/71, age: 18."

Alicia looked at him, horrified.

"Birth mother, A. Musgrave (other initials: A.J.), DOB: 05/11/73, age 15."

Drew closed the booklet and sat back in the chair, exhausted, resting his head on his hand, his elbow leaned on the armrest. His stomach continued to churn as the images of the sex he and Alicia had continued to flash in his mind.

"Drew, you don't think that I'm...no, I am not your mother."

"Really? John had three children; their names were tattooed on his body: Zoë; Benjamin and David. My original name was David Musgrave. I'm his son. My mother is A. Musgrave. I was taken from them when I was thirteen months old."

"Drew, my middle name is Suzanne, my initials are A.S. And I wasn't born in seventy-three; I wasn't born until the late seventies. My birthday is November second, seventy-eight. I would have been ten when you were born. I told you I had been married to John for thirteen years. I only met him the year before. And I kept my last name, Warren, remember?"

As Alicia presented her argument Drew felt a sense of relief and uncertainty at the same time. If Alicia wasn't his mother, who was?

"Alicia, I'm so close to finding my mother it's killing me. Do you have any idea who she might be? Did John ever speak of her?"

Alicia shook her head.

"No, John always said it was part of his life he wanted to forget. I knew he had been previously married and had had a child but that is the only information he would ever divulge."

The two sat in silence for several minutes. Alicia stared at Drew as he struggled with the significance of what he had learned, periodically letting out soft whimpers and shaking his head. His eyes were distant and tired, sunk deep in their sockets. Even his posture revealed the battle he was losing as he sat, slumped in the chair. He wasn't the same person who had left her house only a few months before. He was gaunt and frail with deep hollow cheeks. He was lifeless.

Alicia snapped her fingers as her face brightened up.

"We may be able to get you an answer, after all. John's parents; they would know the girl who John married. I will call them and get her name."

Drew sat forward, obscure relief barely lifting his burden.

"Hello Charu, this is Alicia. How are you?"

There was a pause while Charu answered.

"That's good to hear. Charu, I won't take much of your time. I have an important question to ask you and I need the answer right away. I promise I will call you back with more details after I have passed on the information. Charu, can you give me the name of the girl who John had baby David with?"

Alicia tilted her head back and closed her eyes. She pinched the bridge of her nose.

"Please, Charu, I told you I would give you more details as soon as I can. I need to know the name, please."

Now her face began to flush.

"You need to know right now?" she replied curtly. "Fine! Because his son, baby David, is standing beside me looking for her! Are you satisfied? Now, please, give me the name."

Drew watched as Alicia began writing. After scribbling several lines about what Charu told her, Alicia said good-bye with a promise to call back.

"It will be difficult for you to read my chicken scratch. Do you have a spot to write down what I am going to tell you?"

Drew opened the duotang to the back cover. Alicia handed him the pen.

"First thing she said was she hasn't seen you since you were a young boy; when you visited them.

"Now about your mother: her name is Annette. She was a girl who grew up around the corner from here, but her family has long since moved on. She and John married when they found out that she was pregnant, but when you were taken away from them by Social Services there was no reason to stay together. After the divorce she went back to her maiden name and she and her parents moved away not too long after. Though she can't say for certain, Charu believes they moved down east. But that was a long time ago. She lost contact with them."

"Did she give you Annette's family's name?"

CHAPTER TWENTY-FIVE

The drive home had been filled with sporadic bouts of wretched laughter and uncontrollable sobs until there were no tears left. What Drew had experienced over the past week and a half had left him emotionally fractured and physically traumatized. His world was inescapably controlled by circumstances from a lifetime ago. Circumstances which kept pulling him back. And for all his efforts, he couldn't overcome them.

It was early evening when Drew pulled the car into the driveway of the house. All fight in him was gone. He had no more strength; his tank was empty. Attempting to reconcile with his parents, trying to move forward with a career, the search for his birth parents, all of it had been a mistake. Every new find, every rock overturned, produced another catastrophe. And each devastating occurrence diminished his hope, his desire to carry on. He no longer had anywhere to turn, no one to depend on. Abandoned, abused, lost and conquered.

With the car parked in the driveway, Drew turned off the engine. He sat in silence; his mind in chaos as he began muttering to himself.

"How did a journey which had begun with so much promise, fail so monumentally? I have been nothing but a passenger to so many of my life's events. Everything I have ever thought about my life was wrong. Every person I have ever known and trusted wasn't who I thought they were. Every relationship I ever had was a lie. Jesus Christ, the motives and deceptions, the lies and omissions; one disappointment after the next; all of it."

He let out a quiet whimper as he rubbed the palm of his hand across his forehead, harder and faster, trying to erase all the recent events from his memory.

"Get out. Get out. Get the fuck out," he yelled.

All sense of reason had escaped him as he began hysterically punching and shaking the steering wheel.

"This can't go on, I can no longer allow others to control me, control my life. I have to be the one to determine what comes next. I have to be the driver. There are too many variables in this world, too many things that are beyond my control." He paused and an eerie calmness cloaked him.

"At least in the penitentiary there is structure; there is always the routine. Maybe they control every part of my life but there's a certain safety and security in that. In prison, no one can be trusted so there is never any disappointment because they can't let you down."

Then, with sudden, heartbreaking realization, Drew emitted a cold snicker.

The only person who has always been true to me, true to who he is, is Mickey.

Having decided what needed to be done, Drew cleaned out the car, removing the gun and bag with ammunition along with the accordion file and cell phone, and made his way up to the front door. Quietly he entered the house.

Utter silence.

He removed his jacket and shoes and placed them in the front closet then hung his keys on the key hook. Entering the living room the only sound was that of the ticking grandfather clock standing so majestically at attention in the corner. The only movement it's swinging pendulum.

Jessica walked into the living room from the kitchen where she was preparing some dinner. Seeing Drew standing in the middle of the room, she froze.

In his left hand he held an accordion file and in his right, a gun.

"Hello Jessica," Drew's voice was lifeless. "How was your day?"

"It was fine until this afternoon when I received your message," she replied, trying to appear casual.

Drew let out a tired, inert laugh.

They stood staring at each other for several seconds.

"So, how do you want me to address you? Jessica? Annette? Mom? How about I just call you 'Jam'. That should about cover everything."

The comment would have been funny if it wasn't so tragically accurate.

"Oh Drew, I am so sorry. I'm sickened beyond words by what has happened; if I had any idea. But I didn't, how could I? How could either of us."

"How couldn't you? You gave me up for adoption; you had to have known who my adoptive parents were, you were part of the process; how couldn't you?"

"Because I was sixteen years old when you were taken away from us; I had nothing to do with the adoption other than signing the paperwork. Your father's parents, your grandparents, arranged everything: the lawyers, the arbitrations and court dates, any and all meetings. Your father was slightly more involved but I was left in the dark. That part of my life was very difficult for me and I tried to distance myself from it."

"So giving birth to me was a bad thing? So bad you wanted to forget me. I was the mistake you told me about, the reason you got married. Well thank you."

"Drew, don't be like that. Giving birth to you was joyous. I wept the first time I held you. You were small and vulnerable and you looked right into my eyes; you captured my soul. I needed you as much as you needed me. You were my baby, my gift to the world. Raising you for those thirteen months was an incredible experience. You were a beautiful child and having you changed my life for the better. It gave me a profound sense of being, an ambition that was lacking up until then. I wanted to become something.

"But we had nothing. Your dad, John, had been in trouble with the law and I was still in school. Both sets of your grandparents tried to help but Social Services had been involved right from the beginning, deeming our situation untenable and removed you from us. That was why I needed to distance myself from it, the pain was too much."

"Why didn't you tell me you were married to John?"

"Honestly, I didn't think it was important. Would it have changed what occurred? Would our relationship have been any different? What happened, happened. And you knowing John and I were married wouldn't have altered our course. Besides, as I just mentioned, it was a time in my life I wanted to forget."

Drew put the gun in his waist belt and removed the duotang from the accordion file. He then placed the file on the chair. He opened the booklet and read.

"In the investigation of the adoption of Andrew David Parsons previously named David Colin Musgrave DOB 02/18/89."

"Drew, please don't."

Drew looked up from the pages to his mother. He let the book fall from his hands to the floor, where it landed with a slap.

"Why did you change your name from Annette to Jessica?"

"I was named after an aunt who was a successful businesswoman. When I started out I didn't want to be mistaken for or compared to her. Using my middle name defined me. After a while Annette was a person from my past, Jessica was my future."

Both stood silently.

Jessica nodded towards Drew's waist belt. "Why do you have that gun?"

"I bought it to kill William after he had beaten my mother, I mean my adoptive mother," his voice remained flat. "But when I got to the house I decided that his life wasn't worth my life. If I killed him I'd be no better than he, no better than the sixteen year old who had gone to jail so many years ago. I am better than that. Or so I thought."

"You are, Drew. You are a good person; a person who keeps improving; a person who can make a difference." She continued staring at him, willing him to see in himself what she saw in him.

"But why do you have it here? Now?"

"Don't you see, Jessica, this must end today. I am so tired of the bullshit; all the people in my life who have deceived me. And now I have no one. My father and adoptive father are both dead. My adoptive mother is dead to me. The only one that remains is you, my mother; my lover. And your presence assaults my senses. Your nude image blinds me. Your taste curdles in my mouth; your scents fester in my nose; your words haunt me. We have been together in ways that a mother and son should never be. And I can't get those things out of my head." Drew grimaced and he fought back the nausea that threatened to erupt from him as he thought about what they had done, what they had said.

"I have no one. I have nothing."

Again, he rubbed his forehead.

"But don't worry; I have seen the effects of a bullet penetrating the head. It is quick. It won't hurt."

"Andrew, please, you aren't thinking clearly."

"Please, only my mother calls…" he stopped and produced a disgusted snort, hearing the words he so often said out of habit.

"Jessica, don't you see? My entire life has been a lie; from you and John to William and Jean to Alicia. Every one of you has misrepresented yourself to me. Even your name and mine are lies. And I have had enough. I just needed to know why. Why you did what you did. Now it's clear. And it is time for me to end it; here, now. So, really, I'm thinking more clearly than ever. The crazy thing is the penitentiary was more stable than any other part of my life. Sad don't you think?"

Drew took the gun out of the waist belt and held it to his side. Everything that he needed to say had been spoken. There was nothing more to be discussed; no more opportunities for lies and deception. Jessica gazed at Drew, her eyes pleading. Drew looked back at Jessica, his face expressionless.

Drew checked the gun's clip. Full.

Staring into his empty eyes, Jessica wished, beyond hope, that she could help Drew. He looked so young, so vulnerable; a lost child needing protection; a hug; a mother's loving arms. That was not an option, she knew. Not now. But could she get through to him? Could she make him understand? To see that he had an alternative to the path he hadn't, yet, taken.

"Think about what you are doing," Jessica pleaded, keeping her voice calm, fighting the urge to scream out. *'Please don't do this!'*

She clasped her hands, fingers interlaced, and raised them to her chin, in prayer to a God she hoped would listen.

If I can just get him to say something, anything...I can make a connection... Please, God, please, give me the words....

A mask of anguish began to contort her face; lips slightly parted, teeth clenched and eyes pleading. Jessica fought back the tears. Breathing became shuddered, her head light. Her view of the room distorted, like heat waves rising from scorched asphalt. Taking a deep breath she, again, struggled to calm herself.

Jessica opened her mouth to speak. Drew shook his head slightly and, stepping forward, put his index finger up to her lips.

"Shhh, shhh, shhh."

Then he stepped back. Seconds passed. He kept his vacant eyes locked on hers.

Demanding attention, a kettle on the stove in the kitchen screamed out, shattering the silence. Jessica glanced over to the kitchen door and back. The handgun was no longer at Drew's side. The look in his eyes had changed to one of resolve.

Swiftly, Drew raised the gun. There was no time to move; no time to defend; no time to react but for a scream, drowned out by the sudden explosion. The muzzle flash trailed the bullet as it pierced skin, penetrated bone and brain and exited the skull, stealing with it fragments, and a life.

A single tear trickled down Jessica's cheek as she slumped to the floor.

Drew's body crumpled as blood spilled out, puddling beneath him, covering the duotang. The gun remained, frozen in his hand.

Jessica crawled across the floor and felt for a pulse, knowing the answer before she got to the body.

For a second time in her life, Annette's child, her baby, was taken away from her.

She called 9-1-1 and waited beside David until the emergency services arrived.

Epilogue

It was the anniversary of John's death and Alicia decided it was time to go through the box of belongings which had been handed over to her by prison officials at the time they turned his body over to her. Rummaging through, she found an alarm clock, some photographs of her, Zoë and Benjamin, writing paper and pens, and letters he had received from Alicia over the years of his imprisonment. At the bottom of the box she discovered two envelopes; the first with her name on it, the second addressed to Jessica.

Alicia opened her letter.

My dearest Alicia,

I was so glad to see you, as I always am. I know that I was evasive when we spoke earlier today and for that I am sorry. It's just that I have been going through some very emotional times recently and didn't think that the visitors' centre was the appropriate place to discuss the matter which had so occupied my mind. My reason for wanting to help Drew is not altruistic, you are right. And you are also correct that he can't be my surrogate child. But you are correct for the wrong reasons.

When I said we had both been given a second chance, it was our second chance together. The first time was when I couldn't stop Social Services from taking him away from Jessica and me when he was a baby. Yes, Alicia, Drew is David. I knew it the first time I met him. I had heard his name around when he was transferred in to the pen and had to find out if it was him. Within minutes of meeting him, I was almost positive it was David. He had Jessica's cheek bones and my complexion (though lighter) and wavy brown hair. As we spent more time together and he opened up to me, it confirmed that he was David.

You said I should take care of my family, of my children and that is my goal. I can't do much for Zoë and Benjamin while I'm in here, but I can make a difference in Drew's life. Not as my surrogate son, but as my SON. That is why I said we both were given a second chance; me to teach my son and Drew to learn from his father. I know this will not be easy for you, but I need you to do this for me; for my son. I couldn't save him the first time, but I can save him now.

Finally, Alicia, I need you to keep this a secret from him. I have not told him who I am because I don't want the dynamics of our relationship to change. He simply looks at me as John, an older inmate who has taken him under my wing. If he found out that I was his father, it may cause problems that would undermine what I am trying to accomplish here.

Once I'm released from prison, and depending where things are with him (he has told me he will keep in touch after he is released) I may tell him at that time. Until then I would rather he not know.

Alicia, he really is a great kid who made a bad decision. I couldn't be more proud of him if I had raised him myself.

I want you to know that I truly do appreciate the sacrifices you have made for me and the children and love you more than my simple words could ever hope to express.

Give Zoë and Benjamin a hug and a kiss for me. I look forward with great anticipation to your next visit.

John

When Jessica answered the doorbell, she saw a blue Honda driving away from the house. To her right, protruding from the mail box was an envelope with a yellow sticky note attached to it. She took the envelope from the mail box and went back into the house.

Jessica sat in front of the fireplace and read the note.

Jessica, I found this envelope in John's prison belongings. I am sorry it took this long but I couldn't find the courage to go through the box before today and had no idea that John had written to you – as he had me. I once told Drew that shying away from things that make one uncomfortable is dangerous. No more prophetic words have I ever spoken. Had I looked into John's things earlier, it may have prevented this tragedy. I am sorry.

Alicia

Jessica opened the letter.

Dear Annette,

I know we haven't spoken in a long time and hope this letter finds you well. Thank you for speaking to Alicia who is acting on my behalf.

If you are receiving this letter it means you have considered helping Drew. He is a great guy who is also extremely intelligent and hard working. I have been helping him with his studies while he is in prison and the degree of his knowledge is impressive.

Annette, the reason I have asked you to help is more than simply because of the reasons stated above. Annette, Drew was adopted back in 1990 by William and Jean Parsons. They changed his name from David Musgrave to Andrew Parsons. Yes, Drew is our David. I knew it the first time I met him. I had heard his name around the prison when he was transferred in and had to find out if it was him. Within minutes of meeting him, I was almost positive it was David. He had your cheek bones and, though lighter, my complexion and hair. As we spent more time together and he opened up to me, it confirmed that he was our David.

I immediately made the decision to <u>not</u> reveal my identity to him. He simply sees me as just another inmate who gives him advice to help survive the prison life. I have been making arrangements for him to live with Alicia but didn't tell him about speaking with you as I plan on doing that once you have confirmed your intention to interview him.

I would ask that you keep my secret from him but the decision to tell him about yourself is your choice. I will have no opinion as to that.

Annette, I realize this is probably like a bomb dropping on you but I hope you will find it in you to help our child as he tries to reform himself after some bad decisions (apple, tree huh?). He really is a different, and better, person than the one who walked in here 4 ½ yrs ago and, with the right guidance, I think he will be a great success in life and a contributing person to society.

The decision is yours. But if you can't see to hiring him to work for you, please, try to get him a job with someone else in the industry. He has a real aptitude for art and thoroughly enjoys it (apple, tree huh?).

I appreciate that you have agreed to talk to him. I don't think you will be disappointed. In fact, I expect you will be as impressed with him as I have been. As I mentioned to Alicia, I don't think I could be prouder than I am if I had raised him myself (though, to a degree, I have).

Take care, Annette, and if you have any questions, speak to Alicia or contact me directly at the prison. If you would like, we can arrange a day for you and Alicia to meet me here to work on a plan of action.

Kindest regards,

John

Jessica wiped the tears from her cheeks, placed the letter back in the envelope and threw it in the fire.

Made in the USA
Charleston, SC
06 April 2013